Praise for the Mrs. Murphy Mysteries
by Rita Mae Brown and Sneaky Pie Brown

"As feline collaborators go, you couldn't ask for better than Sneaky
Pie Brown."

—*The New York Times Book Review*

"Enchanting . . . Brown demonstrates once again why she's the
queen of the talking animal cozy subgenre."

—*Publishers Weekly*

"[Brown] successfully weaves mystery, history, real estate and ro-
mance. . . . The blend is unusual but gripping, and combined with
bipedal and quadrupedal characters who constitute old friends, it
shines as imaginative and educational entertainment."

—*Richmond Times-Dispatch*

"This engaging series remains fresh."

—Fredericksburg *Free Lance-Star*

"Fun and satisfying . . . an essential purchase for all mystery collec-
tions."

—*Booklist*

"Clearly the cat's meow."

—*Library Journal*

T0038526

Hiss & Tell

A MRS. MURPHY MYSTERY

Hiss & Tell

RITA MAE BROWN & SNEAKY PIE BROWN

Illustrated by Michael Gellatly

BANTAM

NEW YORK

2024 Bantam Books Trade Paperback Edition

Published in the United States by Bantam Books,
an imprint of Random House,
a division of Penguin Random House LLC, New York.

BANTAM & B colophon is a registered trademark of Penguin Random House LLC.

Originally published in hardcover in the United States by Bantam Books,
an imprint of Random House,
a division of Penguin Random House LLC, in 2023.

ISBN 978-0-593-35756-9
Ebook ISBN 978-0-593-35755-2

Printed in the United States of America on acid-free paper

randomhousebooks.com

1st Printing

Book design by Diane Hobbing

To
Juju and Linda King
The best friends come on four feet;
in Linda's case, two.

CAST OF CHARACTERS

THE PRESENT

Mary Minor Haristeen, "Harry" was the postmistress of Crozet right out of Smith College. As times changed and a big new post office was built, new rules came, too, such as she couldn't bring her animals to work, so she retreated to the farm she inherited from her parents. Born and raised in Crozet, she knows everyone and vice versa. She is now forty-five, although one could argue whether maturity has caught up with her.

Pharamond Haristeen, DVM, "Fair" is an equine vet specializing in reproduction. He and Harry have known each other all their lives. They married shortly after she graduated from Smith and he was in vet school at Auburn. He generally understands his wife better than she understands herself.

Susan Tucker is Harry's best friend from cradle days. They might as well be sisters and can sometimes pluck each other's last nerve as only a sister can. Susan bred Harry's adored corgi. Her husband, Ned, is the district's delegate to the General Assembly's House of Delegates, the lower house.

Ballard Perez lives on a cottage at Lone Pine, his family's large estate in Keswick established before the Revolutionary War. He can't afford the estate but has kept it going with help from the historical society. He owns an Irish Wolfhound.

Deputy Cynthia Cooper is Harry's neighbor, as she rents the adjoining farm. Law enforcement is a career she is made for, being meticulous, shrewd, and highly observant. She works closely with the sheriff, Rick Shaw, adores Harry, and all too often has to extricate her neighbor out of scrapes. Harry returns the favor by helping Coop with her garden. It probably isn't an equal exchange but they are fine with it.

Tazio Chappers is an architect in her late thirties, born and raised in St. Louis. Being educated at Washington University, she received an excellent education, winding up in Crozet on a fluke. Just one of those things, as Cole Porter's song lets us know. Warned off a job at an architectural firm by many people back in Missouri, due to her being half black and half Italian, she came to Virginia, anyway. No one can accuse her of being a chicken. Now owner of her own firm, getting big jobs, she is happy, married for two years, and part of the community. She is also terrifically good-looking, which never hurts.

Joel Paloma owns a large food distributing company serving much of central Virginia all the way to Richmond. He hopes to show his Irish Wolfhound at AKC shows.

Sy Buford owns and runs a large orchard in Crozet. He grows succulent peaches, pears, cherries, and apples. Successful as the business is, it is difficult to find workers, plus Mother Nature is not an easy business partner.

Linda King breeds Irish Wolfhounds at her kennels, Ard Rhis. She is training local owners to really look at Irish Wolfhounds as a judge might look at them. She is much in demand in the Irish Wolfhound world.

Sam Ewing is known as Mr. Irish Wolfhound. His contributions to the breed have been enormous.

Big Mim Sanburne, an outstanding horsewoman born to an avalanche of money, has Tazio's husband, Paul, running her stables. She is called the Queen of Crozet and while not much in evidence in this book, she'll be a bigger part of others. Sooner or later, Big Mim (who is tiny) gets her way.

THE EIGHTEENTH CENTURY
Cloverfields

Ewing Garth owns this vast estate on the north side of the old road to Wayland's Crossing (later named Crozet). Worldly, intelligent, he has the courage of his convictions, risking everything he owned during the Revolutionary War.

Catherine Schuyler is Ewing's oldest daughter at twenty-five. She married a hero of Yorktown, John Schuyler. He is modest, reliable, not well educated, but he can think quickly during a crisis. He was born for battle, having natural leadership abilities. He worships his gorgeous wife and she has helped him modify his hardscrabble Massachusetts ways to Virginia's sometimes comical sense of elegance. Virginia is as close to the Cotswolds as an American can come. A terrific horsewoman, Catherine works with her father, soaking up much of what he knows about business, people, life.

John Schuyler has been put in charge of developing the Virginia militia, as we still don't have a standing army but we do have enemies.

Rachel, younger than Catherine by two years, is also beautiful but it's a warm, very womanly beauty. Catherine focuses on facts, profit, getting the job done. Rachel focuses on easing people's way, caring for them, and struggling with the injustices of the day. She has taken in as her own a little girl, now six, Marcia, who is the product of a brutal neighbor's inflicting himself on the best-looking slave woman on his plantation. He was killed. The unwilling paramour and her true love blamed. Ultimately she died in hiding, with Rachel having full knowledge of all this, desperately trying to save the woman. Bettina and Bumbee really covered the escaped slave's tracks. She and Catherine concocted a story about Marcia's beginnings that used one whopping lie to cover another. She is years ahead of her time in many ways, although accepting of a woman's place.

Charles West is Rachel's husband. John Schuyler captured him at the Battle of Saratoga and Charles was marched to the prisoner-of-war camp on land now abutting Cloverfields. When the war finally ended, Ewing managed to buy much of the POW camp as well as other farms. Having marched through the new land from New York State down to Virginia he realized how rich the land was, how mighty the rivers, and how many. Although the younger son of a baron he had no desire to go back to that life, providing he lived. He did. He stayed and fell in love with Rachel. Following his heart he also became an architect. He is a supremely happy man and a terrifically well-educated one.

Yancy Grant, like Ewing, risked his goods to help finance Virginia's part of the war. His knee was shattered in a duel. He limps, needs a cane, but manages. He, like Garth, is in his middle fifties. He never married, whereas Ewing did, losing his wife ten years back. Yancy, like Catherine, loves horses but, now living in reduced circumstances, he has given her his best horse, Black Knight. He had to stop drinking because it was affecting him in bad ways. He did it and has earned back much of the respect he lost thanks to the bottle.

THE SLAVES

Bettina is the head cook, a woman so creative with dishes that she is known throughout the former colony. She takes no guff from anyone. She was close to Isabelle, Ewing's wife, nursing the woman on her deathbed. Isabelle asked Bettina to look after her two girls, which Bettina did. Now that the girls are grown, have families of their own, she is making a new life for herself emotionally. Bettina misses nothing.

Bumbee runs the weaving cabin. She works at a huge loom and there is a smaller one for her assistants. All intensely creative like her, slave or free. She has a wonderful way about her, plus the patterns she creates, the clothing, dazzles the women. The men are happy with their shirts, no surprise. Her husband, Mr. Percy, is flagrantly unfaithful, bringing her misery, anger, confusion, for she still has a strong draw to him. She's taken to living in the large weaving cabin, while he lives in their cabin. She is approaching middle age, feeling old, but some of that is due to heartache, a heartache women have known for centuries.

Jeddie works with Catherine at the stable. A natural rider with a good eye, he works horses daily and Catherine is teaching him about bloodlines, as horses are being imported from England, a new type called blooded horses (today's Thoroughbreds). He is ambitious, decent, and loves horses more than people. He is nineteen.

Barker O drives the carriage horses as well as being in charge of all carriages. There are different types of conveyances for different jobs, the most splendid being the coach-in-four. He handles it with such ease it looks as though he is doing nothing. He is in hot competition with DoRe at Big Rawly; it's a good competition, as each brings out the best in the other.

Tulli is twelve, Jeddie's shadow. He is such a small fellow. Jeddie gives him jobs, as does Catherine. Tulli often rides with Catherine's son, about four, on Sweet Potato, JohnJohn's pony. Tulli is pretty good and will do anything to shine. His father died in a farm accident when Tulli was five. His mother, Georgia, has ever since been distracted and sad, so everyone takes Tulli under their wing. He is an uncommonly sweet child.

Serena helps Bettina in the kitchen. She does good work, likes to cook, but lacks the creativity of Bettina. Then again, most do.

Mr. Percy, good-looking, smooth-talking, has a way with plants. He oversees the Cloverfields gardens and Ewing allows him to take commissions to design other people's gardens, plant them. So Mr. Percy gets to move around a bit and he has a wandering eye. His body wanders with it.

BIG RAWLY

Maureen Selisse Holloway has a refined cruelty toward anyone who crosses her. Born in the Caribbean to a banker father and educated in France, she has no time for ideas of modern government. She is fine living in the New World but she thinks the politicians naïve. Money talks always and ever. In Maureen's case it whispers, but everyone knows she is one of the richest women in this new nation. And she wants more. She believes in a strict caste system. As far as she's concerned, the Bible countenances slavery and so will she.

Jeffrey Holloway is Maureen's much younger second husband; an Apollo, he is so handsome. The son of a cabinetmaker and that was his profession when he met the new widow. She took one look at this divine creature and determined to have him. Strange as it may sound, he did learn to love her, being dazzled by her education, her worldliness. She built him an enormous work shed where he could design and build coach-in-fours. The results are slowly being seen as far north as rich, rich Philadelphia. He is now swamped with orders and happy, although he tries to mollify Maureen's more savage impulses.

DoRe is the coachman, Barker O's rival. He limps from a long-ago horse accident, tries out each new carriage Jeffrey builds, and is invaluable to the operation. He has found love, being widowed years back, with Bettina, herself having lost a husband. Maureen has agreed to the marriage but she will get her pound of flesh. Jeffrey is doing his best to protect DoRe.

Sulli ran off with William, a self-centered young man who promised wealth, freedom, fabulous clothing. He beat her but did manage to make it to Royal Oak, a large farm in Maryland. So they were free, but they were caught. No one on Royal Oak was part of this, but caught they were, and stolen back, delivered to Maureen, where life is hell. Sulli is eighteen years old.

William, hamstrung during the drive back as he tried to escape, is a beaten creature. He is chained every night and will stay chained until Maureen's revenge is satisfied or she's distracted by something else. He lied, he cheated, he stole, he jeopardized every slave at Big Rawly. He has not one friend but many enemies, including Sulli, who has sworn to herself to kill him someday. William may or may not have learned from what he did to Sulli and how he made life even worse for those at Big Rawly after he ran away. There's no arrogance left and no hope.

Toby Tips works with Jeffrey as his second-in-command. He knows this business. Most importantly he stays clear of the Missus. She'll have people flogged for the slightest offense. Jeffrey has stopped that, he thinks, but if he goes off the farm she has someone battered who she feels is no good.

Martin was a slave catcher but he and his partner have good work now delivering the sturdy work wagons that Jeffrey is building. They deliver goods for other people, too. The money is pretty good, with much less risk.

Shank is Martin's partner. They do their job, are happy to take a bit of money or goods under the table. Neither man has much fear. Violence is part of life and they have little regard for life other than their own.

Elizabetta is Maureen's lady's maid. She paid dearly when William and Sulli ran off, for she was in charge that day. She hates those two with a white hot passion. However, she hates Maureen even more. She covers it well.

THE ANIMALS

The Present

Mrs. Murphy is Harry's tiger cat. She is bright, does her chores, keeps the mice at bay when need be. Harry talks to her but not baby talk. Mrs. Murphy just won't have it.

Pewter is fat, gray, and vain, oh so vain. She irritates Tucker, the corgi. She takes credit for everyone else's work. However, in a pinch the naughty girl does come through. She's also quite bright.

Tucker, the corgi bred by Susan Tucker, runs around everyone. She's fast, loves to greet every person once she has checked them out, and particularly likes to herd the horses. The horses are good sports about it, which is a good thing. Tucker is brave and she loves Harry totally.

Pirate is a not-yet-fully-grown Irish wolfhound who landed in Harry's lap as a puppy when his owner died. Huge, able to cover so much ground, he can be dominated by Pewter sometimes. Tucker has to give him pep talks. Like Tucker, Pirate has great courage, loves being part of the family. He is trying to understand people. The others help. A sweet, sweet animal.

The horses, the big owl in the barn, and the possum aren't in the forefront in this book but they are around and will be their usual selves in future. This also applies to the barn mice, who have a really good deal at the farm.

THE ANIMALS

The Past

Piglet, a corgi, traveled through the war and the POW camp with Charles. He's slowing down, sleeps most of the time.

Reynaldo is a blooded stallion who is proving himself in the breeding shed, along with his half brother, Crown Prince. Other than Catherine, only Jeddie can ride these two.

Black Knight is Yancy Grant's horse, stolen by William. After an arduous experience and injury, he was found and brought back to Yancy, who asked Catherine to care for him. She has and he, too, is proving himself in the breeding shed. He'll never run again, of course, but he gets around pretty good.

Penny is a kind mare that Catherine bought from Maureen for her father. Maureen felt Penny not fancy enough for her. She lost a really good horse thanks to her vanity.

Miss Renata is John's horse. She's 17 hands. He is a tall, powerfully built man and she can carry him. She's a good girl. John can ride but he's not really a horseman. Catherine takes care of all of that.

Sweet Potato is a bullheaded pony. Tulli is in charge of him. He's learning, but then so is Sweet Potato.

Hiss & Tell

1

Friday

A large clear pitcher, filled with credit cards, suspended in the frozen water, sat in the freezer. The American Express card glittered, the Capitol One card shone winter white with green lettering. Bank of America's card seemed patriotic with red, white, and blue on the face of it.

Mary Minor "Harry" Haristeen tried to ignore the frozen cards but they twinkled in the ice. She paused, looked, grabbed frozen coffee beans, and shut the full-length left-side door of the refrigerator.

"I am not defrosting one card. Not one."

Her corgi, Tee Tucker, seemed supportive so the lean woman continued, "I have to practice restraint this Christmas. I'm still paying off the drill seeder."

A farmer, she'd needed a new drill seeder, the old one finally expiring. Cost: $25,000. A wonderful piece of equipment with various size apertures for various seeds, it would make her seeding easier but the price hit her hard.

Pewter, the fat gray cat, had heard this complaining before, during her human's economizing fits. "*She'll weaken.*"

The tiger cat, Mrs. Murphy, advised, "*Let's rub on her leg. She'll take it as a good sign, we want to help.*"

"*All right.*" Pewter agreed without enthusiasm.

Mrs. Murphy picked Harry's left leg while Pewter selected the right as Harry was fetching eggs and bacon out of the refrigerator.

"You are such good kitties. Even though I'm trying to tighten up here before Christmas, you know you'll get buckets of catnip." She placed the food on the counter as she measured beans for the coffee grinder.

"*How about an early example?*" Pewter rubbed harder. "*I've been good.*"

"*At what?*" The corgi raised an eyebrow.

Pewter puffed up. "*I rid the farm of vermin. Death to mice, moles, and even snakes. What do you do?*"

Tucker stepped out of smacking range, then sassed, "*What you do is make deals with the mice in the barn. You have never killed anything and you are afraid of Matilda, the blacksnake.*"

Those kitty pupils widened, a hiss followed. "*Matilda is a python. Huge. She scares everyone. As to the mice, I do make deals. I neutralize them. Harry hates blood.*"

True enough, Matilda was huge. Apart from being an old snake, she had a sense of humor. In the summer months she went out of her way to terrify the gray cat. Currently, she was hibernating in the basement and would awaken late April. The technical term is *brumation*, but Matilda in her hidden den was blissfully asleep.

Harry put the freshly ground coffee into the top of the pot, hit the button. Then she turned to fry bacon and eggs. She woke up hungry.

The bacon provoked rapt attention.

Pirate, a young Irish wolfhound, now almost fully grown, wanted to put his head on the counter to snatch the bacon. His manners

forbade it but what a temptation. He wondered if people could smell the bacon as well as he could. Perhaps not, or they'd eat it all in a gulp.

Tucker sat close by Harry, now in front of the stove. "*Do you remember Christmas, Pirate? Last year was your first.*"

The gentle fellow replied, "*I remember a tree. Big. The house smelled like a forest.*"

The cracking of an eggshell captured more attention. Then another frying pan was put on the stove as the eggs began to sizzle, slowly. Into that Harry peeled off strips of bacon, carefully filling the pan, which already released the magical bacon odor.

Pewter repaired to the kitchen, jumped on a chair, waiting. "*I bet I get bacon before you all do.*"

"*Pig,*" Tucker snapped.

"*With a butt like yours I'd watch what I say, especially to your betters.*" Pewter swept her whiskers forward and back, turning her head in disdain.

Watching this at a distance, because Pirate knew how testy the gray cat could be, he asked, "*What are credit cards?*"

"*The handiwork of the Devil.*" Mrs. Murphy, now on another kitchen seat, uttered this in the voice of doom.

"*Not if she buys us presents,*" Pewter announced, waiting impatiently for Harry to sit down.

"*Pirate, credit cards mean you can take what you want. You don't have to start paying for a month. Mother goes overboard, especially at Christmas, so January, February, and March she tries to pay her bills. Upsets her.*" Tucker expanded on the reality of credit cards.

Harry carried the plate, put it on the table. Walked back for her coffee and picked up the plate of nothing but bacon, lots of bacon. Her four friends were enthralled.

"*Bacon.*" Pewter closed her eyes. "*If the credit card is the handiwork of the Devil then this is the work of angels.*"

They all agreed.

Pirate, trying to understand this bizarre concept, asked as he stared at the food, "*Can I get a credit card?*"

"Sure." Pewter delicately put her paw on the table, inching it toward the plate of bacon.

"*Bull. Pirate has no credit,*" Mrs. Murphy said.

"*Neither do half the people who get them.*" Tucker laughed. "*I don't see why Pirate can't get one. Pirate Haristeen. I can see it now on a card.*"

"*Oh, I am starving. Starving,*" the gray cat wailed.

"*Over the top, Fatty.*" Tucker sniffed.

"*You're lucky I'm on this chair or I'd give you such a smack.*"

"*Yeah. Yeah,*" the small dog responded.

Any dog looked small next to Pirate, who had moved to sit closer to Harry. If it worked for the others it might work for him.

"I don't know why I do this." Harry plucked one strip of bacon, tore it in half, giving a half to each cat. She repeated the process for the dogs.

"*I love you, love you, love you.*" Pewter licked her lips, eyes on Harry.

"*Can you buy bacon with a credit card?*" Pirate also hoped for more.

"*Sure. You can buy anything.*" Pewter reached over but did not touch the plate.

"Don't even think about it," Harry warned as she, too, ate a piece of bacon.

"*Do all humans have cards? If you can buy bacon then I really want one.*" The youngster felt deserving of such a wonderful tool.

"*Worth a try.*" Mrs. Murphy thought, why not?

"*I'm famished. I'm perishing. I need more food. Only bacon can save me. Don't let me die.*" Pewter raised her voice.

"*What a ham. You don't need bacon.*" Tucker now sat next to Harry's chair.

"Pewter, calm down." Harry handed her another bacon strip then realized she had to give one to everyone else.

The bacon plate was diminishing.

"*Gimme that.*" Pewter hopped on the table to snag Mrs. Murphy's bacon.

"What is wrong with you?" Harry stood up and pushed the fat gray cat back in the seat as she wisely grabbed the last of the bacon for herself.

The sky lightened but remained sunless. November meant the sun rose later and set earlier. Harry stared outside the kitchen window over the sink as she sipped her coffee. The diminishing light didn't affect her as it did some people, but she knew she had less time to get outside chores done. Checking the large clock on the wall, an old railroad clock belonging to her late mother and father, she finished her cup.

"If you have more bacon in the fridge, I can help you get it," Pewter offered.

"Don't listen to her," Tucker grumbled.

"Really, if I had a credit card I could buy all the bacon in the world." Pirate promised this with a smile on his handsome face.

Harry, carrying the plates to the sink, turned on the hot water, set the plates in the sink then reached down to stroke the wolfhound's prominent mustache.

Pewter immediately hopped on the table to check for any crumbs. No crumb was too small.

Mrs. Murphy instead sat in her chair and watched Harry wash dishes.

Harry, in her mid-forties, kept her figure but then farmwork burned the calories. She looked younger than her years but given vitamins, good dentistry, and modern health practices so many people radiated good health but not always a good body. It always seemed to Harry, though, that farm people remained the strongest, the fittest. She finished the washing, grabbed a towel, and dried the two dishes, her cup and saucer.

"When we go to Coop's," Pirate remarked, "she has a machine that washes dishes. Why don't we?"

"'Cause Mom likes to do things by hand. She tries not to use electricity. She's real careful about money." The tiger cat loved Harry, thought her prudent, as she herself was.

"And Coop is a cop. She has no time. So a dishwasher makes sense," Tucker chimed in.

Cynthia Cooper rented the adjoining farm, which was the old Jones place. The Reverend Herbert Jones loved it but as he was the pastor at St. Luke's Lutheran Church he lived there in a quite beautiful home, the church and pastor's lodging having been built immediately after the Revolutionary War. Crozet was then called Wayland's Crossing. It changed, of course, in many ways, but in others not so much. People made an effort to know one another, to preserve the beauty of the mountain views and the rolling hills.

"*Would you really buy everyone bacon?*" Tucker smiled at Pirate, whom she still considered a puppy . . . a one hundred fifty pound puppy.

"*Sure.*" Pirate wagged his tail, which hit the table, making a loud sound.

"Honey, come over here." Harry called the dog to her to get him away from the table. Not that he would break anything but Harry was keenly aware of Pewter's dramatic temperament. Another thump like that and the cat was capable of jumping down to smack Pirate's face. The dog, too sensitive to snarl back, would flop down with sorrowful eyes.

"*When is enough enough?*" Mrs. Murphy asked. "*Maybe we'd be with bacon like people are with money and things.*"

"*Greed.*" Tucker licked her lips, thinking about bacon.

"*It's not greed. It's enjoying food.*" Pewter was a testimony to her attitude.

"*Well, Coop has to deal with greed crimes.*"

"*Greed is a sin, not a crime,*" Mrs. Murphy corrected Tucker.

"*If someone got Mom's credit cards out of the freezer, stole them, would Cooper find them?*" Pirate wondered.

"*Sure. If it's a theft or a murder, that's her job,*" Pewter airily replied.

As it was, Cooper was at a van wreck. All the occupants had fled. When people escaped their accidents it often meant they had some kind of criminal record, or had stolen the vehicle.

2

Sunday

"It was the damndest thing." Fair Haristeen, lumber-jack cap pulled on his head, stood outside with Coop, notebook in hand.

In front of them a van leaning against a tree, doors open, wheels spinning, gave evidence to sloppy driving.

"Okay." Coop felt the cold air on her bare right hand. "Fair, let's sit in your truck. I'll write better. There's nothing I can see having walked around the ancient van. Three empty wooden crates inside. Maybe they used them for seats. Called the boss. The wreck team will be here in good time."

He walked to open the truck door for her but she was already in. He then opened the driver's door and got in, closing it behind him. The cab's heat felt wonderful.

"Okay. What time? Six-thirty?"

"Yes. I'd finished up at Big Mim's early call. Colic, nothing too terrible. Was on my way to the clinic." Big Mim owned a spectacular estate filled with equally spectacular horses. "That van pulled in front of me, down where the new bridge was built. It still has some lean to it despite being widened."

"Yes, it does," she agreed while writing.

"Anyway, the driver was over the speed limit. I could see heads in the van. Knew there were passengers but that was about it. I kept my distance as the driver dropped a wheel off the road, then corrected. I just wanted to get to 250." He cited the route, east–west, much traveled. "Early morning traffic, but not clogged."

"What do you estimate his speed to be?"

"I was going fifty. He was pulling away so he had to be sixty or more."

"Okay."

"Reached the stoplight. I was going to turn right but then I noticed he ran the light, careened across 250, avoided a car, the van started to tip over, and where you see it is where it landed. The next thing I knew, because I crossed the road to see if anyone was hurt, the doors flew open except for the one jammed against the tree. Men flew out everywhere. No one I recognized, and they were dressed like men who work outside. There must have been ten people crammed into the van. I mean they burnt the wind. Running into the fields, behind the few houses on the south side of 250, off Miller School Road. It was like the Keystone Cops."

"Did anyone look hurt?"

"If they were they could still run."

"Do you think they were migrant workers? That's unusual at this time of year."

"That's what I thought. It could be that these fellows, all men, have long-term employment at some of the vineyards, but what can you do in the dead of winter? Fix fences. Half the time you can't dig. Why do you think they ran?"

"They could have police records, or they could be here illegally. No way to know without identification."

He crossed his arms over his considerable chest. Fair at six four was a powerful man, muscular. He had to be. Even a pony can weigh near a thousand pounds.

"We've never talked about this, but do you handle a lot of illegal entry cases?" Fair asked.

"No. We don't, but the Immigration Service raids farms. Not often, but when they do it's a mess. And it's a mess that appears not able to be resolved anytime soon."

"You're right about that." He sighed. "As you know, I visit farms in a lot of counties. I specialize in equine reproduction, so I travel. If I didn't have a specialty, I doubt I would see as much as I do. I see a lot of workers from south of the border."

"That doesn't necessarily mean anything, many of them could be here legally." Cooper stopped writing, folding her notebook. "But breeding operations, cattle, or horses, yes, they need labor, usually men. And the apple and peach orchards, as well as the vintners, also need labor. I doubt all of those workers are here legally. Usually they leave when the harvest is over. That's why this accident is a little peculiar. What were these men doing in central Virginia in November, and why did they run from the crash?"

"Here comes your crew."

She opened the door. "Go on to the clinic. I know where to find you."

"Good luck getting to the bottom of this. I mean, it really was like the Keystone Cops."

She was going to need that luck.

3

Monday

"Why did I let you talk me into this?" Susan Tucker, Harry's best friend since birth, moaned.

"I didn't talk you into it." Harry tightened the old cashmere scarf around her neck as Tucker, Pirate, and Owen, Susan's corgi, trotted along with them.

Mrs. Murphy and Pewter stayed in the old truck. Harry liked to run it at least once a week. Pewter refused to get out in the cold. Harry tossed old coats in the truck, a few old fuzzy horse pads. The old 1978 Ford F-150 tottered on its last legs. She and Fair found a used 2018 Ram last year. After torturing herself, Harry agreed they should purchase a better work truck for her. As it sported an extended cab with a nice, padded bench seat, she was surprised at how useful it was. The animals loved it although Pewter bitched and moaned constantly about Pirate taking up so much space. The sweet fellow actually sat up the whole time so as not to take up so much space. But why take Pewter's moment of offense away from her?

The truck sat in a small parking area about one hundred yards from the top of the ridge, a ridge one level lower than the spine of the Blue Ridge Mountains, about 2,172 feet at this point.

Susan's late uncle left her over 1,000 acres of black walnut. Harry had a much smaller stand around which Susan's wrapped. Harry kept her eye on the timber, which made sense; she was right there.

"*Got hateful cold.*" Pewter wiggled deeper down in the saddle pad.

"*Did. Bet we have our first snow soon. Feels like it.*" Mrs. Murphy looked out the window.

"All I did was say I hadn't seen the stand since October. That didn't mean I wanted to see it today. But you threw me in the truck. It's too cold to walk."

"Means you have to walk faster." Harry picked up the pace, the dogs now ahead.

Huffing and puffing, streams of breath shooting into the air, the two women, both in shape, reached the top of the ridge, a narrow elongated meadow offering some respite. If one climbed higher you would soon be on Route 250 and above that Route 64, the big interstate. They were far enough away that they could barely hear the traffic and in the summer with the leaves on the trees, you only heard a muffled sound. The pines couldn't absorb as much sound but it wasn't offensive. A lone dirt road zigzagged down from an abandoned farm near the top of the ridge. No road ran off of 250 and none, of course, from the big interstate.

Both women stopped, turned to look back, as it offered a good view of much of the 1,000 acres.

"Slow growing." Susan stated the obvious.

"Hardwoods are, and especially this hardwood. But the wood is incredible whether it's walnut, red oak, or even Deep South stuff like cypress. I love hardwoods."

"Me too. What do you think? Another ten years and then I harvest twenty acres every few years. And replant right away?"

"Depends on the weather. If it's too wet it's a god-awful mess. If it's too dry you can timber easily enough but replanting is difficult. Mother Nature needs to give us the right balance."

"In every respect," Susan agreed.

Tucker lifted her nose. The other dogs followed suit.

"*Dead,*" Owen declared.

"*Not long dead,*" Tucker added.

"*Let's find out.*" The three dogs followed the scent. Tucker was in the lead as they came to a deer, shot but not harvested by the deer hunter.

"Hey, you all, get back here," Harry shouted.

"*All right.*" Tucker agreed mostly because the carcass, frozen, was of no use to them. Had to have been a clean death. Not a lot of bullet holes.

"*I hate hearing the shots,*" Pirate confessed.

"*It will be over the first weekend of January. And think of it, Pirate. The deer population is exploding. The humans want to manage it. It's their fault the deer are all around.*"

As they walked back to Harry and Susan the two corgis discussed this. Their version of animal husbandry differed from most people's. They reached Harry and Susan before exhausting the subject.

Walking back down the steep incline meant the humans stepped sideways. Walking directly, feet in front, invited a stumble especially as roots protruded in many areas.

Harry opened the door, then flopped her seat forward so the dogs could crawl into the space behind.

"*Watch where you're going, Bubblebutt,*" Pewter complained.

Tucker bared her teeth but nudged next to Mrs. Murphy while Pirate sat motionless on the end.

Harry backed out, shifted to the lowest gear, and carefully drove down the hill. Better to be under power than simply coast.

The timber road zigged and zagged. They neared the bottom.

"Why don't you turn left? Go on the old road at your pasture and come out on the macadam. Let's swing right around through Aunt

Tally's old road and come in your front drive eventually," Susan suggested.

"Okay. Haven't been that way in a long time. I hardly see Aunt Tally anymore. What is she now . . . 104, 105?"

"Think so. I saw her briefly at Halloween. She uses a cane but she still walks. Skinny. Well, she was never fat."

Harry slowly drove along the old farm road, then turned right off of it, sliding at the edge of Aunt Tally's large farm, the old barns with their elaborate cupolas shining in the distance.

"She has never failed to keep this place pristine," Harry said admiringly.

As they neared the state road where they would turn left, Susan ordered, "Stop."

Harry did.

Susan opened the door. Harry cut the motor as Susan's boots hit the ground. The two corgis squeezed out to join Susan. Pirate, too big to squeeze through without someone holding the door open, watched, frustrated. The cats watched also.

Harry, knowing Susan as she did, realized something was important or amiss. She, too, got out of the car.

Susan knelt by the side of the farm road, a narrow ditch alongside. "Dead. Frozen."

Harry came by her friend. "Good Lord."

"*A hint of blood.*" Tucker posited and Owen agreed. "*Underneath.*"

The dogs were right. For the man had been shot, falling forward. Susan and Harry couldn't see the bullet hole.

Harry was shocked to find him, middle-aged, in a ditch this far out from Crozet.

Harry pulled out her cellphone, called Cooper. Gave her the information. "She says to wait here. She's driving by St. Paul's. Will be here in twenty minutes."

St. Paul's was the Episcopal church off 250 and the Owensville Road.

"Poor fellow," Harry murmured. "I hope he didn't truly freeze to death, maybe he had a heart attack. Just 'boom' and you're gone. I didn't recognize him. Then again, if he worked for an orchard, I doubt I would know him. If he worked with horses, maybe."

"*Shot or stabbed. There's blood,*" Tucker informed her.

As she'd predicted, Coop arrived in twenty minutes. She did not turn on her sirens. Parking nose to nose with the old Ford, she jumped out. Walked over.

Then she looked all around, pulled on her thin rubber gloves, cold, turned over the body. A bullet hole showed in his short but thick jacket, over his heart. She rifled his pockets, including his jeans' pockets.

"Nothing. No ID." She stood back up.

"Is that unusual?" Susan asked.

"Not if a person is here illegally or has a hot record. Usually they have no identifying papers. That's why if there's an accident, they run. Like the bump into a tree that your husband saw. Everyone ran."

"He mentioned it in passing." Then Harry filled in Susan.

"Could this be one of those men?" Susan wondered.

"Possibly." Cooper tugged off the thin rubber gloves, pulling on her warm ones.

"Maybe someone thought he was trespassing in the night and shot him," Susan thought out loud.

Cooper knelt again, close to the corpse. "He was shot face-to-face. Whoever killed him meant to do it."

"Do you want our statement?" Susan asked.

"Yes. Let's sit in the squad car so we'll be warm while I write it out. The ambulance ought to be here soon. After you called me I called them." She opened the door to her car as Harry opened the door to the truck, lifting the corgis to get them in faster.

"*What's going on?*" Pewter insisted.

"*Why should I tell you?*" Tucker turned her head away from Pewter.

Harry closed the door as the two started to argue. Once in the warm car both women told what they knew.

"What made you notice the body?" Cooper asked Susan.

"I thought there was something in the ditch. When we got closer I saw it was a body."

As there wasn't much to tell, Cooper checked the clock in the car, wrote down the time. "You all can go on. Might as well get out before you're stuck here. I'll call you if I need you."

Harry backed out, then drove around the squad car. "Sometimes I think violence is what people do best."

Susan sighed. "I hope not. Who's to say? A lover's quarrel? An infuriated spouse? Maybe he owed money? You never know but there's always a reason."

She was one hundred percent right.

4

Tuesday

Midday, the sun beat down. Thanks to a six-mile-per-hour breeze, the heat was endurable. If one sat under a shade tree it was even pleasant.

Catherine Schuyler and Jeddie Rice, her nineteen-year-old slave and a young, gifted rider, sat on two stools under a large chestnut.

"If we start before the heat comes up I think we can finish the course by tomorrow."

"Hope so," the slender young man replied.

"We'll have time to review our work. I've set the date for September 12." She looked toward the west, the Blue Ridge Mountains thirteen miles away covered in lush summer foliage. "Here comes my father."

Ewing waved as he approached.

Jeddie rose. "Please take my seat."

Ewing Garth studied the low stool, decided standing would be easier than descending to that level. In his mid-fifties he was enter-taining more aches and pains than he would wish.

"You stay put. I'll enjoy standing under the shade. I do find the chestnut tree one of the most impressive." He added, "Daughter, our apple orchard should have its first harvest this fall. To date, the weather has been beneficial."

"It has. We're finishing the course."

"It's such an interesting idea, my dear. Then again, if the Irish can do it, so can we." He grinned.

She grinned back. "Well, I think we will be close but no one ex-actly knows what they have been doing. Running from steeple to steeple, leaping obstacles in between, so we'll do better. We've built some jumps, as we don't have their fencing or brush fences, so we've made our own. We should make a bit of money, Father. I still don't know what to charge for an entry fee. Then again, people will bring horses to sell."

"Mmm. It is tempting to ask for a wee bit of the sale's profit, but you know, I think it better to create good feeling. It always comes back to you in the end."

"Can I get you anything?"

"No, thanks. I just walked down here to get fresh air. Sometimes the library is stifling. I'm feeling hopeful. I do think Hamilton's program of assuming the states' war debts will bring foreign invest-ment to our country. The bonds are tempting, I would think, low interest. Potential large profit. We need investments, if for nothing else to build roads and bridges; we need to get our timber, hemp, tobacco, apples to the markets and the biggest markets in England. France . . . well, perhaps France will return in time. Here I am, dot-ing on."

"Father, you have broad vision," she complimented him, having learned a great deal working with her father, which she discreetly kept to herself in public.

Catherine, apart from her astonishing beauty, had inherited her father's business brain. When her mother died ten years ago, she was in her early teens but she vividly remembered the two of them working in the wood-paneled office. Isabelle never mentioned her knowledge or assistance to her husband. She worked in the shadows. Once Catherine was old enough to do the same, her teaching by tutors over, she took over that function, astonishing her father with how quickly she grasped fundamentals. How she could think of ways to create profit. Even though many were fanciful when she was young, his older daughter showed great promise. She, too, worked in the shadows. People noticed her beauty, of course, and her natural horsemanship. In some ways the horses proved a good cover.

Rachel, younger by two years, lovely to look at, sweeter, was certainly intelligent but not driven. She married a prisoner-of-war, Captain Charles West, who had been in the POW camp, that land now owned by Ewing. They always referred to it as The Barracks, many of the haphazard log structures giving way to the elements.

Both sisters married for love. They were successful, happy marriages. Rachel had two children. One her own, one presented as a cousin but really the child of a beautiful slave who fled a neighboring estate, Big Rawly, dying while being hidden at Cloverfields. She had been beaten so severely, she lost an eye. She forced herself to live despite her injuries until she could give birth. The child, Marcia, looked white. Rachel passed her off as a cousin's child, hinting that the infant was born out of wedlock. That was all people needed. It was gossip so juicy they never suspected the truth. That was three years ago; little Marcia had inherited her mother's refined features, even her smooth way of walking, small though she was.

"I'm going down to your sister's. I promised to take a walk with her, that fat little dog, her two children, and your son, who is growing like a weed."

"He is. They love being with you. John imitates everything you do."

Ewing beamed. "I think he imitates his father, but perhaps I have some small influence."

"A large influence. Actually, you do better with my son than I do. I'm not sure I understand him."

"Well, boys can be more trying perhaps. I don't know, but I do know that unbridled energy gets them in trouble." He turned to view the mountains. "What a fine day." Then he took a breath, swung his elegant walking stick, and bid them goodbye.

"Father looks down the road. I wonder if we will create goodwill. I think that's the term. I hope so but some people are perfidious. They take. Don't give back. What about you?"

"I stick to horses." Jeddie laughed.

"Smart." She laughed back.

"I wonder if Mrs. Selisse will have a horse in the race? DoRe and Barker O say she's concentrating on driving horses because of her husband's coach-building business." She'd mentioned two men well known for their driving abilities.

"I can't get used to calling her Mrs. Holloway, either. Guess she'll always be Mrs. Selisse except to her face. Who knows what she's about? I know Father and Yancy Grant," she named a close friend of her father's, "are waiting to see if she moves some of her money from Italy to here. She took it out of France. She was educated in France and has aristocratic connections thanks to that and her great wealth. That's when my father figured out we would not get paid for the last tobacco shipment to Paris. We'll manage, but Jeddie, sometimes things come down like a bolt from the blue."

"I do know that."

He did, too, having had his arm and shoulder damaged during a flat race over a year ago when his rival bumped him at top speed then yanked him off his horse. The rival, William, Maureen's slave, fled the state, was free for a time. Foolishly, he came back to steal a pretty girl, Sulli, from Big Rawly and to woo her to steal jewelry. Both were caught in Maryland, returned to Maureen Holloway, and are now living hellish lives.

She stood up. "Let's check Sweet Potato. It will soon be time to find another pony for Marcia. She's big enough to be led around on a lead line."

"Do you think we'll ever be able to bring in horses from England?"

"If business improves, I do. It's always good to find new blood but we have fine blooded horses here now. Takes time and travel to see them. We know the good horses here and in Maryland. I don't want to breed to a mare unless I see her first." She headed for the riding-horse stable, which had two cupolas on the top and a large weathervane, a trotting horse on the spine of the roof.

"We'll learn a lot from our steeplechase," Jeddie said with conviction.

"I hope so."

"Miss Catherine, you will have the best horses in the colony, I mean Virginia. No one knows as much as you do."

"That's very kind. If you don't want to be the best, what's the point?"

5

Afternoon

"Look underneath." Jeffrey Holloway knelt down to peer underneath a work wagon just built. "Look at the axles."

John Schuyler, Catherine's husband, knelt down. "Heavy. Be hard to break." He stood back up. "Our roads are so bad, wheels break and so do axles."

Jeffrey, also standing now, nodded toward one of his men, Caleb. "They have all learned and in the beginning it was the hard way. Once I got my hands on that Studebaker wagon from Pennsylvania, I could study how it was rightly done. We've mastered it."

"I can see that." John smiled at the workers, both white and black; all men, as it was heavy work.

It was also hot, as the small forge was near the wagon shop. All doors open. The huge carriage shop rested perhaps twenty yards away and was much fancier, as all of those customers were rich. Some of the wagon ones were, too, but Jeffrey wisely built for those with funds and those bumping along hoping to make more money.

He'd started life as a cabinetmaker, learning from his father to do hard work, and learning how people buy things.

"You've been traveling." Jeffrey smiled. "You know the condition of the roads in Virginia better than I do."

John grimaced. "Can make every bone in your body ache. It's good to see you, Jeffrey. I have been traveling so much. Being back is a joy."

"How are the Missus and your son?"

John smiled. "My wife, my angel. JohnJohn is growing. He tries to read. He opens a book and makes sounds."

"You are fortunate. As you know, my wife and I can't have children. It troubles her more than me. Big Rawly has children racing about. One sees them develop. And the little blind child in the upper cabin, she tugs at my heart. Sulli, you remember Sulli, is in charge of her."

"Well, good for them both, I would think." John did not mention that Sulli, having run away with William, then was caught and returned, would have been miserable in the house with Maureen.

"Would you like a drink? A cold soup? My manners are a bit shaky," Jeffrey apologized.

"No, thank you. I'm here to ask for your help."

"Come, let's sit outside on the bench." Jeffrey led John, almost half a head taller than himself, to a clever bench built around a pin oak trunk.

The trunk had room to grow but one could lean against it if needed. Jeffrey directed all outside building, cleaning, laying brick walkways, leaving the inside of the house to his wife, who changed the arrangement of the furniture monthly, or so it seemed to him.

"Big Rawly is a hive of activity. I admire your ability to keep everything running." John meant that.

"Ah, well, thank you. I like to work and I know that when I married the widow Selisse . . . still called that sometimes, I'm sure." He paused. "I knew people thought she married beneath her. A cabinetmaker. I am not an educated man."

John quickly replied, "Neither am I."

"We have much in common, John. I always feel I can speak freely to you. However, I am not a war hero and you are. I have heard General Washington . . . forgive me, President Washington . . . has asked you to be in charge of the militia in our state, of modernizing it. Our standing army is tiny. Shall I assume our president wants to make sure if we should again be invaded we will be ready?"

"Yes. The British underestimated us, plus they didn't know how to fight on our territory. An infantry square is only useful if the ground favors it."

"I was a bit too young. I wanted to go but my father forbade it. Then again, I don't know as I would have been much of a soldier."

"Ah, there you are wrong. With your abilities, you could have built temporary bridges, repaired wagons. You can do things with your hands. Well, let us hope you are never tested. But we can't believe we will not be pushed now and then."

"How so?"

"The Ohio territory. The English made alliances with our Indian enemies and remember the Indians were drawn into the French War with England. We can't truly settle in the west until we have forces that can defend against raids and foreign powers."

"Do you think the British will be back?"

"I pray to God, no. But what of Spain, Jeffrey, or France? If any of those powers had a large land holding, say on the other side of the Ohio River, we would be imperiled. Not only can we not let our guard down, we also have to build a true army and a navy. Congress will blather. Getting anything resolved in Congress is something I will never understand. I don't have the temperament for it."

"Neither do I. On the other hand, my wife keeps current. Being raised in the Caribbean, educated in France, her net is wide. She believes our trade with England will again be strong and profitable. She is far more educated than I and having a father who was a banker for Spain in the Caribbean, she met everybody, watched money being made and money being moved. All those ships from Spain, France, Portugal, England stopped at their port. All those lavish parties and fetes. I marvel at her abilities."

"I think many do. My father-in-law has always mentioned her financial skills. Well, she understood what you wished to do."

"She did. I bless the Lord every day that I make a profit. I would be humiliated if I did not make money. I know people think I married Maureen for her money." He paused again. "As I said, John, I can talk to you. But I did not. When I attended Francisco's funeral, I fell in love with her. I don't know why. She is a woman whom many men admire, want to hold. I know that. But I don't think I had ever felt that way just by looking at a woman."

John laughed. "Jeffrey, when I first saw Catherine, I couldn't breathe. I couldn't talk. I came here on a mission from General Lafayette to speak to the commandant of the prisoner-of-war camp. It was fate that I was directed to Cloverfields. And you know, I still sometimes can't breathe when I look at her."

They sat in silence; finally, John slapped Jeffrey on the knee. Jeffrey laughed. "Perhaps we aren't the most logical of men." John smiled, changing the subject.

"I am here to ask for your help. We need forges. Large forges. We need to build wagons, caissons to move artillery, sturdy coaches to move people if we need to do so. Most of our officers rode and a few even walked but sometimes I think we need strong carriages and wagons. Just in case. If for nothing else, to move the wounded."

"Yes."

"I am hoping you will build such a forge and allow me to send you our engineers to work with you. We have good men making a pittance, Jeffrey. You know a great deal. You can get along with anyone. It will be costly. Will you consider it?"

"I would be honored. Allow me time to ask my wife. She may want this at the edge of the property. I would like to meet with your military people before I embark on this."

"Of course."

Jeffrey replied, "The cost of funding an army and a navy will be high."

"Yes, but I swear to you, Jeffrey, if we don't have armed forces, we will be bedeviled sooner or later. Sometimes I think all the world knows is war."

"I am afraid you're right."

As Jeffrey spoke, Olivia, the older slave in charge of the log building on the hill, housing those born with some affliction, walked by with Sulli, carrying the blind child.

"My wife, who can be strict about her servants, is kind to those who are missing a limb or can't hear. She is a complex woman." Jeffrey stopped himself. "Perhaps all women are complex."

"I don't know. Sometimes Catherine comes out with something I had no idea she was thinking about. She has insights I do not." His eyes followed Sulli and Olivia. "Will the blind child learn a craft? I have seen blind people build chairs, weave, things you wouldn't think they could do."

Sulli put the little girl down while holding her arms above her head, slowly walking her a bit. Tiny steps. Sophia screamed in delight.

"I'm sure she will master something. Sulli is devoted to the little thing. People find one another, do they not?"

John smiled. "One hopes so."

Caleb walked down to the tree. "Excuse me, Master. What color did Percy Ballard wish his wagon to be?"

"Caleb, I've asked you to not call me Master."

"Oh, if I do not, your Missus will have my hide."

Jeffrey knew that to be true. "All right. The color. He wanted dark green."

"Thank you." Caleb left.

"Percy Ballard. My comrade?" John was surprised.

"He sent his aide-de-camp, you know the fellow who runs the farm, to me with specifications. A new set of people will see the work we do here. Maybe even Mr. Madison. Percy is not all that far from Montpelier. What, twenty miles?"

"A long day's ride, but you are right, Percy moves in exalted circles. I think he harbors political ambitions, but while I am in charge of raising and training this militia, he is my aide-de-camp. He, thanks to his connections, is raising the money. He has tried to call on Governor Randolph, who eludes him. Percy thinks the governor fears we will ask to raise money through a tax. You know the Randolphs and Washington are a bit strained now."

"My wife keeps up with this. Edmund Randolph is our attorney general. I think he supports Washington. Beverly Randolph, our governor, feels that Washington is too much under the influence of Hamilton. He believes the states have a right to tax and the federal government does only for a few specific things. That's the problem with this whiskey tax. It's over my head."

"Mine, too, but one way or the other, Percy will get money. He's gotten muskets pledged. We've both called upon old brothers-in-arms. I mean to get this done."

"And so you shall, John. I will build that forge, one way or the other."

After a bit more pleasant chat, for the two men did get along, John mounted Miss Renata, the 17 hand horse his wife had found for him, and rode back to Cloverfields, perhaps four miles, if that. Along the way he listened to the birds, busy, especially the bug catchers, and wondered what Jeffrey would need to do to bring his wife around to the idea of a large forge. He decided not to think about it.

6

November 19, 2021

Friday

"Not that again." Susan took off her fleece-lined winter jacket, hanging it on one of the shaker pegs inside the kitchen door.

"Well, I have to free my American Express card." Harry chipped at the inside of the plastic frozen pitcher, which she positioned in the sink.

"You do this every year. Stop freezing your credit cards. We all overspend for Christmas. Why should you be any different?"

Harry stopped for a moment, removing her heavy gloves, which she wore so she wouldn't cut her hands. "Look, if I think I have a lot to spend, I will. I have a good credit rating and the cards entice you to max out, you know. Anyway, I didn't ask you here for a lecture."

Susan dropped onto a kitchen chair as the two dogs and two cats, lounging in their plush beds, opened their eyes. "All right. What do you want?"

"I need you to help me get a new set of golf clubs for Fair. Thanks to you he got hooked this summer."

"Blame it on me," Susan shot back but with humor.

"You've been club champion for three years now. Three years. And how many times were you runner-up before that? So playing with you, he watched, listened, and you flattered him. Now he thinks he can play golf. And I didn't help matters by caddying for my husband, who didn't know one club from another."

"As I recall, every time you caddied for me, I won. You really are good, so don't put the whole blame on me."

"Got it!" Harry delicately wiggled out the frozen but free American Express card. She put the pitcher back in the freezer and sat down at the table, flipped the card in the center, then rose again. "Need coffee, tea? Have a special kind of Assam tea thanks to Sara Bateman." She named a friend living outside of Richmond.

"Let me try the tea." Susan picked up the card then dropped it.

It really was cold on her bare fingers.

Filling the teapot, setting it on the burner, Harry hummed to herself as she selected two heavy mugs. Each one had a special meaning. Had you asked her, she would swear she was not superstitious. She leaned against the counter until the pot whistled, having already measured out the delicious tea in two mesh tea balls, which she hung inside the mugs. Susan's mug, an ochre color with flowers painted on it, was from Provence. The mug Harry selected was white with a checkerboard pattern under the lip. That was from England. She thought checkerboard patterns lucky.

Pewter perked up hearing the cups placed on the old table. *"Maybe she's going to eat."*

Mrs. Murphy stretched out one paw. *"Not time for lunch."*

"That doesn't mean she can't put out cookies and then those little fishies for us. I could ask."

"I wouldn't do it."

"You're not me." The gray cat stretched, stepped out of her circle bed

filled with something close to the fleece lining in Susan's jacket. She sashayed to sit by Harry. *"A cookie would be nice."*

Harry looked down at the luminous green eyes so contrasting to Pewter's gray fur. "Beggar. All right. A fishie."

Harry got up, pulled open the treat drawer and gave fishies to both cats, walking over to Mrs. Murphy. Then she put that back, pulled out two bacon strips, fake but delicious, tossing one to Tucker and the other to Pirate.

"You spoil those animals."

"Susan, I have watched you spoil your husband, your two now grown children, and Owen, my wonderful Tucker's brother. Don't give me the lecture about spoiling."

"Okay. We're both pushovers. Back to golf."

"You've seen his clubs."

"I have. They are old, but no need for anything too fancy when starting out. Also, he is so tall and powerful. Took a bunch of us at the club to find those old used ones for him."

"He was so grateful and so was I. How do you outfit a six four man who can pick up three hundred pounds over his head if he has to do so? And no fat. He looks the same as when we were all in high school."

Susan batted her eyes. "So do I."

Both women laughed.

"Well, okay. We all have a wrinkle here and there, a little gray, but Susan, we do look pretty good. I think it's because we do what we want. We are active. You are obsessed with your gardens and your golf. We aren't sitting on our nether regions, as my grandmother used to say. So how do I get clubs? And will they improve his game?"

"That's the sixty-four-dollar question. So many people think that the latest technology is the answer. The answer is developing your strokes until they're second nature. Will great equipment help? Only if you practice. When I was a kid my father took me to the golf course, had two clubs made for me, I was maybe eight. He handed me a seven iron and a putter. He told me to use those first. And I did.

I played . . . as best I could, but he did get me lessons . . . with those two clubs until I was nine. Then he added a wedge so I could learn to get out of sand. I didn't have a driver until I was eleven. Daddy was with me every step of the way." Her voice was warm with memory and love.

"Isn't there proof or some kind of studies that fathers determine girls' success? Mothers do the same for sons."

Susan took a sip, perfect temperature. "Think I've read something way back when or heard it, but I do think a father helps a daughter. He doesn't know exactly what she's up against but he wants her to go to the top. I think it's through their daughters that men learn about sexism. Just a thought. On the other hand our mothers don't want us to rock the boat. They know the price that can be paid. It's better now, and I can't say that I have been trammeled and trod upon. I sure have listened to a lot of mansplaining though." She burst out laughing.

"God, haven't we all?" Harry laughed with her. "Fortunately neither of our husbands go that route."

"Well, they don't want to walk around black and blue." Susan laughed again then switched the subject. "This really is good tea."

"Sara likes tea as much as I do. Okay, back to clubs. What do I do and how much will this cost?"

"The truth? A great set of clubs fitted to you personally can cost thousands. But if Fair does what the fitter asks, he will get what he needs. By that I mean you don't go in and try to swing like a pro. You need to warm up then go to the fitter and swing your normal swing. He or she will fit you according to your physical dynamic, for lack of a better word. And that will help you improve. A few years down the road you can adjust your clubs for your improved swing. That and take lessons. Golf is notoriously difficult."

"Like hunt seat in riding. Looks easy. Takes years to master. I still struggle when I'm out on one of the horses to keep my weight over the center of gravity. Fortunately my horses are saints."

"You have always had good horses."

"*Oh, they are big dumbbells.*" Pewter wanted another handful of tiny fishies.

"*No, they aren't,*" Tucker called from her bed, which had four raised sides, whereas the cat beds had sides but they weren't as stiff.

"*What do you know?*" Pewter swept her whiskers forward.

"I hear grumbles." Harry put her cup down, got up, and tossed out two more bacon sizzle strips and poured two handfuls of those fishies just outside the cat beds. "They love this stuff."

"Owen loves the bacon sizzles. Okay, how about we take Fair's clubs to the club? You and I can talk to the pro, and the fitter. Then bring the clubs back until you're ready to tell him."

"Maybe I could buy one club, even if it isn't right, to put under the Christmas tree."

"Not a bad idea. And seeing what he is using now will help Deke," she named the pro, "pick something that might be useful. Ready?" Harry walked down the hall, lugged out her husband's golf bag while Susan put on her coat then grabbed Harry's goose-down jacket, which was quite thin. Worked. Kept her warm.

The two dogs and cats followed the friends outside. Clicking the button, the rear hatch of Susan's Audi station wagon opened. Harry lifted the clubs in. The animals climbed into the back seat. Tucker needed a bit of help. Susan had a heavy seat cover for her dog, whom she had left home, not anticipating driving anywhere.

"Getting so cold." Susan turned on the motor and pressed the button for heated seats. "Let me warm this up a little."

"You've gotten your money out of this wagon."

"I have. The next vehicle I buy, though, will have a heated steering wheel."

"I never put much store in stuff like that, but the Ram has one and I am now dependent on it," Harry confessed. "That and the rear-view picture when you back up. How did we live without it?"

"Don't know, but all these improvements jack up the cost. I am pushing 150,000 miles on this thing but I can't afford a new car now. The prices have skyrocketed."

"Yeah. It's crazy." Harry enjoyed being in the passenger seat so she could see. "Did Ned say anything about those men without IDs?"

Susan, now going down the long gravel drive, shook her head. "He felt terrible that we found a dead man in a ditch. I called him in Richmond and asked if he could see what the status or number of undocumented workers might be. As our delegate he can get information quickly. Anyway, we talked today; he'll be home tomorrow, but he said there is no way to accurately find that number. He did say there are 710,000 green cards currently issued in America. Whoever hires one of these men, and some women, has to do all the paperwork, pay the fees, as it is the only way to get into our country legally. It's easier and cheaper to hire workers off the books. It takes seven to thirty-three months, usually, to get a green card."

Harry really had never thought about this issue. "I mean, in the summers you see all those workers in the orchards, on ladders, or walking along the rows of grapevines held up by wire. It is wire, right?"

"Yeah, but it also depends on the age of the vine. And let us not forget the horse industry. Migrant laborers."

"So Susan, the advantage of undocumented workers is you don't pay any of those costs. No finding a lawyer or a service for this issue. There have to be people who make a career out of getting workers into our country."

"There are. But the trick is hiding them. And if you are discovered, you wind up in court."

"I would think. If the employer got caught, the legal bills alone would be punishing enough. Your name in the paper. Nothing like our Immigration Service to spread fear and dread. I think Sheriff Shaw will have anyone who asks if a missing man has been reported brought in and questioned."

"You'd think." Susan nodded.

"No one will do that," Harry correctly said. "None. That man had not a scrap of ID on him. No cellphone."

"And he'll eventually be put in a pauper's grave. That gets me. I really believe everyone should have a burial service. It's only respectful."

"Susan, lots of people don't think that way anymore. I mean, there are people who will spend and leave behind millions so they can be frozen at death, to be thawed out later when whatever killed them can be medically cured or fixed or whatever. It's ghoulish."

"I don't know. There is an element of curiosity to it. I mean, to come back. Sort of like Rip Van Winkle. How would you find the world?"

"Rip Van Winkle fell asleep. These people will be brought back from the dead." Harry sounded final. "Creeps me out."

"If you go first, I promise not to freeze you." Susan sounded so understanding.

"How do you know you won't go first?"

"You can freeze me. I won't know the difference." Susan laughed.

"Has it ever occurred to you that in the times in which we live, it's un-American to die?"

"That's a thought." Susan pulled into the big parking lot.

"Well, let's hope no more deaths." Harry was resolute.

It was a vain hope.

7

Tuesday

Harry read from the handwritten menu, "Grilled young squab with seared fois gras nesting on rhubarb compote." She waited while the waiter wrote this down. "No wine for me, thank you."

Susan next ordered. "Prosciutto wrapped tenderloin of veal with orange-glazed sweetbreads, morels, and raclette ravioli." She paused. "Masseri Li Veli."

As their husbands ordered, and their friends Joel Paloma and Ballard Perez, the two looked around the simple room, a huge fireplace at one end.

"Well, ladies," Joel smiled, "how do you like it?"

"It is lovely. I wish Jodie could be here." Susan mentioned his wife.

"Me, too, but she couldn't miss her William and Mary Alumnae meeting. Those girls are dedicated." He looked happy when his wine was set before him. Li Veli Askos Susumaniello, reasonably priced.

Ballard . . . an old friend, whereas Joel was newer . . . groaned. "The thought of a reunion, any reunion, strikes terror in my heart."

They sipped their drinks. Harry joked, "If I had your party record in college, I'd be terrified, too."

They all laughed, as Ballard had been a hell-raiser.

This was the third gathering of their restaurant group, which met erratically. They'd decided to visit the best restaurants in Virginia, the grand finale to be the Inn at Little Washington. They currently were in a highly recommended establishment in Fredericksburg. As Joel had a business supplying frozen foods, vegetables, and fruits, he said he wanted to dine at restaurants he supplied, as he meant to check them out, but time being what it was, too much to do, too little time, he rarely went out of town. He would be a customer. Gives a different viewpoint.

Harry evidenced no great interest in cuisine, but Fair, like many men, loved to eat. So when Joel suggested a group to sample some of the best of Virginia, Harry readily agreed.

Ballard, no stranger to the finer things in life, readily agreed as well.

"How's business?" Joel held up his glass after they all sipped to the first toast, which was "To our health."

"Our black walnut grove is spectacular and this was the best year yet for my Italian sunflowers," Harry chipped in.

He listened with interest. To Joel's credit, he knew agriculture was Virginia's biggest moneymaker.

"Don't forget to tell him about your ginseng." Susan was proud of Harry's hard work, a trait she recognized early in their childhood together.

"Oh." Harry smiled. "Did okay. You know, Joel, you have to guard it, as it is so easy to steal. I have my Irish wolfhound, as do you. They scare the bejesus out of everyone."

Ballard added, "I've thought about ginseng, but don't have enough help."

Harry said, "It's not difficult, except you need to have moist soil. Pretty easy, really."

Joel savored the wine. "If there's money to be made, people will steal: ginseng, the copper off your roof, your car."

"They'll steal horses, too," Fair joined in.

"Do you really like being our representative?" Joel asked Ned. "Theft made me think of legislation to reduce crime."

"Most days, I do. So much of the polarization is for show. Cheap theatrics. Thank God not everyone behaves that way, but we have our media whores." He winced. "Sorry."

"Oh, don't be, honey." Susan beamed at him. "The difference between a political whore and a true whore is the latter provides a needed service. The former emits clouds of hot air."

Ballard raised his eyebrows in jest. "Susan, you shock me."

"Young people aren't attracted to long hours. We see that even at the state house," Ned added. "The workload is overwhelming. Some of it spurred on by the ease of email. Everyone has a complaint."

Joel took a long sip of his Russolo Refosco. "How have I missed this wine?"

Susan said, "I'm not sure Americans are as educated about Italian wines as, say, French."

"With all the vintners now in Virginia, that's changing." Ballard then said, "We still have a lot to learn."

Harry, loving agriculture, including vinery, jumped in. "Argentina, South Africa, there is so much to learn. German wines. I know nothing really but the duration of many of the Old World vineyards fascinates me. Or the newer ones, like ourselves or South Africa."

"Now, there's big business." Joel held up his glass again. "For over two thousand years. I remember when Jodie and I sailed on the Rhine, we looked at vineyards carved into the high banks in places. The Romans did that work."

Ned nodded. "It's hard to remember how young we are. We can be deluded by our technology."

"Young, yes, but don't you think we learned from history?" Harry enjoyed discussions with her friends.

"Up to a point," Susan chimed in. "You and I went to the same schools until college. Public schools, but we did get a good education. Good history teachers and good civics classes."

"Gone now." Joel waved his hand.

"My Lord, they don't even teach cursive writing," Ballard huffed. "How stupid is that, or lazy?"

"Sure seems like it." Fair smiled when their entrees came.

"Try to teach history and someone will sue you. It's crazy." Ned waited for everyone to be served. "Doesn't matter where you are or what exactly you are focusing on. Someone will go after you. If you don't know where you came from, you don't know where you're going."

Joel inclined his head. *"Bon appétite."*

"Who is the head of the table?" Harry asked. "I think at each meeting we should appoint one of us as the head of the table. That way we know when to start eating."

"You have a point." Ballard picked up his fork. "You know, my mother, who was within her rights to head the table once Dad died, always asked a man to do it at her big dinners. A different time."

"We can draw straws," Joel teased.

"Sounds fair," Harry teased back. "Anyways, just saying if we are to be well mannered, there has to be a head of the table." She paused. "Male, female, in-between."

"All right, honey. I'll bring straws next time." Fair grinned.

They consumed their food, marveling at how interesting, original, the entrees were. Being a chef for a high-end establishment pushed one to creativity.

Fair returned to the original subject. "Joel, how is your business?"

"Fortunately, even terrific restaurants like this one still need some frozen foods, depending on the season. Small markets, too. Business is steady. And I can get some fresh foods flown in weekly. Brazil, some of Latin and Central America, grow succulent fruits and vegetables."

"Think COVID will affect you?" Harry wondered.

"Who would know better than Ned?" Joel responded. "It can hit my restaurant customers but I think the small markets will be okay."

"I can tell you what our state government will do, but I can't predict how long this will infect and affect people. My hope is cases have dropped because of the cold and the masking. If they spike again in the spring, it will be the same fights all over again." Ned grimaced. "People are using this to advance their political careers. In my job I realize the old saying 'Never let a crisis go to waste' is depressingly true."

"I'm afraid of that, too," Harry agreed. "We live out in the country. We're pretty safe but you have to see more people every day than we do. It only takes one. Then others declare how they became infected. The great game of faultfinding drags everyone in."

"Does," Joel agreed. "But some people have COVID and don't know it. I think we have to approach herd immunity."

Ned half laughed. "Those are fighting words."

"Yeah, I've read the speeches or seen them on television regarding our state house." Fair finished his fabulous meal.

"When you politicize a disease, nobody wins." Ned meant this. "And why is everyone stirring the pot? So their face will be on the media. This is really about getting reelected, not helping the citizens of Virginia. Thank God, I have some sensible colleagues, but with some of them, their IQ would make a good golf score."

This brought everyone's eyebrows up and at that moment the waiter swooped in to remove their dishes.

"We can return to this later. Dessert is more important." Susan had no patience left to discuss COVID. She ordered mousse Napoleon. The others stuck to various sorbets, except Harry.

The wood in the fireplace gave off a pleasant smell. Winter brought its own delights, the odors, the darker colors, and heavier fabrics, drawing close to others.

The small group drank a digestif. Fair had a weakness for Fernet-

Branca while Joel downed Chartreuse. Ballard joined him. The ladies passed.

Susan, feeling stuffed, leaned back in her chair. "How was your
dessert?"

Harry replied, "Unusual, they glazed sweetbreads. Somehow it
was really good paired with the crème brûlée. Who would have
thought it?"

Harry looked toward the back of the restaurant as the door to the
kitchen opened. Some of the workers in the kitchen looked stressed
to her.

She asked the others, "Are there a lot of people from below the
border working in restaurants? The kitchen has people in there that,
well, look Hispanic."

"It could be. Sometimes people who come here for work find
jobs in kitchens." Ned filled her in. "But they really don't look alike,
Harry."

"I suppose you're right, I'm lumping everyone together." Harry
paused. "I never really thought about it but now that I do, I think we
treat them badly, lumping everyone together. I know I have, and I'm
wrong to do it."

Ned smiled at her. "Right now there is super sensitivity to these
issues and rightly so. Are the Venezuelans different from North
Americans? It's a different culture, but we are all New World people.
So many people are desperately trying to get into our country, as
their economies have collapsed, violence in the streets."

Joel interrupted. "You don't have to go to Guatemala or Venezuela
for that. We have it here."

"Yeah, we do," Fair ruefully acknowledged as Ballard nodded in
agreement.

They openly talked about this, low voices, and the fact that they
were friends helped them introduce ideas or thoughts perhaps a
person not much inclined to working outside their own field might
not consider.

The Haristeens and Tuckers drove home in Ned's car, chatting the whole way.

"Did I put my foot in it in the restaurant?" Harry asked.

"Not with us," Ned said soothingly. "And there are people off the grid, so to speak."

"I am still upset by finding the man who was shot," Harry confessed. "We've all seen unpleasant things in our life. I'm not in need of counseling." She said that with an edge. "But here is a man, killed. No ID. And he looked foreign to me. Are these people risking their lives to come here?"

"That's hard to say, honey." Her husband held her hand. "Could he have traveled here illegally? Sure. Could the men running out of the wrecked van be here illegally? Also a possibility. But we don't know for sure. And that still wouldn't explain why he was killed. We'll probably never know."

"I suppose." Harry sounded unconvinced.

"Life does not go according to plan," Susan wisely said.

8

Monday

Unshucked peas rolled over the green grass. Bettina, the cook, had fallen asleep in the midday heat as she sat in a chair at the back of the house. A full bowl of peas rested in her lap, but slid to the ground as she nodded off.

Roger, the butler, had also fallen asleep, only in the front hallway. All the doors and windows of Cloverfields, wide open, allowed a hint of westerly breeze into the house.

Virginia summers tried the patience of all the giving saints. The only reason Ewing wasn't asleep is he walked outside to receive a letter, paid the postman, then looked down toward the stables. He could make out Catherine standing in the aisle. The letter was from Baron Jacques Necker in Paris. He held it and walked down to the stable, where huge trees offered shade. Usually Ewing wore a jacket even on a hot day but today he did not. A cotton scarf tied around his neck helped catch the sweat.

"Daughter." He waved the envelope. She looked up from a bit in her hands, which she was rubbing to see if she could feel any pitting.

"Father. Come sit in the aisle. The breezes float through. It's cooling. Jeddie, pull up the old chair in the tack room for my father."

"Yes, Miss Catherine."

"Thank you." Ewing dropped into the old but still serviceable chair.

He had gained weight but not terribly much. Still, he felt it; twenty pounds perhaps. It irritated him but when one has a cook as good as Bettina, not eating her latest creations took more discipline than he evidenced. He started to put his thumbnail under the flap.

"Wait." Catherine again called to Jeddie in the tack room, cleaning stirrup leathers. "Bring me my little penknife. It's on the shelf, I think."

A minute later, Jeddie handed her the small knife used to slit pages in new books, open envelopes, as well as cut small pieces of thin leather.

"Here, Father."

"Ah, yes." He cautiously cut the envelope flap and side.

It had been closed with great care, sealed with a large wax daub, Necker's coat of arms imprinted in it. No mistaking who sent it.

"Do you have your glasses?" Catherine asked her father.

He looked stricken. "No. Sometimes I think I would forget my head were it not attached."

She smiled, reached for the letter. "He has written in English."

Ewing smiled. "I wrote him in French. From time to time we test each other. Jacques is far better at languages than I."

Catherine began to read, her alto voice soothing to the ear. Jeddie edged closer to the open tack-room door, as he wanted to hear, too.

"Mr. Dearest Ewing, friend of my youth, I write to you under extraordinary circumstances."

Ewing immediately sat up straighter. Catherine continued, "On July 11 of this year, my gracious king dismissed me, egged on by those most conservative elements at the court. My ideas about representative taxation, curtailing the centuries-old privileges of the First and Second Estates, were met with unremitting hostility. They convinced the king that I was too sympathetic to the Third Estate.

"When the people learned of this they marched on the Bastille on July 14. Thirty thousand pounds of gunpowder are stored in that grim building. To the people this is a symbol of the monarchy's tyranny. Nothing of this nature has ever happened in Paris before. The people are enraged.

"Although the king has at his disposal troops, should he have deployed them en mass during and after the storming of the Bastille, I truly believe the violence and anger would have greatly increased. As it was, the governor of the Bastille was stabbed and shot.

"A thousand Parisians marched on the Bastille. Ninety-eight people were killed. Seventy-three wounded. Many were captured, possibly over one hundred.

"Swiss mercenaries and regular soldiers, although invalids, no longer able to fight on the field, battled the furious people.

"Seven prisoners were released.

"My enemies lay the fault at my feet, telling the king my economic reform ideas emboldened the people. They will never take responsibility for their rigidity. I cannot believe this hatred on either side will dissipate.

"The confusion, no clarity other than the First Estate's greed is seconded only by the clergy's greed, might finally cause the king to perhaps reconsider events, even those in his own family. The Duc de Orleans is still presenting himself as a friend of the Third Estate. To an extent, dear Ewing, I am a friend of the Third Estate. Best I not write how I consider the duc's behavior. We must radically reform our taxation.

"How many letters have I written to you citing the crushing expense of the war from 1756 to 1763? The drain on our treasury was punishing and then our costs in financing your war at my urging was added to that. While I urged our assistance to you, I also urged a reforming of our taxes and hereditary privileges in my account, which I sent to you. The outrage at court was sulphureous. It never truly resolved but rather became as most things at court, hidden behind a veil of polite intrigue, rigid adherence to the old ways. How could I propose taxes anew under the burdens?

"Remember your Cicero? How he lamented the times changing? For us, the times must change. We teeter on bankruptcy. So I was dismissed.

"I do not have all the details or who worked in secret but the king recalled me to duty on July 20. The finances of France are again in my hands. My enemies can't kill me but they dream of ways to disgrace me. If I could not reduce the crown's expenditures in the past or reform the way royal finances are administered, I do not know if I can do so now. Except. Yes, except that perhaps the events of July 14 have shaken the First Estate as well as the king into realizing they must change, reforms must be enacted. The tax privileges from feudalism must go.

"I can advocate loans but who will risk them? England? Now, that would be a complete shock. Of course they won't. They will relish our financial crisis. Sometimes, I think this really started when we lost Quebec.

"You are once again receiving a letter from your friend who is the Director of Finance for France. I fear my efforts to reform French institutions will fail. The conservatives of both estates will work tirelessly behind my back to undermine me. The Third Estate will grow weary of waiting for an end to their crushing burdens. The king will hesitate and I fear all will be lost.

"My dear wife continues her Friday salon entertaining politicians, financial people, and those with crown posts, as well as France's writers. My darling has no fear nor does my daughter. Suzanne says she must go on as though all is well. My beloved Suzanne continues to encourage me. Germaine, at twenty-three, continues to delight her mother and I with her wit.

"I will write when I can and, as always, I eagerly await your letters. I send my fondest regards to you, your engaging daughters, and the grandchildren.

"We have lived through a great deal, have we not?

"With my deepest admiration,

"Jacques Necker."

Catherine rested the letter in her lap. "How extraordinary."

Ewing's face registered his concern. "Never forget he is a Protestant. The monasteries and the church will use that against him." He took a deep breath.

"The church in France must have a fortune greater than the crown, considering they have never paid taxes."

"Yes." Ewing sighed again. "It is a difficult question whether to tax churches. As they are responsible so often for the poor, the lost souls, the crown should not need to create institutions for those unfortunates. But over time the church has failed the people."

"Surely the crown sees this." Catherine found this cruel, ignoring suffering.

"What happens, it is so different there. Say a mistress of a king feels deeply for the suffering. She may create a convent for poor girls and fund it. Things like that help, but as it stands, this is not enough. I do know that Jacques feels if the First and Second Estates are taxed, more can be done for the poor and those cast out. The crop failures have been borne by the Third Estate. The brutal winter guaranteed hunger and death. There will be poor harvests this year. The state must offer relief."

"But no one wants to give up their privileges." Catherine looked at her father.

"Does anyone ever wish to do that? Think of the old families in Rome, the Julians, the Flavians, the others. Did they want to make way for new men? Remember, Cicero was a new man."

She nodded. "The way of the world."

"I believe it is." He half smiled at her.

"Do you think there will be more stormings, Father?"

"The king has troops. The people, nothing but sticks and rocks. I doubt much can be done. I do not envy my friend."

"We turned violent." Catherine stated the obvious.

"Well, that too had taxation as a provoking issue. But had King George made any effort to provide us with protection, assistance in building roads, maybe we would not have so resented those taxes. England took and gave back nothing. We weren't French peasants, my dear. We were Englishmen and expected to be treated as such. I don't think a peasant in France has the same attitude."

"But maybe they do now, Father."

He considered her point. "Well, perhaps. What I do know is we will not be selling any tobacco to France for some time." He threw up his hands. "Too many forces arrayed against my dear baron."

"I would imagine Baron Necker and our Alexander Hamilton would find a great deal to discuss." Catherine watched a barn swallow swoop low then go to its nest in the stable rafters.

"Indeed. One of our great advantages as a new country, a new way of governing, is we have no feudal past with its centuries of privilege to overcome."

"What I want to know," Catherine said with a gleam in her eye, "is does Maureen Selisse know any of this yet?"

"She must," Ewing responded. "She's probably moving more money around. Her money is now in Italy. Perhaps also in the Caribbean. Her father's old bank. She has a nose for where money travels and how to profit. My real concern is, what do our congressmen, our secretary of treasury as well as secretary of state know? And will these events create problems here? What if France and England go to war again? Will we not be called to the French, who helped us?"

"Let's hope it doesn't come to that, Father. With France bankrupt, how can they afford to pay their army and navy?"

It was that thought that struck Ewing. "I never thought of that. If men can't be paid, they won't fight." A long pause followed this. "Why should they protect the king?"

"I don't know, but I am glad it's far away." She paused. "On the other hand, Maureen is right here. She has a variety of ways to make trouble. If so, there will be dollar signs."

"I sometimes think, everything comes down to money. All other considerations are aroused so we won't watch where the money is going and who is profiting." He held up his hand. "Mind you, I am not averse to profit, but I truly believe there are things more important in life." He looked up to see JohnJohn being walked to the stables with John. "Like my grandson."

9

Friday

The target, pulled up to her, made Harry smile. She had two bullets in the bull's-eye and one in the next circle, three more in the one beyond that.

"Thanks. That will be it for the day." She carefully laid her pistol in its case. She'd clean it at home.

Seeing Harry finishing, Coop wrapped up, too. Harry was a good shot but Cooper was lethal. Being a law enforcement officer taught her she needed to keep in shape, keep her skills sharp. Much as she hoped she would not need to use her Glock, given the law of averages, someday she would.

The two walked to a table in a room off the shooting range, ordered a beverage.

"Wicked out there. Glad you suggested coming to the range." Harry reached into her pocket to pay for the drinks.

"No you don't."

"Coop. It's my turn. It's mine." Harry looked up at the young male waiter. "She's a bully, don't listen to her."

This provoked a laugh out of Cooper, who then said to the fellow, probably a college student, "Let her pay for the teas. How about two hamburgers, medium rare. She'll have Swiss cheese on hers, lettuce, of course, and I'll have American. Fries. Catsup on the side, and bring the mustard." She then waved a twenty-dollar bill in the air. "Here. We can settle up later before Dead-Eye Haristeen has a moment."

Laughing, for she adored Coop, Harry said, "Okay. You win."

They both glanced out the window. The snow was starting again, not heavy but the sky showed all the signs of snow picking up as the day wore on.

"It takes me time to adjust to winter, then I do." The tall woman held the warm cup in her hands. "But there is something soothing about the shooting range." She looked at Harry. "Take your earplugs out. Otherwise I'll have to shout."

"Oh." Harry took them out, dropping them in the shirt pocket of her heavy flannel shirt. "Damn things. I thought you and that fellow sounded funny. Yeah, I have to adjust, too. Foxhunting and beagling help but when the weather turns bitter or we get a lot of snow, they cancel. Too tough to drive, but I like moving about. I mean, I can go to the gym but it's not the same as being outside."

"Know what you mean. What I really like is going up to the Homestead to shoot skeet in good weather. If you bring a group you can order a picnic lunch. But I love to shoot skeet. My dad was good at it and so is Mom. There're good places close by. Flying Rabbit is good. The Homestead would be extra special." Cooper sighed.

"Country life." Harry smiled. "Our pleasures tend to be vigorous and outdoors. I know one stands still to shoot, but you have to be able to swing your arms up, hold the weight of the rifle, and some of these pistols can get heavy. It's good for my eyes, too."

"It is. Teaches you to concentrate. Focus on what's important."

She smiled as the food arrived. "Before I forget. Got a call from Sy Buford asking did we know who the shot man was?"

"Buford?"

"Yes. I was surprised, too. Anyway, I said nothing. We sent the body to the medical examiner just to be sure. Pretty simple. He was shot and that was it. Sy paused then asked could we describe him. I said we could send him a photo but I would describe him anyway. Medium height. Maybe mid-forties. Thick mustache. Receding hairline. Anyways, I sent the photo to his computer and waited for his reaction. It's amazing what you can do with computers. Sy said he didn't know him. So I asked why he was curious. He said he lost two workers, and workers with green cards, from his farm. They simply disappeared. He was concerned but wasn't sure whether to file a missing person's report. He did say the boys could go on a real bender from time to time."

"Maybe they decided to take an unscripted vacation."

"I don't know. What I do know is our government isn't welcoming people coming from south of the border. They are hired, and in time some bring their families or marry here, but they aren't accepted into the larger community."

"True." Harry slapped mustard on her burger. "Has to be hard for them to fit in. We must seem cold."

"Harry, we are cold." Cooper squeezed the fat hamburger sandwich and took a bite. "Mmm."

"Mine, too. Okay, I accept that we can seem cold, but there is the language barrier. And we aren't that close to the white laborers in our country, either. I mean, Coop, there is a class system not just in Virginia but in this country. People want to ignore it but it's there. The equality dream."

"One way to put it." Coop often thought of these things while cruising around in her squad car listening to whatever mayhem was transmitting. "It is a dream but I think we have gotten closer than many. I don't know. Maybe Australia, New Zealand are ahead. Haven't been there. But they have to be even more divided in France than we are. All those places that had counts and dukes. Different."

"Yeah. But it gave them stability. Better to be on top than on the bottom."

"True anywhere and in any century." The tall blonde finished her hamburger in record time.

"You were hungry." Harry was behind.

"Forgot to eat breakfast this morning."

"I never forget breakfast." Harry laughed. "Maybe if we went to Catholic church we would be closer to the people working on the big estates. Maybe they even have services in Spanish. I'll ask Reverend Jones." She named the pastor at St. Luke's Lutheran Church, her church since childhood.

"That reminds me, this spring I want to plant an Italian lilac by the gate of his family graveyard."

"He'll like that."

"I've been saving my money. I love that place. I want to buy it."

This stopped Harry for a moment. "That would be perfect. He's never coming back to the old home place. He'll die in the traces at the church. It is his life's calling, his joy."

"Reverend Jones has done a lot of good for a lot of people. Do you really think he would sell it?"

"Go talk to him. Can't hurt to ask."

"You're right."

"Just thinking. Did Sy say anything about seeing new faces at his big farm? People visiting his workers who live there."

"No. Maybe I should drop by and ask him a few questions. He runs a big operation. A lot of people."

"I don't think Sy would hire undocumented workers, but who knows. What do you do? Ask to see a green card? A work permit?"

"At the least, you would ask to see a driver's license," Coop said.

"What if the van Fair saw go off and hit a tree, then you came, what if those men worked for people who were not vintners, orchard people? Maybe they ran not because they were here illegally but because they were involved in an illegal business. What if they had the job of, say, stealing silver? Remember when there used to be those silver gangs? They'd come through every few years. Hit up the country clubs, rich in-town neighborhoods. Clean them out."

"It still goes on, but not as much. The silver they stole would get resold or melted down. The precious metals markets have changed. But I do remember." She leaned back in her chair. "You might be on a new track. Maybe they had another plan. Like selling illegal booze and cigarettes north of the Mason-Dixon line. There is a big market for stolen cigarettes and distilled spirits. Can't say *moonshine*." She smiled.

"What about hard cider?"

Coop looked at Harry. "Good one. People will pay a fortune for the stuff in Manhattan, Boston, the big cities. But still, a van full? Wouldn't it make more sense if they were working, driving a big truck?"

"It would, but maybe they were recruits."

"You've identified big profits."

"And what about stealing women? Sex slaves. We have them." Harry grimaced.

"Young women lured to this country or smuggled in. Promised work and then, bam. Or poor girls from our own country. Sex trafficking is another big business. I guess that's true for domestic workers, too."

"People as commodities." Cooper sighed. "We haven't advanced very far, have we?"

"In ways we have, but the vices of the human race will never disappear and the weak will always be preyed upon. You can pass all the laws you want. Someone has to enforce them, and that's you."

Cooper finished her drink. "When I was young I had no knowledge of such things. Children shouldn't, I think. Then I got my degree and wanted to go into law enforcement. I grew up fast. There is always someone who will lie, cheat, steal, and kill. Always. And a lot of times that person looks fine, a member of the community, so to speak. The lure of profit or easy sex. Bank accounts can tell you a lot."

"Don't the smart ones know how to hide their money?"

"They do, but Harry, what if the biggest thieves are the corporations?"

Harry smiled. "That's what Bernie Sanders says. I think that's what he's saying."

"A thought. Those crimes are not my territory. Congress and government agencies are supposed to handle that. Can we really go forward without a profit motive? I don't think so, but how much profit is enough?"

"Coop, I have no idea but I truly believe if you profit from human suffering you are evil. And perhaps in some fashion those men who ran from the van were part of that as perpetrators or victims and I have a hunch that whatever they were doing, they weren't getting rich doing it."

"True. And one of them is dead. I figure he was one. In time, it will be clear."

"Does that mean I should keep sharpening my shooting skills?"

Coop smiled at her. "Sure. Anyway, what else are you going to do on a snowy day?"

"Organize my closet."

"What a terrible thought."

The two walked out, climbed into Cooper's SUV from the sheriff's department. Given weather conditions, Sheriff Shaw would often let his officers take their SUVs home if it was a late day. Today was a long day for Cooper, but not late. She had gone to work at five-thirty A.M., as one of the officers was sick.

It was starting to sleet.

"Know what I love about riding in this or a squad car?" Harry watched the road. "I like seeing what drivers do when they see you."

"Yeah, to amuse myself sometimes I will follow someone. Makes them nervous as hell."

"Brute," Harry teased her.

Cooper left Harry off at the farm. Although only four-thirty, it was darkening, the sleet falling harder. Harry opened the door to a rapturous greeting.

Cooper drove down to her adjoining, rented farm, thinking about the ideas Harry had come up with for illegal profits. It occurred to her that one unknown murder victim could presage something much bigger. But what?

10

Saturday

Rolling her cart through the Farm Co-op, Harry stopped to read the contents on a box of Miracle-Gro. Coming down the opposite end of the aisle was Sy Buford. He stopped as Harry looked up.

"Well, Harry, you've got a big box of dog biscuits in the cart and," he leaned over to look more closely, "cat treats. Living must be good on your farm."

She smiled. "It is. I figured this is the four-footed version of chocolate chip cookies."

"You might be right." He looked down into his cart. "One crimper for my shed tin roof, a pain to do especially in the cold, but the winds curled up the tin."

"That's a job. Do you have to replace the roof?"

"No. I was lucky. That roof has held for over thirty years but we've had so many storms lately that somehow the wind snuck up under the top seam. Peeled it back, but I can fix it."

"You don't trust your insurance company?"

"Actually, I do. I've used Hanckle-Citizens for most of my adult life. Dad used them, too. But getting a new roof isn't going to solve the problem. I have to go over the seam, re-crimp, then I'm going to put in a two-inch screw every five inches. Won't peel up then."

"I expect after that the shed will blow to bits before the roof goes." She smiled up at him.

"Tell you what, I have never seen weather like we've had these last few years. Remember three years ago when temperatures rose to the mid-seventies in February? My forsythias bloomed. Looked out over the orchards. I could see the buds swelling. The next night it was in the twenties. We were all lucky that our trees didn't open. Would have destroyed peaches, and pears. Maybe apples. Maybe not. Have a little more time on the apples."

"I don't see how you do it. Your orchard is huge. There's so much to do. I can't imagine your fertilizer bill."

"I can't, either." He laughed.

"I've gone to your beautiful place so many times to carry off huge baskets of whatever is ripe at the time. And I've never asked you, is it difficult to get labor?"

He took a deep breath, leaned over the handle on the cart. "Is. Yes, it is. I have a good crew and I have good housing. They can stay through the winters if they wish. There's always work on the farm, although not as much. Most go back to Mexico. Some have brought their families here. Lost two workers, oh, maybe a month ago. Didn't really need them over the winter, and they were just up and gone. Don't know if they'll be back. Actually, I don't know who I can hire come spring. Crazy times. Every Sunday morning I watch the over-winter families drive out of the farm, children without a speck of dirt, everyone dressed up as they go to St. Mary's. Don't see much of that anymore and I am guilty of it. All I want to do is sleep in, especially as I get older."

"I'd like to say I'm virtuous but I can't sleep late. I go to St. Luke's. Herb gives the best sermons. I'm not sure that counts as virtue."

"Can't believe he's eighty. He is, isn't he?"

"Looks the same as he did at sixty. I think those who do what they love don't grow older like other people."

"I'll remember that when I get up in the morning and it takes me a half hour to straighten up." He patted her shoulder. "Always good to see you. Give my regards to Fair."

"I will."

Twenty minutes more of patrolling every aisle, getting what she needed and a few things she didn't. If Harry spied a new tool, she had to have it. For one birthday, Fair bought her a four-foot-high, multi-drawer tool cabinet. Bright red, it did brighten wherever it sat. She kept it in a corner of the basement with a smaller version in her tack room. Not finding the right tool for the job put her over the edge. Since she had most everything, Susan, Coop, and friends might stop by to borrow something or ask what they need for the problem. To everyone's credit, they brought whatever they took back.

Finally out in the parking lot with her goods, she lifted up the back of the aging station wagon, carefully arranged her purchases while Pirate and Tucker peered over the backseat.

"Looks like treats," Tucker mentioned.

"Did she use a credit card?" Pirate was fixated on the card.

"She has an account. She doesn't need her credit card." Seeing confusion, Tucker explained accounts.

Talking to her dogs, Harry peered out the window. "That sky is so gray, if I lowered the window I think I could grab some of it." She then looked at the thermometer reading on the dash. "Thirty-one degrees. And it's not nightfall yet."

"If you had a double fur coat you'd feel better," Pirate suggested.

"She has her jacket with the fleece lining. Keeps her warm." Tucker liked to snuggle in the jacket when Harry left it open in the backseat.

"Why doesn't she wear something long?"

"She can't move as well. She has her scarf, gloves, and her socks are wool. When she's done with them, we get the socks."

"Oh." Pirate didn't think this was such a good deal, but then again, Tucker kept the socks for herself.

Cars parked around the old school that Harry and her history group were rehabbing. Three framed buildings with floor-to-ceiling windows, paned, built originally in the 1880s and finally discontinued in the 1950s. While in use, called the colored schools, they served black, mixed race, and tribal children. The group, led by architect Tazio Chappers, was determined to save them, rehabilitate them, and have them available for special classes. Tazio did not believe in burying history, but in preserving it, celebrating those who lived it. Harry, as part of the group, managed to get the third building to use for training Irish wolfhounds; it originally was used for an auditorium for both grade-schoolers and high schoolers. Once the schools were no longer used, the old big building was used for some storage, which Taz cleaned out.

All three buildings kept the original wood-burning stoves. All three had been electrified, so a heat pump served the classroom buildings. But this building used the old wood-burning stove, which still worked. The preservation group locked their tools in the building, plus one riding mower. All were along one wall, the old bleachers along another. Linda King, a breeder with many champions to her credit, arrived early with Joel Paloma, fired up the big stove, set out a few water buckets for thirsty dogs, as there were faucets in the classroom buildings. Harry had given Linda the key.

By the time Harry, Pirate, and Tucker arrived, walked into the inviting space . . . walked into another century, really . . . the room felt warm.

"Just in time." Linda smiled as Harry put on Pirate's leash. "You have to sit on the bleachers, Tucker."

The corgi did as she was told, sitting on the bottom bleacher. One Irish wolfhound was impressive enough, but here were six with their owners for training.

While Harry did not think she would ever show Pirate, she wanted to learn what a judge looked for, how to handle the huge animal.

Along with Joel, two other women and their dogs and one man Harry didn't know well and Ballard Perez completed the circle.

Veronica Cobb with Bugsy, Alice Minor with Marvel and Isadore Reigle with Jumpin' Jack, Ballard had Lafayette. Linda brought one of her show dogs, Lacey.

Joel had fired up Harry's curiosity to participate; good thing, as now the small group of people and wolfhounds had a place to learn together. Given the size and stride of the breed, they usually worked outside, suspending class in winter. Now they could continue on with reasonably warm conditions. Joel wanted to show his dog. He had gone to a big AKC show at the Richmond Raceway to watch. It fired him up.

For a half hour the people were instructed how to hold their leashes and where to position themselves to show off their dogs to best effect.

"Walk," Linda instructed them.

Pirate walked but thought the leash ridiculous. He would have been fine without it.

"All right, change direction." Linda carefully observed each animal.

They walked, trotted, then loped. No indoor space is big enough for a wolfhound to really run, but the people were panting.

"Joel, well, everyone stop. Okay, Joel run along the outside. Stop, then trot through the middle."

As he did so, Linda called attention to the animal's movement. "Notice how the hound reaches. He looks good from the side in both directions. Now, Joel, bring him here to me."

The obedient dog walked and stood in front of the good-looking woman wearing a turtleneck, which was almost beginning to feel too warm.

"Watch as I feel from his shoulder down. Then I'll glide my hand over his back and then under his stomach. You can see the movement but you want to feel the muscles in his shoulder, and his leg to the ground. If a bone is offset it may not be possible to see it, but you will feel it. As to his stomach and sides, he should be a bit filled out, but not portly. A fit wolfhound will be more lean than fat. Lodestar is fit. Okay, now Joel, I want you to run down the middle again, and then back to me."

"*Do I get a cookie for this?*" the dog asked.

"Come on, big boy." Joel enjoyed being with his dog.

"Now look at him coming at you from the front. Okay, Joel. Thank you." She scanned the room, her eyes fell on Pirate. "Harry, come down the middle with your hound."

Harry trotted with Pirate, knowing she wasn't doing such a good job but she was game.

"All right, stop." Linda looked at the group. "Can you see the difference?"

Alice spoke out. "Bigger."

Linda nodded, so then Veronica spoke up. "He's huge."

"He has an impressive front. But I'm now going to feel him as I did Lodestar."

As he was being felt, Pirate looked up at Harry.

"*When you do this, it's personal grooming.*"

Tucker wanted to run to the center and join her pal, but being a truly good dog, she sat, ears pricked, eyes bright.

"He has good bone, is well muscled. He runs with the horses, right?"

"Yes." Harry nodded.

"But he's not as full as I would like. He's young. It's possible he will fill out some. If he were female and had a litter, that often pushes the ribs out a bit more. They don't look ribby, they look fuller." She then said to Harry, "Run him around the group."

She did. No one said anything.

The dogs sat as Pirate ran. He hoped he would get to talk to them, as he had never seen a member of his own breed.

Lafayette, Ballard's dog, called out, "*Your human can run better than mine.*"

"Thank you. Our next class will be next week. Same time. Same station." Linda looked to Harry, who nodded, then returned to the bleachers.

As the class disbanded, Alice Minor, maybe mid-fifties, walked over to Harry, Marvel in tow. Harry was already at the bleachers where Pirate and Tucker were talking. Alice's Marvel pulled to get to the two dogs.

"Will the little one bite?" Alice asked.

"No. That's Tucker. She herds cattle, horses, and people, but she won't bite you."

As Alice laughed, Tucker jumped off the bleacher to chat with Marvel.

"Do you show your dog?" Harry asked.

"No. I hope to. My husband died two years ago and I'm just coming back to, well, being social again. I want to do something different. Meet new people."

"This seems like a way to do it and if you go to dog shows, you meet all kinds of people." She looked at Tucker. "Including corgi owners."

Joel came over, as did Veronica, they all chatted then dispersed. Ballard, Harry, and Linda closed the building, swept the floors, turned off the lights, and locked the door. The stove would burn out but the room would stay warm . . . large, with high ceilings as it was . . . for maybe two hours after the wood turned to glowing ashes.

Linda gave her the key, and Harry remarked, "There's a lot to know."

"We probably never know it all." Ballard plucked his gloves out of his coat pocket. "Mother had Irish wolfhounds and Scottish deerhounds all her life. Grew up with them, as you know, Harry. And I still look at a wolfhound as though seeing him or her for the first time."

"I love to look at hounds. It's a passion." Linda petted Lacey, who pushed her head under Linda's hand.

"What do you think about the restoration?" Harry asked the two.

"You all have done so much work. The buildings were so well proportioned and thought out to begin with. I believe our ancestors had more sense than we do when it comes to building."

"They did," Ballard said with finality. "Lone Pine's first section was built in 1744. Still solid as a rock."

"Those two heat pumps cost us seven thousand dollars apiece when we put them in this fall. And that was with a discount. Tazio worked her magic. I've never worked with an architect before. Makes a huge difference. But the old way kept everyone warm if you attended to it."

"I know."

"Let's go to the Mudhouse for something hot."

"Sure." Linda was already opening the door to her van. "I'm glad Joel talked you into this. You'll enjoy it."

"I'll pass. Have to stack wood, speaking of the old ways, for the cabins," Ballard excused himself.

Once at the Mudhouse in downtown Crozet, which is no bigger than a minute, the two ordered hot drinks and sandwiches. Tucker and Pirate cuddled in the heavy blankets left in the back. Lacey had toys, a bed, her own blankets in the van.

The two humans chatted about Harry going to a restaurant in Fredericksburg.

"Fair decided we were going to do this. In a way, it's history. Culinary history. Another of Joel's ideas."

"Sounds interesting. Before I forget, when will the schools open?"

"Next fall. We'll have a big ceremony. We hope people whose ancestors went to the schools will come."

"I like that you all left the gas lamps hanging. When there is a power shortage and there will be, you'll still have light."

"Have them at home. We lose power all the time out there."

"Read in the paper about you and Susan finding the man who had been shot. That had to be a jolt."

"It was. No papers. No phone. No ID. Coop thinks he was an undocumented immigrant. She says we have a lot of them in the county but they rarely get caught and they rarely cause trouble."

"I'm sure she sees everything."

"She does," Harry replied forcefully. "I don't know how she does it but she really likes law enforcement. I wonder about undocumented immigrants though. No social services. How can they go to a doctor if they need one?"

"Well, if they are housed by their employer, I bet the employer can bring the doctor to them." Linda thought that possible.

"I never considered these things. Well, who would think about this if you didn't have workers from other countries? Maybe we make everything too complicated," Harry wondered.

"I know. If people sat down and talked, really talked, I believe a lot of this would be solved, but you can't make a political career today by being reasonable."

"Yeah." Harry sighed. "But now I'm alerted, sort of, so I find myself looking around to see if I can identify migrant workers or people from other countries. You know, like an Indian student at UVA. Just never ever crossed my mind what they go through."

Linda nodded then pointed to the window. "Look."

"Snow." Harry grinned. "We're together for the first big snow. That's good luck."

11

The morning early, the heat not yet suffocating, proved delightful as the two neighbors rode over Big Rawly.

"Where did you get that horse? So well made," Maureen Holloway asked Catherine.

"Zachary Thigpen sent her down from Leesburg. He fought with my husband at Yorktown. He would like me to decide whether to breed her to Reynaldo or Crown Prince."

"Ah. Half brothers. Well, what is her temperament?" Maureen, a highly intelligent woman, was also intelligent about horses.

"Quite mild. Then again, she's not in season and won't be for quite some time. But I like riding her. I like to take time to figure out a horse. Zachary is fine if I do take some extra time."

"He's quite rich, is he not?"

"Yes. He inherited money, then after the war he started a stage-coach line. He has been wonderful to John. He's raised money from men up there for muskets, he's found drilling areas, and currently he is finding men for the militia."

"Your husband has taken on a very large task."

"He has. I'm glad for it. John is not meant to be a businessman. Working for our defense, well, he is passionate. Then again, he saw battle and I have not."

"Yes," Maureen murmured. "I pray we will be left in peace." She glanced up at a large flock of starlings overhead. "Do tell your husband that Jeffrey and I will build a forge. I thought I might ride to the spot so you will see it."

Catherine beamed. "How gracious. How can we thank you? A forge is an enormous project."

"It is, but we can use it for many things apart from military matters. There is a paucity of forges. We have enough water mills. More than enough men to saw timber and sell it; but iron, steel, not much. The forge my husband built for axles, and other small things, has taught me a man must know a great deal to fashion useful things. It's brutal work."

"John said the government would send us engineers."

Maureen smiled. "Good."

Older than Catherine by perhaps fifteen or twenty years . . . Catherine was twenty-five . . . Maureen kept her looks. She was a testimony to the effects of lavish attention to one's body, hair, teeth. She ate carefully, tried to ride or walk daily. It was no secret that her husband was almost a generation younger and beyond handsome. No one knew the exact number of years, but her concern for appearance escaped no one who knew her. Whatever she was doing, it worked. She wasn't as beautiful as Catherine, but then who was? Still, Maureen was a good-looking woman, with an ample bosom she used to devastating effect. Her voice, modulated as only a lady's voice can be modulated by time among the aristocracy of France, lulled those who listened to her. Even women found it a lovely voice.

"Your mares look splendid," Catherine complimented her as they passed the mares' field.

"Thank you. DoRe overseas all the horses. He is training, as you know, younger men. But the young are flighty. Your English word, *flighty*."

Catherine smiled. "As young men I believe their attentions do not wholly focus on horses."

Maureen returned the smile. "My workers are worse than my indentured servants." She squinted in the sunlight. "One must keep track of the years with those from Europe."

Neither woman would readily use the word *slave*, preferring terms like "*worker*" or "*our people*" that allowed them to paint themselves in a better light. Catherine avoided that subject with Maureen, whose attitude and cruelty were well known. Her lady-in-waiting, Sheba, had disappeared a few years ago. She stole a fortune in Maureen's jewelry, and she spoke perfect French, although a slave. She had come to Virginia with Maureen when she married. Her outlook was not at all English. She was never found. Most people felt she made it to Philadelphia, boarded a ship, and was living in splendor, possibly even in Europe. Few people would think her enslaved, because she had escaped with precious stones the size of pigeons' eggs. If anything, people might assume she was a rich man's mistress. But one avoided the subject with Maureen.

"Keeping track of the years, once I had my son I began to lose track of time. It flies." Catherine laughed.

"Ah, Catherine, you are the center of male attention. The years are of no concern. You will be wherever you go." Maureen meant that.

"You are too kind. I don't like it. I want to concentrate on the horses. I have never been interested in men. Until I met John. We can talk about anything. Well, sometimes I believe I talk and he listens."

They both laughed.

"The good Lord means for us to live in pairs," Maureen, who thrived on male attention, posited.

"I expect he does." A downy woodpecker flew close then landed on a tree quickly, twisting around the tree trunk; those bird claws are so useful.

"This must be the spot." Catherine looked as they approached the flat pasture above fast-running Ivy Creek below. The sides of the creek were quite high.

"It is. If we put the forge here, we can pump up water. The building . . . stone, of course . . . can face the northwest. The winds will help, for it will be sweltering in the forge. Jeffrey says he knows how we can build a pump for the water. He says oxen can turn it. I said why can't we build a higher pond, use the creek to fill it? Would this not dispense with another device needing so much labor, as even oxen must be supervised. He says he is not opposed, but he has to figure out can we build it so the water runs down to the forge. Again, dispense with as much labor as one can." She sighed audibly. "Even if one has reliable workers, they sicken, they age, they die. I dream of a day when there are no workers. It will never happen, but can you imagine? All your resources can be focused on what brings profit."

"I can't imagine it." Catherine paused. "This is perfect here. And it's far enough away so noise will not disturb you."

"Indeed." Maureen turned her elegant gelding toward the stables, a mile in the distance.

"I am hoping you will have some horses in my steeplechase."

Maureen brightened. "I will. I expect all manner of people will come, exchange the news of the day, perhaps even find new paths to profits. Since the war has ended, we are recovering . . . slowly, but recovering. Even our cities, although few streets have cobblestones. I hope someday, my dear, you can visit France, Italy, England, and see civilization. I miss it, but Francisco," she mentioned her late husband, "said vast fortunes would be made in this raw land."

"Father feels most of our business will be among ourselves. He hasn't abandoned tobacco. All those acres he has in North Carolina and southern Virginia produce excellent burley tobacco, but the huge market of France is no more. England is increasing its use. You must be thinking about France." Catherine said this in a manner that was not intrusive. "Speaking of civilization and profit, it's confusing now."

"It is." Maureen, always careful in disclosing her business deals or financial exchanges, tilted her head. "Your father has powerful friends remaining, but they are imperiled should new taxes, taxes on the First and Second Estates, come to pass. I would hope some rough accord could be reached so everyone can settle down to business. I realize the crown does not truly do business." She raised her eyebrows. "But of course they do. Much as I recoil from these ideas of equality, the time and money that will be squandered on elections, the lack of old ways, ways used for centuries, allows us to create all manner of profits in all manner of ways. My father was adamant about profit. And as I said, so was Francisco. If nothing else, it was a bulwark against destruction. You can buy your way out."

"Yes. It does seem to me that the Church in France lives off profits and pays no taxes on their holdings; the special things the monasteries create surely make money. But I have not lived there and you have."

"Not a sou. Not one sou do they pay. Then again, the life of the spirit is to be free from the life of the mind and body. Do you think it is?"

"No," came a forthright reply. "I would like to think so but I don't. I have often wondered about your education, your life in the islands and then France. Did you see Versailles?"

"Oh yes. My convent school, Pentemont Abbey, was founded in 1217, we were often taken there, as the abbey also had a close association with the late Louis XIV. Versailles stinks to high heaven. However, it is beautiful. So many people lived there. Being the seat of government, people were in and out. I have heard three hundred live there now, but ten thousand were there as officials, minor royalty. You name it. I don't know. I was young. But I do know there were many, many people. You had to be correct. Our mother superior so feared we would misstep that she always accompanied us. There will never be any place like it, especially here."

"Ah." Catherine's voice faded.

"I don't mean that as criticism. There is no need for such grandeur here. The new government is a government of the people. It really shouldn't be overwhelming . . . the buildings, I mean. Once a site is agreed upon."

"You don't think our government will stay in Philadelphia?"

"I don't, although I'm sure Pennsylvania hopes so. It is a big city, bigger than many European cities. I am curious about such things, but mostly I listen."

Catherine knew Maureen had her hand in many political issues. With her wealth, she could buy and sell people as she chose.

"I envy your travels in Europe and your education."

"You have had a good education, especially for a woman of Virginia."

"Father and Mother hired tutors. Rachel and I had to learn Latin, French, and some German. So many Germans in Pennsylvania, and now the Shenandoah Valley."

"Your parents were wise. As we ride, and it is so pleasant to be with you, as always, what do you think of Fearnought?"

"Excellent blood. You know he died three years ago. But outstanding blood," Catherine, who studied equine bloodlines, answered.

"I knew you would know. Do you know where his progeny is? Stallions. I have a few mares to breed. I want to bring one to your Reynaldo, of course, but I was thinking of Fearnought, having heard so much about him and John Baylor." She named the man who imported the stallion to Virginia.

"Then you also hear he spent one thousand guineas on the horse," Catherine replied.

"Shocking. Then again, he must have made some of it back on stud fees."

Maureen half smiled. "Would anyone make the price back in the twelve years he lived here, at a stud fee of eight pounds per mare? Fearnought lived a remarkable twenty-one years."

Catherine answered, "A hopeful thought. Of course, as his son has some of the progeny, it is possible that stud fee will be paid in full eventually. Colonel Baylor succeeded in being the talk of the colonies and then the new nation."

"He did. A fool with money though," spoke Maureen, who was anything but. "Yes, and I have heard his son is even more excessive. His father's debts could be paid with land sales, so John the fourth was not a pauper, but I believe he will eradicate his fortune. He will possibly be left with some acres. To think his father had 12,000 acres with another 6,500 adjoining Mr. Madison's land. How old is the son?" Maureen couldn't imagine failing to capitalize on the land.

"Thirty-nine." Catherine spoke his age with authority, then changed the subject. "Isn't it odd what money does to some people? Having it can possibly be as bad as not having it." Catherine knew her father made a great deal of money as a young man, money he managed brilliantly, making more.

"About our Mr. Hamilton. He married well." Maureen mentioned Hamilton's fortuitous marriage into the Van Rensselaer family outside of Albany, New York.

"That he did. I hear the Van Rensselaers have over two hundred slaves." Catherine marveled at the number.

"So does Mr. Jefferson. Another person whom I believe imprudent about finances. An important man, a man who has accomplished much, but not prudent. If we added up all the cost of slaves over the years, the cost of building and managing his two great estates, we would question his wisdom."

"Perhaps financial prudence is a quality rarer than we realize," Catherine diplomatically said.

With that sentence, Maureen knew, cleverly, that Catherine worked with her father, and was learning a great deal about money.

Riding home, Catherine considered her time with Maureen. There was no question the woman was highly intelligent, shrewd, too, about most people. She would never trust her but she would work with her. Catherine believed they could generate profit by their association. She wondered, would the price be too high?

12

Sunday

People were putting on their winter coats, getting their gear together as Linda walked over to them. The class having ended, Linda mentioned to them they would have an important guest next time, the leading Irish wolfhound breeder and shower, Sam Ewing.

Harry knew Ewing, not a common name, but Sam Ewing was a Pennsylvanian.

Veronica put her hand on her three-year-old hound, Shamrock Kennels' Celtic Queen. "Bugsy, you are going to be seen by the great Sam Ewing."

A buzz of anticipation filled the auditorium, the heat emanating from the burning stove. The warmth made everyone happy, for it was another bitterly cold day. The group sounded small, but given the attention to detail that Linda focused on with each hound, it was a lot.

As they filed out, everyone in their coats, Linda and Harry checked the floor, the benches by the wall, turned out the lights as they left the old school building.

"Stop!" Veronica, outside, yelled as two men, caps pulled low, grabbed her purse from her car and left in their ancient Chevy Blazer, which they'd kept running, speeding out of the school parking lot.

Everyone hurried to Veronica.

"They stole my purse."

Harry, now outside, cellphone in hand, as she had it in her coat pocket, called Cooper. "Ancient Chevy Blazer, blue and white. Two men, baseball caps, heading down toward the Exxon station."

"Are you all right?" Ballard reached to touch Veronica's shoulder.

"Was your car locked?" Joel asked.

"Yes." The distressed short lady slumped against her car, a nice Mazda, then she answered Ballard. "I'm okay. Thank you for asking."

"They knew what they were doing." Alice Minor, thin, holding the leash on Marvel, who picked up on all the excitement.

"I remember when we didn't lock our cars or our doors at night," the older gentleman of the group, Isadore Reigel, announced as his hound, Jumpin' Jack, watched the Blazer disappear. "But who would think of locking here? There's nothing around us but orchards."

"If we'd come out a minute earlier we could have scared the daylights out of them." Lodestar relished the thought.

In the distance they all heard a siren, then another, then silence.

"Given the looks of their getaway car, they won't go far," Ballard predicted.

Harry's cell rang, "I was coming in the opposite direction and turned around just as they came out of the school road. Pure luck. Ran them off the road, as Pete Hollis was coming in the opposite direction. Got them. Got the purse. I'll bring it to you." Cooper made a decision violating protocol, knowing she could get it back if needs be.

Harry slipped the phone in her coat pocket and told everyone. "Bad luck followed by good luck. Officer Cynthia Cooper apprehended the thieves."

"I can't believe it." Veronica clasped her hands together.

"*Can I get in the car?*" Bugsy asked, tugging slightly in that direction.

Veronica opened the back door, closed it, then looked at the front door. "How did they get in?"

"New cars are essentially computers on four wheels. If those thieves were geeks, they could get into any one of our cars. If you drive an old car, unless the thieves are old, they'll have more trouble breaking in. If you leave a car by the side of the road in some parts of the country, usually when times are really tough, you'll come back and that car will be missing four tires." Joel folded his arms across his chest as the sheriff's department SUV could be seen in the distance.

Cooper pulled up, got out. "Who had their purse stolen?"

"Me." Veronica raised her hand.

"Is this your bag?" Cooper handed it to her.

"It is."

"Check to see if you're missing anything."

They all watched as Veronica dutifully took everything out of her voluminous purse, placing cosmetics, pencils, sunglasses, and a large wallet on the hood. She left the small box of Kleenex in the bag. Sorting through everything, she smiled.

"All here. They didn't even get my credit cards."

"You were lucky. Really lucky." Joel, gloveless, felt the cold, which made his hands sting.

"Officer, thank you."

Cooper smiled slightly. "Give me your number in case I need a statement from you."

"Better yet, here's my card." Veronica pulled a business card out of the big bag.

"Ah. Roy Wheeler Realty. You'll be easy to find." Cooper's smile broadened.

People began to leave, as the cold was punishing, once they thought Veronica was settled, not shaken up.

"Veronica, it's a good thing you didn't come out two minutes earlier." Ballard pulled his lad's cap down farther over his close-cropped gray hair.

"*I would have brought them down*," Bugsy predicted.

"*We could have pinned them to the ground*," Lafayette bragged.

"*Had their throats in our jaws*." Bugsy liked the thought.

"Come on, big boy." Ballard clutched Lafayette, who followed.

Linda looked at Cooper. "Joel mentioned new cars are easy to hack by geeks. Veronica's car is brand new. Makes me want to buy an old heap."

"Well, I hear you." Cooper laughed. "Harry, are you on your way home?"

"Yes."

"I'll stop by."

As Cooper drove off, Harry, Isadore Reigle, and Linda stood there for a minute.

"Those guys couldn't have been too bright." Isadore shook his head.

"Maybe they drove by and it looked easy. What's the expression? Opportunity makes a poet as well as a thief." Harry shrugged.

"I'll see you next week." Linda headed for her van, her wolf-hound vehicle. "I hope it isn't quite as dramatic."

With a knock on the door . . . the screened porch was closed in with solid wood, waist high, windows above that, for the winter . . . Cooper announced herself and walked inside the kitchen.

"Last winter was mild. Not this one," she grumbled as she removed her coat, hanging it on the hook.

"Sit down. Fair will be home in all of ten minutes. Have supper with us."

"I would love that. It's been a long day. One damn thing after another," Cooper, in uniform, complained. "We really need to hire more people. The county is growing but the department isn't growing with it."

"The bad thing is, you are exhausted. The good thing is, all the overtime."

"You know, Harry, I'd rather have the time. I can't even buy new boots because I don't have the time. The money sits in my account." She stopped. "Well, that is a good thing, but before I forget, the two thieves. Middle-aged. Not young. No idea who they are. Not a scrap of ID. Like the dead man. No cellphones, either. If they had gotten hold of Veronica Cobb's credit cards, who knows how much they would have spent? They'd need to have a woman to help them. Neither could pass as Veronica."

"Can't they buy IDs?"

"You can buy driver's licenses, passports; if you have the money, you can buy anything. Some of the work is quite good. Anyway, Pete took them to the station, they'll be processed and put into jail. But I note, no ID, and the Blazer had been stolen from Virginia Beach. Forgot to tell you and Fair, the van, the wrecked van, was also stolen. Two wooden crates in it with a few seeds. Fruit crates once. Junk, but it ran. You'd think a newer car would be more appealing to steal."

"Maybe there's some kind of gang," Harry thought out loud.

"Well, if no one claims these two, if we can't find out identities, they'll be in the jail until we can. It's getting really overcrowded."

"Is there that much crime?"

"No. But there are people who are out of work, have no place to live, winter is hard, and they don't want to freeze on the streets. Even here in Virginia, we have many homeless people. So they commit some small crime, find dope, sell it to an officer. The real dealers can always tell who the undercover officer is. So whatever the small crime is, we arrest them, put them in jail. They get three hot meals in a warm place to sleep."

"I never thought of that." Harry was surprised.

"The expression is 'Three hots and a cot,'" Cooper informed her.

"But our two thieves, that's not the motivation."

"Credit cards. Or cash, too," Cooper said. "It's the lack of ID that gnaws at me."

"So they steal credit cards and buy IDs. What you were talking about."

"They could. Having no ID in its own way is a form of action."

"How?"

"Perhaps they need to hide. The Blazer wasn't theirs. It's old enough that information would go out about a stolen car, but we would be more alert to a new car. You might be sitting in the squad car. That old trap would go by. You might not notice. Maybe I would. I don't know. But with the van. Older. Worn. But I still think a newer theft with some work to obscure the released description would be a better bet."

"Maybe this was a crime of convenience?"

"I don't know. The two men we just picked up are middle-aged white men. Doesn't mean they aren't out-of-work farmhands, gas station attendants, who knows?"

"Well, here comes my middle-aged white man. He doesn't look middle-aged, though, does he?"

Cooper watched Fair walk to the back door.

"He looks cold."

Happy to see his neighbor as well as to smell the soup Harry had made for supper, he caught up with the events.

"Maybe those people are scared. Scared to the point where they hide their identities." He looked at Cooper.

"They are all frightened of cops." Cooper shrugged.

"No. Something else. Maybe being in jail is safe. Like for the men that ran out of the van. Maybe the van was safe. Now they have to find other places to hide. Just a thought."

Dessert was candied oranges and vanilla ice cream.

"Did you invent this?" Cooper asked.

"No. When Fair, Susan, Ned, Joel, Ballard, and I went to that fancy restaurant in Fredericksburg, I ordered orange-glazed sweetbread for dessert, with crème brûlée. Well, I am not making anything that complicated, but I didn't think that of the oranges. So this is my concoction."

"It's wonderful." Cooper relished the mixture of textures and tastes.

"Bet you'd think more of oranges or lemons if those fruits could grow here." Fair also liked the dessert.

"True. Peaches. Pears. Apples. Now that I think about it, most of my desserts are what we grow here."

"Keep oranges in mind." Cooper smiled. "Delicious."

13

Monday

"I hate this," Harry grumbled as she drove around and around, looking for a parking space at Stonefield.

The last week of November pushes people out for shopping and nervous breakdowns. Some people, like Susan, knocked out all their Christmas gifts by the end of October. Drove Harry crazy. Susan was overorganized.

A space appeared in the back of the beyond. She turned the nose of her high-mileage, aging Volvo station wagon into it. The thought of her dogs and cats, left at home, made her feel guilty as she cut off the motor. All four of them loved to go wherever she went, not minding sitting in the wagon or the truck, so long as there were plush covers on the seats, piles of warm blankets. The cold intensified. She couldn't see bringing them along, leaving them in the Volvo. Many times she did take them, but not for Christmas shopping. It was not an activity that improved her mood.

Stepping outside, her breath immediately crystallizing, she

clicked the lock button on her fat key fob, large enough to trip over if dropped.

Looking around, Harry muttered, "A branch of Hell."

Hell or not, she walked across the lot, her gloved hands jammed in her pockets, until emerging on the main street of the shopping center.

She crossed the thoroughfare, glad to open the door and feel the warmth inside L.L.Bean. Susan needed a new pair of work boots. They needed to be supportive and warm, but flexible enough so she could kneel for her gardening.

The choices overwhelmed Harry. Dutifully, she picked up each model, lifted the front of the boot from the bottom. Too stiff. She picked up another one, lighter, worked. Then she rubbed her hand inside. Sort of thin, not enough warmth. Thinsulate helped. So she put that back, moving through the entire two rows.

"Aha." A light brown pair of work boots, rubber soles designed to prevent slipping, lined in Thinsulate.

Looking around, she saw that every salesperson was busy. Many of them looked quite young to her. Perhaps students working until they left for home for Christmas. She remembered the long, long trip from Smith College in Northampton to home. How glad she was to step out of the car of whoever she shared the drive with, to see the barns, the house, and to hear that light, refined Virginia accent. True, one Virginian knows where another Virginian is from the minute they open their mouth, a bit like England. However, the class baggage here proved not as restrictive. She took pride in that, although she wasn't sure why. Snobbery is ingrained in the human animal, whether from Virginia, California, or Massachusetts. You open your mouth, people know.

Harry finally caught the attention of a saleswoman, young, tidy, had to be from what Harry's mother called Other Parts. Harry figured the other part was maybe upstate New York. Harry, a Smith graduate, spent time at Cornell when in college and loved upstate

New York. She also quite liked the young men at Cornell. Even the winters did not temper her affection.

"Do you have an L.L.Bean card?"

"I do." Harry handed her the green card with mountains and a lake on the front.

The line at the cash register was long. Well, she'd known it would be this way; she recited poetry in her head. "The Charge of the Light Brigade" was a poem she remembered from middle school. Her teachers made them all memorize famous passages from literature. Boring as it seemed at the time, she used those lessons in times just like this. She also learned from them. Discipline never hurt anyone.

Finally, boots in hand, she walked out the front door and was hit again by the frigid air. Turning left, she headed for Brooks Brothers. While she arranged for Fair's fitted clubs, his big present, she needed a few small things, plus a stocking stuffer; in his case, toe warmers and cashmere socks.

Brooks Brothers, like L.L.Bean, was jammed. She found the merino wool sweaters. She pulled out a caramel-colored one, turning as she heard a voice call her name.

"For your husband?" Veronica Cobb smiled.

"Hello." Harry remembered her, of course, from the handling class and Veronica having her purse stolen.

Holding a dark navy cable knit in her hands, Veronica looked at the caramel color. "Is he blond?"

"He is. He can wear colors I can't."

"Well, at least your husband still has hair. Bob, my wonderful guy, started thinning in his late twenties. Still handsome though." She grinned.

"What do they have to do? Shave, get a good haircut, or trim their beard. That's it. No heels. No nail polish. No streaks." Harry laughed. "Well, every now and then I actually streak Fair's hair. We giggle over it, but he sits in that chair just like one of the girls. A six-foot-four girl."

Veronica laughed. "I envy their clothing choices. The money I spend on clothes, but Bob has to go to fundraisers, and I better look decent."

"You always look sophisticated. Even with Bugsy," Harry complimented her.

"Thank you." Veronica smiled. "We are fortunate. Bob is head of the accounting department for GM here. When we married, we didn't have a penny. But he worked, I worked. I went back to work when our youngest entered first grade and I was lucky to be able to stay home as long as I did. Large corporations made no provisions for child care when we were young. You and I don't know one another well, except we both love Irish wolfhounds. But women can't compete, truly compete, without child care."

Harry held the sweater to her chest. "Maybe the real question is how much will this cost corporations, and maybe the old guys that run them want to be retired before large numbers of women are really competitive. Know what I mean?"

Veronica nodded her head. "That's one of the reasons I like showing Bugsy. Anyway, when I am in the ring with her, the world drops away. Bob loves it, too. He attends the weekend shows. Middle of the week, no, but it takes time and money to campaign any dog."

"I'm beginning to discover that. My big baby isn't going to show. But I want to learn about conformation, handling. He is so big, I don't think I can leave training to chance. Training my corgi was easy. Not that Pirate is difficult, just a different canine mind."

"Yes, it is." Veronica changed the subject. "That's all you're getting?"

"It is. I fry my two brain cells every Christmas and always forget somebody or something and run out Christmas Eve. By which time my list is crumpled."

"Know what you mean." She paused a moment. "The sheriff's department asked me if I wanted to press charges." She shrugged. "They didn't get away with anything, so I dropped it. Anyway, Officer Cooper said the jail was overcrowded."

"Cooper said the homeless sometimes try to get arrested to get out of the cold. We have the Salvation Army but that's not enough, and some homeless people don't want to hear religious stuff."

"Ah." Veronica thought a moment. "I don't see why we can't have those mini houses or even rehab old trailers, or even old shipping containers, for the homeless. The county would have to find a place, a place where people wouldn't complain."

"That's always it, isn't it?" Harry responded. "I don't mean to sound harsh and I am not a medical person, but I think so many of these people have mental illness. Maybe the prevalent alcoholism is a way to feel better. I don't know, but I know this isn't a new problem, but maybe we can come to it with new energy. No one should be left on the streets regardless of condition."

"Yes. But there is a percentage of the homeless that trust no one. They'll slip away. Forgo the housing, the food. The two men who stole my purse, according to Officer Cooper, were well-spoken, white, middle-aged. And she made it clear they had no IDs. So I wondered, why? Whatever I imagined came with more government departments badgering the men and the sheriff's department."

"You can bet Coop sent out photos, plus the information on the stolen car. Amazing that the old thing ran. Obviously no one responded. It's a frantic time of the year."

Veronica smiled. "My car is loaded with computer chips. My owner's manual is larger than *War and Peace*."

"Mine too. It's nudging 200,000 miles, and it's five years old. But again, the owner's manual. I'm not reading that thing. Never have."

"Does your car beep all the time, lights come on the dash?"

"Does. Unless it's the engine light, I ignore it. Actually, I make my husband look at it and we have a talk about women's equality." Harry laughed. "I'm not bad with machines, especially tractors, but a new vehicle, can't do it. I tell him that's what men are for."

"Tractors?"

"I farm. Used to be the postmistress, but when Crozet built the new big post office, I couldn't take my cats and dog . . . then I had only Tucker, the corgi . . . to work. I quit. So I became a full-time farmer. Mother Nature is a demanding business partner."

"I'm sure she is. Can you repair riding lawn mowers?"

"I can," Harry replied with a hint of pride.

"I'll remember that come summer. Well, let's troop to the check-out. I'll buy this sweater. You've got yours."

Finally home, Harry hid the sweater and the stocking stuffers in the library. She sat down at the simple heavy wooden kitchen table, which had also served her parents and grandparents.

"*A snack would help. I've been here all day while you were away.*" Pewter batted her eyes.

"*Milk bones.*" Pirate put his head on the table, which Harry did not encourage, but she was too tired to bother about it at that moment.

"*I feel faint.*" Pewter flopped on her side.

"*You look like a used rabbit-fur slipper.*" Tucker blew air out of her nostrils.

Pewter leapt to her feet, swirled around, and hit Tucker on the nose. "*Wretched creature.*"

"All right. All right." Harry wearily rose, went to the cupboard, taking out enough treats to satisfy them. Then she dropped back down.

Looking at the clock she thought she might take a nap, which was unusual for her, but the cold, shopping, and early sunset made her tired today.

As she stood up, the phone rang.

"Hi, Coop."

"I'm at Wegmans, I bought three chicken pot pies. I owe you a supper. Anyway, I'll bring them by. I get off work, mmm, in an hour."

"Great." Harry was pleased. "Fair will be home by then."

Within an hour, Cooper came in. Harry popped the pies in the oven just as Fair drove up. Twenty minutes after, they sat at the table, each with a hot chicken pot pie, a loaf of bread on the table, Irish butter, and iced tea, even though it was winter.

"I ran into Veronica Cobb." Harry repeated their conversation.

"We discharged them. Last I saw, they were walking toward Charlottesville. If she had pressed charges, we would have kept them and we would have had to spend hours trying to find out who they are. We are swamped as it is, plus all the traffic accidents. People are stressed to the max over the holidays. They don't pay attention when they're driving."

As the animals also ate supper, the conversation was not interrupted by bad table manners.

Cooper's cellphone rang. "The boss." She answered. "Hello."

Harry and Fair continued eating, then slowed down as Cooper was listening intently.

She clicked off her phone. "Well, our two unidentified thieves are still unidentified. But now they're dead."

"Did they try to steal someone else's purse?" Harry blurted out.

"No. They were found on the wooded hill behind the BP station on the corner where Keller and George is. Someone, one of the kids at the BP station, thought they heard a shot. Walked up there and found them."

"Why up there?" Fair wondered.

"Every now and then, a few homeless people camp there. It's not visible from the road or the shopping center. Plus they can come down at night and go through the big garbage dumpsters. There are two restaurants, a McDonald's, and the supermarket. We check the place maybe once a month. When it's busy like this, we really don't."

"Do they have shelter from the elements?" Harry asked.

"There's an old lean-to up there. We've found tents, plastic sheets for the bottoms. Pretty rough, but you can get out of the rain and snow. We've never had any trouble with these people."

"Two dead." Fair shook his head.

"Three," Harry corrected him. "Remember the man we found in the ditch?"

"Do you think that's related?" Fair put down his fork.

"Could be. Could not," Cooper stated. "But we have three corpses, no IDs, all three shot. The men on the hill were shot."

"I would think there would be more stealing during the holiday but less murder." Fair added, "I don't know, but I bet you do."

"If there is a murder, it is generally inside the family. The holidays expose every fracture there is. Fortunately, this doesn't happen often but we do get calls where a man, almost always a man, loses it, or an old boyfriend smashes down a door." She paused. "Christmas usually isn't a big killing time."

"Is now." Harry looked down at Tucker, looking up at her, having finished her dish.

"I doubt this has anything to do with Christmas," Coop replied.

"But Coop, wouldn't Christmas be a great time to, I don't know, commit fraud, steal, carry illegal cigarettes across the Mason-Dixon line? Everybody is distracted."

Cooper knitted her eyebrows together. "Well, that's a thought."

"Who knows what you could get away with." Harry then stopped. "Ended the sentence with a preposition. Miss Kimball would dock me a grade."

The other two laughed. Cooper hadn't known Miss Kimball in high school, but Fair did.

"Maybe if Miss Kimball knew what this was about, she would have left town," Fair suggested.

"Oh, that would have been a huge Christmas present." Harry smiled.

14

Saturday

Standing on the heights above Shockoe Slip, shielded by parasols, Georgina and Deborah looked down at the activities below. Skiffs, mid-sized schooners, a variety of boats, were tied up at the docks. The James River, miles wide at that point, allowed goods to be brought to Richmond. Housewares, beautiful furniture, expensive clothing, as well as rich fabrics, would be offloaded from the big clipper ships making port where the James empties into the Atlantic. Other goods, mostly agricultural, arrived from the other direction, the west. Those ships, flat-bottomed, were smaller.

Sailors' voices, stevedores, floated upward. Mules, horses whinnied. Wagon wheels clattered over the cobblestones as men came to pick up their goods. The slip could handle heavy wagons. Others came to load goods. Even in the darkness if a ship came in, men ran to the dock, catching the tossed ropes, tying the ship up. Richmond, not a great port city like Philadelphia, New York, Boston, Charleston, and Savannah, still burst with activity. Anyone watching the people working down below could see commerce enriching those who took a chance on supply. If Richmond was any example, the new nation was growing. Money was being made. Money was being spent.

Close to four thousand people lived in Richmond. Being made the capital in 1779 fostered growth. The river did the rest. Many single men, young, had not found wives. Many older men had. Georgina and Deborah knew their business, men, would keep growing along with the city.

"Most excellent," Georgina uttered, her voice pitched lower than her natural timbre.

"Every man I see below has money to burn. Even the slaves have money, if traveling with their masters." Deborah, a black woman, perhaps late twenties, uncommonly beautiful, lifted her soft pink parasol higher.

The two women had evolved into unequal business partners, but partners nonetheless. Deborah had escaped slavery. Her beauty brought the men to Georgina's tavern. The food was excellent. The rooms comfortable and the woman awaiting a man in the rooms, should he request her, provided comfort. No patron of The Tavern was ever met with a scowl. Radiant smile, low-cut dresses, easily removed, were worth every penny. Married patrons may have loved their wives but every man needed a wife. A man without a wife rarely rises unless he is born to wealth. Georgina had some of those, too. Men wanting a good time. Wanting a woman to exclaim with wonder when he disrobed. The thrill intoxicated them. So many wives, bearing children, keeping house, forgot about the thrill, if they ever knew it. As for the girls, they made more money than they could have ever imagined on the farm or in a shop at some dusty crossroads. Few were ashamed of their profession. Most accepted it, wanted the money, and had learned the secrets of how to please a man. A woman who knows that will not fail in the world.

Deborah, like most of the black women working at The Tavern, has escaped her bondage only to discover she knew little about how to survive in a situation where she knew no one, had no future. Many of the girls, as they called themselves, felt marriage was another form of bondage. Deborah was one of those. Her extraordinary beauty, refined features, allowed her to spurn men who would pay up to one hundred dollars a night for her. A fortune. Over time, Georgina observed Deborah's viewpoint. Deborah loved money. She made a few suggestions to Georgina about perhaps a different hairstyle for one of the girls, a way to buy foodstuff for a bit less. Where a good seamstress lived. Deborah began monitoring the girls. In this way, Deborah lorded over the others, white and black, but they also came to understand she shielded them from the boss's wrath.

A leading banker in town, Sam Udall, wanted to take her from The Tavern, set her up as his mistress. He was, of course, married, but were he not he still could not marry a black woman, legally. The law forbade it. Deborah immediately went to Georgina, revealed all, and suggested that eventually she would sleep with him. Her refusal made him all the more determined. Deborah would weasel financial information from him useful to Georgina. What a perfect fit.

Georgina, early forties, a bit more padding on her body now, but still attractive . . . after all, looks were her business . . . listened intently. When she asked Deborah what she wanted, the cool thinker said to be her business partner. A junior partner, of course.

After taking a week to consider this, the two sat down again. Deborah declared she would pay rent, and her food. She would buy her own clothes, which she had been doing anyway. As most of the black servants had been runaway slaves, Deborah knew their fears, how to handle them. In the past, some of those women ran off again. Others accepted marriage proposals. Many servants harbored the hope of a marriage. Deborah said she could handle that. Any woman who wished to marry had to give The Tavern six months of her time or money before leaving. Often the man paid the six-month fee. Deborah would take care determining what clothing a girl could take and what stayed. Georgina had an eye for a lady's dresses herself, but Deborah swore she could get alluring clothing made for much less.

The deal was made. Georgina took seventy-five percent of the earnings, Deborah the rest. After all, Georgina had bought the house, paid the cooks and stable boy. Bought the food, linens, furniture, and so forth.

Now standing at Shockoe Slip, they formulated a new deal. Deborah would open her own house near the slip. It would serve whoever wished to come but mostly her clientele would be men of less means than those attending Georgina's. Working men whose pockets jingled once their work was done at the docks, or on the ship, needed entertainment. For those back from long journeys, the company of a woman was paramount.

Georgina would buy the property. She would also buy the furniture. Both women would find a cook, a gardener, and a stable boy or boys. The house needed a carriage house for those not coming from the ships. Many men now drove, sailed, or even walked into Richmond. They wanted a bath, a good time, and a decent place to sleep after a good time.

"Grace Street?" Deborah looked at Georgina. "Too," she paused, "respectable. If we could find something closer to the Slip but up high. Something the men could walk to from below."

"Yes." Georgina turned to walk back to her tavern. The walk even in the heat lightened her spirits. A breeze off the river helped.

"Laundry, sheets, it adds up."

"It does."

"Every lodger wants a clean place to sleep, a bath, food, drink, and a girl to hold him at night. Some have the odd woman tucked away here and there but this will bring them to us. I want to double our profits. Whatever we pay for food, grain, I want to double what comes back to us."

"First we have to find a house. Deborah, when Sam is drooling over you, see if he knows of any house being claimed, going into foreclosure."

"Of course."

They walked the twenty minutes back to The Tavern, the large shade trees and grounds welcoming all who walked through the iron gate. Georgina cleverly planted boxwoods, bushes, and flowers, but especially bushes that would shield a man coming from the road. While she did serve good food, the other dishes were known to many men. Why let someone see you come in? She also provided a back entrance and a side entrance, both of which saw more use than the front entrance, which was lovely. Best the wives be kept in the dark.

Georgina opened the door, stopped. The front hall mirror over the elaborate sideboard, Louis XVI, Georgina's favorite period, very modern, was smashed. She heard screams from an upstairs room.

Quickly she hurried into the dining room. Tables had been up-turned. She rushed through to the kitchen. Untouched. Eudes and Mignon were down at the market buying food for tonight. Every-thing must be fresh. The quality of the food was a big draw.

Her voluminous skirts swished as she pushed the door open from the kitchen back into the dining room. The screaming upstairs continued.

Climbing the stairs by the back stairway, the one used by men who had decided a lady would provide an excellent dessert, she reached the top. Three of her girls stood outside a locked door.

"Miss Georgina. Thank God you're here." Lily, a young newcomer to the trade, wide-eyed, reached for Georgina's hand. "Livia Taylor attacked us." She indicated the three. "She was trying to leave The Tavern but we stopped her."

Jocelyn, mid-thirties, a veteran and beginning to show it, leaned against the door. "She's crazy. She was trying to leave. Said you owed her money. A lot of money."

"I pay all my girls on time." Georgina listened to the raging inside the room. "Was there anyone waiting for her?"

Milady, not her real name but her professional name, black, a fabulous lady, replied. "There was a wagon, half-hidden, but we could see the rear of it. We couldn't see who it was. We only looked out the window. But she had a man waiting for her, I'm sure."

"Said he was going to take her away from all this." Lily had heard that line many times, as a fellow after satisfying himself, feeling somewhat grateful, made promises.

"I'll kill you. I'll kill you all. I want out of here," Livia bellowed.

Georgina, voice calm, replied, and she knew Livia could hear. "When you've made two thousand dollars for the house, you can go."

"I've made more than that. The men love my red hair."

The three women looked at Georgina then back at the door.

Milady folded her arms across her stupendous bosom, one of her leading features. In fact, some of her customers probably never looked at her face.

Jocelyn reached for the door. "She'll break it down."

"Not if we move the hall table against it. Pile it with whatever we've got. She'll come around."

"You're right. Get the other girls out here to help."

Milady asked Georgina, "What are you going to do?"

"Think on it. Whoever her fool of a customer is, he may come back. I'll make a decision by tomorrow. If he wants her, he should pay for her."

Deborah came upstairs. She had stayed outside in the back to admire the crepe myrtles starting to bloom. "Livia?" She was not surprised.

The three women filled her in.

Georgina quietly said, "She can go if her john pays."

Milady spoke plainly. "She swore that those of us, black, are runaway slaves and she would make sure we were returned to our masters if we didn't let her go."

Deborah, who had handled this before with a male customer who threatened her if she did not give him an exclusive relationship, stepped toward the door, put her back to it. "I'll take care of this. Do the other girls know?"

"Those still in the house heard her. And when the others come back from their constitutional walks, as the boss calls them, they'll all know."

Georgina, in control, said, "Secure the door. Deborah and I will talk this over. If she's here she will only make more trouble. She'll be calm by tomorrow and I'll talk to her. Let me find Christopher. He can help."

Christopher was the stable boy.

Georgina and Deborah walked downstairs.

"The mirror is ruined."

Georgina replied, "The frame is good. I'll get the glazier over by the church to put in a new mirror. We've got enough chairs in the back to replace the ones she's broken. They'll do until I can find matching chairs. Shall I leave her to you?"

Deborah smiled. "Yes. Let her go. I'll take care of everything. She'll cause more trouble."

"I am sure you can pacify her unreliable nerves."

With that Georgina smiled and left by the back door to find Christopher.

15

Friday

"Six people." Harry stood with Cooper in the still operating department store at Fashion Square.

"How much do you want to spend?"

"I knew you'd ask that." Harry zipped open her coat. It was warm inside. "Fifty dollars. I don't want to be cheap, but I want to be careful."

"And which credit card did you thaw out for this?" Cooper stopped at the bedding section, fingered some thick towels. "This is a good price."

Harry stopped to do the same. "It is. I think anyone can use new towels but it's kind of personal, isn't it?"

"Yes, plus, you need to know the color of everyone's bathroom, guest bathroom, too."

"Okay. What about a portable toolbox? Kind of the size of a briefcase. Would have different kinds of screwdrivers, nails, screws, a hammer, and wrenches. I always find I need wrenches or needle-nose pliers."

"Well, you aren't going to find that here. We need to go to Home Depot or a Lowe's."

Harry grimaced. "I hate those big box stores. Make me dizzy. No windows."

"Gets me, too, but this is clothing and house stuff. Let me get some towels. Mine are threadbare."

"The navy ones are nice. Won't show the dirt."

Cooper picked up bath towels, hand towels, and washrags, which she piled onto Harry's outstretched arms. "Navy."

After paying for the towels, both women walked back out to the jammed parking lot. Once in Cooper's car, Harry leaned back, happy not to be driving.

"Where to?"

"Oh." Harry thought. "Well, if you go up the road, there is a Sam's Club, but I'm not a member."

"Me neither. Keep forgetting to do it. How about I head south and we go to Lowe's or Home Depot?"

"Six of one. Half a dozen of the other." Harry clicked on her seatbelt as Cooper's car talked to her. "I hate that."

"I do, too."

"How many miles do you have on this?"

"Twenty-five thousand."

"After two years living out in the country. How did you do that?"

"I'm usually driving squad cars."

"That does save the miles." Harry had a moment of envy.

"We got back the medical examiner's report. All three of the men killed had fentanyl in their systems."

Harry turned toward Cooper. "So they were drug addicts?"

"Mmm, not necessarily. Did they inhale or ingest this? Sure. But if someone is loaded with this stuff and I lift them up or get close, it can knock me out. No joke. The stuff is lethal."

"Yeah, but I thought it was mixed with heroin, cocaine, stuff like that. So they were drug addicts?"

"Harry, you jump to conclusions. What if someone gave you something? A drink? Pills? It's a bit unlikely but possible. If they were committed drug addicts, I would think there'd be more evidence in the autopsies. One fellow had cancer but probably didn't know it. Lung cancer. Crummy at Christmas, isn't it?"

"Crummy that no one knows who they are. They must have families somewhere."

"Now I get to addiction. So many people who are addicted are estranged from their families. Think about Ballard Perez. He finally got clean but if he didn't have family money, maybe he would have stolen. The two white men who stole that purse could be hitting the bottom with no one to bail them out."

Cooper stopped for a light. "Traffic is so heavy. It's one thing I hate about Christmas."

"Me too."

"How did you know Veronica didn't press charges?"

"Ran into her at Brooks Brothers. We were both buying presents for our husbands. You might want to go in there to get something for your boyfriend."

"Good advice. Well, yes, Mrs. Cobb didn't press charges. We let them go. We probably should have tried harder for an ID, but everyone is exhausted. COVID doesn't help. It's whipping through the jail and some of those guys refuse shots. What is wrong with people?" Her voice rose.

"Constant conflicting information. Look, I'm college educated and so are you. Half the time I don't know what to believe. I rely on Fair. He's a doctor; a vet, but a doctor. He said we are getting the shots and so we did. So what if someone gets really sick at jail?"

"Hospital." A long pause followed this. "Which gives them an opportunity to escape if they feel better. Plus it costs the county a bundle. You know, Harry, this stuff has got to stop. I am a county employee. Give me a clear order."

"I hear you. But back to fentanyl. Is it odd that all three men, seemingly unrelated, had this in their systems?"

"Well, not as unusual as I would like it to be."

"Parking place right over there. I'm assuming you want to go to Home Depot and not the bird store." She named a store that had everything for birds, which she quite liked.

"Good eye." Cooper nosed into it, cut the motor.

As they walked through yet another huge parking lot, Harry said, "Maybe drugs are a way of life. Older people take doctor prescribed painkillers. The young take anything, especially if everyone else is doing it. Maybe COVID made people anxious, isolated, receptive to drugs reversing those emotions." She picked up the pace, as she was cold. "So maybe three men, not kids or old people, needed a hit. Or what if they were smuggling people? Take drugs to focus, to blunt the fear. It's possible. I've been focused on laborers. What if they were smuggling in women?"

"You think they'd do a better job. A van full of men. Where are the women?"

"Stashed somewhere. Anything is possible."

"Where do you get these ideas?" Copper laughed at her as she pushed open the door, which made an oomphy sound.

"I read history, especially our history here. And back in the eighteenth century, there was smuggling of slave women and poor white women, good-looking and young, to a house of ill repute. Every city had them."

"A profession that will never go out of style."

"If you're smart, you can make good money. It is a business, after all."

"Harry, is there something about you I should know?"

Harry laughed. "No. But the things women had to do, dependent on their age, race, and background, does fascinate me. We only got the vote in 1920, which if you think about it in terms of history, was yesterday."

"Right. The problem with the vote is what are your choices? Bad or worse?" Cooper smiled. "Okay. Here." She started down an aisle, stopping at the toolboxes, chests, big metal cabinets.

"Wow." Harry found the choices daunting.

Cooper picked up a metal toolbox. "Handle. Will be a bit heavy but it isn't big." She looked at the price. "Seventy-nine ninety-nine."

"That's a little high. I need six of these." She scanned the display, grabbing a plastic colored container about the size of a large brief-case.

"Over here." Cooper walked to a counter, where Harry plopped the plastic case, opening it. "Hey, this has a lot of stuff."

Cooper picked up a hex wrench. "Kind of cool because you can change the head size. Same for screwdrivers, too. How much?"

Harry flipped up the one side, all the tools secured within. "Fifty-three seventy-nine."

"Let's see if there are six." Cooper walked back to the display. "Not all the same color."

"I don't care." Harry this time piled three onto Cooper's out-stretched arms, cradling three herself.

Once checked out, back in the car, Harry was relieved to have knocked off a big item on her list. "Okay, what do you need?"

"Got Mom and Dad's. Bought them a big outdoor grill. Dad will use it even in sub-zero weather."

"What is it about men and grills?"

"Genetics," Cooper said with finality. "I need something for Jessica at headquarters."

Jessica was the secretary for law enforcement officers. Paperwork slowed everyone down so finally the department had hired secretaries, all of them having compliance training.

"Lots of nail polish."

"What?" Cooper questioned.

"Have you ever looked at her nails? She changes the colors constantly. Buy her that and one or two lipsticks. Jessica has a big investment in cultural femininity."

"You know, if I had more time maybe I would, too."

"Cooper, the last thing you would do is the nails, the pedicures, the facials. Add to that tight sweaters to expose proof of one's femininity."

Cooper really laughed at that. "I would be happy with less proof. Gets in the way."

"Does." Harry laughed, too, then returned to fentanyl. "Is fentanyl hard to get?"

"Unfortunately, no. It can be inhaled, sniffed, eaten. Mixed with other drugs. It's an opioid. It can even be taken as a lollipop. You can get it on the internet, or social media."

"Is it possible the three dead men didn't know they were taking it?"

"Yes."

"How do you get it?"

"Drug dealers. But fentanyl is also a legitimate medicine. It kills pain. A cancer patient might have it in their meds. Your husband probably has it in vet meds. It is more powerful than heroin. And it often is mixed with heroin." She continued, "All those platforms, Instagram, Facebook, Twitter, Snapchat, TikTok, Reddit, Twitch, Discord, Telegram, and what is being started even as we speak? You can order drugs from all of them."

"What. You just punch in an order?"

"Yes, but it's coded. Sometimes the emojis will advertise a deal. Often it's a high schooler or college kids. Older people know the codes but they are more clumsy about it. Let's say there's an emoji for painkiller. A high school football player wants that. Thinks he's ordering Percocet. The pills come. Laced with fentanyl. One swallow. He's dead. The young are especially vulnerable."

"That's awful."

"Awful and growing. People think they can order Xanax, Adderall. It's not so much cocaine and heroin, it's painkillers and mood elevators. The uproar over COVID, wear a mask, don't wear a mask, the shutting down of classrooms and some businesses have affected people. Young people want to be together. To party. Older people want to forget their troubles. I think. It's social media and counterfeit pills."

"Can you test for it?"

"Not if you're someone buying what you think is a pill. You'd have to be a doctor or chemist to know how to do it. People say they can test for it but it's not that easy. Remember this stuff costs money. It makes money. You can sell it as an inhaler, as a patch you put on your body, as a drug, in a drink. There are all kinds of ways to make it part of a drug cocktail. Whoever is selling it or stealing it isn't paying taxes. Illegal anything, drugs, booze, sexual services, makes big money."

"Ah." Harry buckled up again, as they were back in the car.

"Well, the three who have been shot most likely weren't selling it. They didn't look like they had a lot of money. But who is to say they hadn't been paid yet?"

"Cooper, I would never have thought of that."

"You're not a cop. It is unlikely they were selling but I have to consider everything and I still miss things." She fired up the car. "Criminals come in two classes. The stupid, who react emotionally, and the truly intelligent, who can plan, wait, and cover their tracks. There is a bell curve for crooks, too."

"Not a happy thought."

"You asked. Let's focus on Christmas, which is supposed to make us happy." Cooper smiled.

"Right."

16

Sunday

The clink of plates mingled with male voices. The Tavern's meals outdid every other establishment in Richmond. Only men enjoyed the food. They never discussed this with other men, women, and most emphatically not their wives. Some men rejoiced in the food even more than the women. The pianoforte played outside the dining room and the parlor where the ladies sat, impeccably dressed. To chat, flirt, and Fiona, getting on in years but blessed with a haunting alto, sang.

"She'll never be out of work." Desmond Duff leaned toward Hale Van Vlies, captain of Duff's ship, which had just come in.

Not only did it come in, the graceful, masted vessel sat low in the water; the goods were being removed. As the two men ate, listening to Fiona, they counted their profits as the furniture, silver, even horses were unloaded.

Tasting good bourbon, Desmond looked toward the sitting room. "Be easy for someone to steal goods while unloading. Small stuff."

Hale folded his hands together. "My first mate will watch everything, plus two other men assist. Luther would break a thief's jaw, crack his head, and throw him in the water. Maybe the man would swim out. Maybe he would drown. If he lives, he'll have a hard time finding work. It also instills fear in anyone shipboard with ideas."

"Ah." Desmond exhaled. "Fear always works."

"It's easy to understand. The law isn't."

Desmond smiled at Hale. "You're a good man to do business with. If you'd like a special dessert, allow me to oblige you."

They rose, walking into the sitting room. Hale wasted no time. He selected Lily, young and pretty, while Desmond, weary, listened to the music.

The ladies, whose attributes were generously displayed, talked to him. It was all very pleasant. He indicated he was tired but thought they were pretty girls.

Georgina sometimes walked back to the music room, as she euphemistically called it. Usually on a big night . . . and this one was, as so many ships had come in . . . she stood in the large front hall to greet her patrons.

Before Punch, her eleven-year-old slave, a bright young man, could take a gentleman's hat, cane, and gloves, Georgina had dispatched one of the girls to escort the man or men to the table, wishing them a good evening. She always wore a low-cut dress, leaning over to hand them menus when they sat. Georgina never missed a trick, literally.

Every man who walked through that door was made to feel important, unique, and most welcome.

One of those most welcome men, having eaten an early dinner, performed upstairs on the second floor. Livia Taylor happened to be working in the next room, but she could hear the thump, thump of the rocking bed.

Deborah, walking the hall, had made a quick $100, a large sum for forty minutes' work with Sam Udall, who was besotted with her. Sometimes he became so excited he didn't touch her. He lost all control. She babied him, played with him, would get him ready again, and tell him how exciting it was to watch him. One hundred dollars barely covered how fabulous this made him feel.

What Deborah felt at that exact moment was curiosity. She knew Beatrice Harbor's customer was rich, peculiar, and oddly secretive. A large man, overweight, people would have assumed a man like that would pay for a woman one way or the other. A wife could collect unto eternity. A lady of pleasure would profit for a night, or as often as he wanted to see her.

But thump, thump, thump.

Standing outside the door, she wondered. Beatrice didn't sound as though she was in trouble. Nor did Livia, whose bedsprings provided counterpoint to the thump, thump, thump.

A large "Ah" escaped Beatrice's room.

"Let me open the door. You're overheated," Deborah heard Beatrice offer. The door opened to reveal Bayard Ernst, swathed in a fine silk dress, low-cut bodice, a wig with massive curls, shoes made for such large feet, a telltale drip on the floor from underneath the skirt.

Deborah walked past him to check the window, which she opened farther as Beatrice ran downstairs for a drink for her customer.

Recovering a bit, Bayard sank into a chair. "Oh please, Deborah, don't tell anyone."

"What I want to know is where did you find that fabric, that apricot color?"

Brightened by this question, he beamed. "My sister imports fabrics from Milan. She helps me." He reached for the drink that Beatrice, having dashed up the stairs after running down, offered him.

"Precious lamb, thank you," Bayard gasped.

Deborah, turning away from Bayard, mouthed silently, "Precious lamb."

Beatrice pinched Deborah's forearm then focused exclusively on Bayard. "Take a deep breath. Drink more of Georgina's cool wine. You outdid yourself, lovie. I need a sip of your libation myself."

This was too good to leave, so Deborah put her hand on Bayard's shoulder. "We all like you here. You need to take care of yourself."

"Nobody knows." His voice quivered.

"Of course not," Beatrice quickly said. "The only reason Deborah knows is I opened the door to get you some air. You overexerted yourself and physical congress was not made for wearing a full gown on a hot night."

Deborah checked the door, which Beatrice had closed on her way back. She couldn't be too sure. Bayard handed out money freely, often asking Fiona for special songs. A large man, a tidy beard, seeing him in women's clothing was startling but Deborah and many of the girls had learned to handle anything, including raising the dead, which took skill and diplomacy. No man wants to fail at getting an erection. A good lady can usually fix that unless someone is falling ill and doesn't know it.

Another deep swig from the good wine. Georgina only served good stuff, and the heavyset man brightened.

Beatrice put her hand on his exposed shoulder, the gown was low cut. "Would you like me to help you out of this beautiful gown?"

"Yes, thank you." Bayard looked at Deborah, who headed for the door then stopped.

"Who is your seamstress? She's very good."

He smiled. "I have a woman on Shockoe Slip. Sworn to secrecy." He smoothed his skirt. "I love to touch my clothing. The fabrics feel so soft against my skin, and the colors . . ." He paused. "I'll fix an appointment for you. She is very discreet."

"I can see that. Well, I'm glad you are recovered." Deborah left.

As she approached the stairs, Livia came out of her room so the maids could change the sheets, the water, and the water bowl, plus anything that needed scrubbing.

The two women stared at each other then Deborah broke the silence. "You are wise to stay here. Wait until you get enough money for a house."

Livia sniffed. "That's what men are for."

Deborah smiled, did not respond, started down the stairs. Livia trailed her, reached the bottom, the music provided soothing tunes.

A short man, mid-forties, stood upon seeing her. She walked to him, kissing him on the cheek. Some of the girls laid claim to their richer customers in similar fashion.

"Let's listen to the music for a little bit."

"Of course."

Mignon, a tiny woman, peeked into the room. She took a break from working in the kitchen with her husband. Ducking back, she motioned to a young girl, perhaps fourteen, not yet working but learning the trade, and the customers. "Sally, see that the drinks are refreshed."

A half curtsy. "Yes, Miss Mignon."

Mignon looked back, counted heads, noting that Livia, who had torn the place apart, was now docile. She walked back to the kitchen.

Eudes, her talented husband, looked up. "Busy night."

"It is." She put her hands on her hips. "Livia is sitting next to Nestor Tilton. She is smiling, chatting with the other girls; swooning over Nestor takes imagination."

Eudes laughed. "His business must be doing well. People need grain. He spends so much time here. What we need in Richmond are more mills . . . big mills and more bridges."

"There are a number of grain dealers." Mignon usually accompanied her husband as they bought fresh food for the day.

"Middlemen. Middlemen always make the money. It's better to go to the mill, but who has the time?" He finished turning the edges of the pastry. "You are the baker. I'm the chef."

"Here." She stepped to his side, expertly flipping the paper-thin crust.

Outside the kitchen, the talks sounded louder.

"A lot of people," Eudes noted.

"Keeps the boss happy."

"That it will."

Men crowded the dining room. The music room was also crowded and some men and their escorts sat outside in the long backyard filled with lilac bushes, crepe myrtles in full bloom, and dense box-woods to hide patrons from view. One would have to walk into the back alleyway, open the garden gate, and come in to see who was really there. Even the stables had bushes to obscure the view. The men could rest assured that a wife would not be tiptoeing in the alleyway. Then again, so few even suspected their husbands' enter-tainments. But just in case, best to make sure no one knew anything.

Georgina, wearing a thin long-skirted dress, a light scarf over her shoulders, walked back in from outside. She'd needed a breath of air, but the air wasn't moving.

Turning for her office, Deborah left the music room to tell her in a low voice, "Nestor is here. Livia's next customer."

"Tell Christopher to be on the alert. Nestor's rig is in the stable, along with his horse."

"Yes."

Neither woman needed to say more. If one were to make an es-cape, a night when many ships were docked at the slip, or a Sunday, which created crowds and diversions, was perfect.

Beatrice, walking with Bayard, squeezed his hand as he prepared to go out to the stables. "You must bring me some of your fabrics."

"Yes, of course."

"You do have a rich sense of color. If I might make a suggestion. You need more comfortable shoes."

His eyebrows wrinkled. "Where can I go? Someone discreet."

"Try Isaac Berg on Broad, near the slip. If you will permit me, I will tell him you will pay a call and would like to be measured in private."

"Oh, would you?"

"Of course I will, Bayard. You are my favorite," she searched for the right word, "caller. Such excellent taste."

He bounced down the stairs a happy man.

Beatrice came back into the music room, where Deborah sat in a corner with Sam Udall. Upon seeing Beatrice she rose, excused herself, took Beatrice by the arm, walking her down the hall.

"How can he get through those skirts," she teased.

Beatrice smiled. "It is time consuming, but more interesting than buttoning britches. He is a gentle soul."

"Does he want to be a woman?"

"No. But he likes the clothing, he likes to lavish the clothing, textures, colors on himself."

"His jewelry is impressive."

"His mother's."

"Ah." Deborah walked to the front bar. Picked up a glass of lemonade. She didn't drink while working.

"He plucks it out of his wife's jewel box. He presented her with the jewelry after his mother died."

"Old Mrs. Ernst wore big stones." Deborah appreciated anything expensive. "I do wonder what would happen if Bayard's wife wanted a necklace, opened her jewel box to find it missing?"

"He has an excuse for that. If it happens, he'll tell her he took it to the jewelers, as the clasp was loose."

Deborah tilted her head. It was as good an excuse as any. She was more curious about the expensive clothing and jewelry than what he desired from Beatrice. Deborah felt she had seen or provided any manner of desires. The stranger the desire, the bigger the bill. Some of the girls specialized. Fiona, in her prime, would tie up and beat her customers with riding whips. Hard to believe that violence came from a woman with such a haunting voice. Fiona said what was pleasing to her was the money. Most of her customers wanted to be whipped until their cheeks were red. Some wanted their genitals tied up. But all wanted some form of humiliation or release. Or so she believed.

The night, heat slowly subsiding, provided typical entertainment. A few men passed out, were placed on chairs outside. Others became louder. Some, deep in the grape, would leave their girl, come down the stairs with their britches unbuttoned, their equipment exposed. Usually one of the girls back in the music room would point to the offending article. If he was too drunk to tuck it in, she would do it for him. Buttoning his britches. Rarely, a fight would break out.

Mostly, Georgina's gave the men escape from their daily lives. The place meant a good time. Good food. Pliant women. Then, too, business deals could be made. A happy man is generally a more optimistic one.

By three in the morning, the night dark, some of the customers slept with their girls. Others went home. Deborah, wide awake, as was Georgina, turned off the lantern in the office, the door being closed to the back door. They heard steps, quietly, coming down the back stairs. Steps in front of the office. The back door opened. Deborah silently slipped out of Georgina's office. She ducked back in.

"She's on her way."

"Christopher will follow to the corner, then get in our wagon, Michael driving." Georgina shrugged. "Fool."

"Many are." Deborah shook her head slightly.

"Yes," Georgina agreed.

Michael Raines, a carter, knew every road into and out of Richmond, every place you could hide yourself, too. A man in his position needed to escape thieves and the revenue man from time to time. He had carried goods to and from Georgina's for years, including girls. Those coming into the business, those retiring mostly due to age or infirmity, and a few brought and bought against their will. Georgina treated her girls well. She taught them how to dress, to speak, good manners. She took fifty percent of their earnings. The men paid directly downstairs. Never paid the girls. But Georgina kept honest accounts, giving each girl her earnings once a week. A smart young woman could set money aside for the future, the vain ones spent a lot on themselves, but that was their choice. Many sank into poverty when their beauty faded. Others moved far from Richmond, setting up boardinghouses, became seamstresses or cooks. Others managed households. No one had any idea of their former employment. Some married. For a girl to leave in her prime meant something was wrong.

In the distance, Michael and Christopher could see Livia and Nestor.

"Christopher, drive the wagon. I'm going on foot, he's heading for the west end. I can reach it before he does if I go through alleyways, back of the houses. Meet me at Grace Church."

"Yes, Sir."

Michael, glad for the darkness, covered the ground quickly, emerging as Nestor and Livia passed by the Episcopal church. Sprinting, he came up behind the wagon, pulled a scarf up over his face, easily reached Nestor. He pulled the startled man out of his seat and onto the road. The horse stopped. Livia had the presence of mind not to scream as Nestor tried to climb back in. Michael knocked him out, hitting Nestor with the heavy butt of his knife. Livia picked up the reins. Before she could duck, Michael grabbed the reins from her with his left hand, held on to her arm with his right.

"You can't stop me. I didn't steal anything."

"Whoa," he called to the horse.

The horse obediently stopped.

"Out," Michael ordered.

"No."

He turned sideways on the seat, placed his right boot on her side, kicking her out. Then he jumped out. Pulled her up.

"Walk with me."

First he tied up the horse by a water trough, while holding on to Livia with one arm. He was a strong man.

The mare stood by the water trough, drinking, as Michael pushed Livia toward the church.

"I am not going back to Georgina's."

"I know."

They reached Grace Church. He tried the chapel door. Open. He pushed her in.

"What is this?"

"Sit in a pew." He pushed her down, standing beside her. "Pray."

"For what?"

"For mercy. You threatened to expose some of the girls at Georgina's as escaped slaves. That was unwise."

Livia was figuring out that she was in more trouble than she'd thought. She figured she'd be dragged back to Georgina's to be beaten and locked in a room.

Voice shaky, the redhead murmured, "I wouldn't have done that."

"Pray."

As Livia started, "Heavenly Father—" Michael slipped into the pew behind her. Reached around, cupped her chin with his left hand, and in one smooth violent motion, slit her throat with the big sharp knife.

He left her slumping in the seat, blood spurting from the jugular. Walking outside he saw Christopher right where he told him to wait. He climbed up, took the reins, drove to pick up Nestor's horse and wagon. Then, both back to Georgina's, he left without speaking to anyone.

The next day the news of a woman murdered at the church galloped through Richmond. Neither Georgina nor Deborah said anything. The other girls spoke of Livia's fate, for they knew who it had to be, from the description. People noted the murdered woman was a flaming redhead, young. And Nestor had been found in the street, a crack in his skull, but alive. Young Sally, black, asked Milady, who was standing with Beatrice, "Is this because she tore up The Tavern?"

A long silence followed this, then Milady, in a low voice, counseled, "Sally, sometimes one must take justice in their own hands."

Another silence.

Beatrice, white, seeing the youngster puzzled, gently took her hand. "Years ago a handsome, arrogant, young man was crazy in love with Deborah. She refused to run off with him. He threatened to tell the constable, lawyers, whoever would listen, that Deborah was an escaped slave. He also threatened to tell on many girls here. He was found dead for all to see, propped in a doorway."

Sally's eyes widened.

Milady, again voice low, took Sally's other hand.

"Do you understand? Livia made the same threat."

Sally nodded.

Beatrice smiled. "We shall never speak of it again."

17

Saturday

"Great that you opened up the school building for us. You all have been working on that project for years." Joel Paloma smiled. "I keep forgetting to thank you."

"Tazio has been a terrific leader." Harry complimented the young woman behind the restoration.

"I never even knew about how the segregated schools worked. Did we have segregation in Ohio? Sure. But it was more subtle. Glad those days are gone."

"Me too. But I have learned how well built those old schools, houses, and commercial buildings are. You'll be surprised at the natural light. There is lots of room, too."

"Did you grow up with segregation?" Joel asked.

"No. But like in Ohio, there were ways for people to keep apart, be kept apart. Maybe that never ends. Wherever you are in the world, there is a vertical hierarchy. Here in North and South America, that hierarchy is easy to see."

"Is." He paused. "You are bringing Pirate, aren't you? To change the subject."

"He's still a puppy. About one and a half years old. I'm not going to show. I just want to learn."

"You might change your mind." He reached into a display of shiny apples. "Here. Try one."

"Thanks."

"Glad you stopped by." He smiled. "I try to use local growers. Sy Buford is good. Very good produce. Given the volume that I sell to small specialty stores and restaurants, I still have to use Washington State apples. It's often easier to buy volume from the states that produce large quantities of something. Like maple syrup from Vermont or even Canada. You'll find all that in my store, obviously, but I stress locally grown produce."

"You always have fresh vegetables and fruits. I remember when you grew Fair Market foods. I thought it was too fancy for us. Little did I know it was exactly what we needed."

"Americans are becoming more sophisticated about produce." Joel reached over to another display, plucking an orange. "Citrus. Big item. Florida and California mostly. Can tell the difference. Most people can't. Sy and I were talking about that. He said it's like when the soil, the sun, the temperatures, rainfall, those things differ from state to state. It's a tough business but I love it."

"Well, you deal with a shelf life."

"I do. That's why you need to learn how and what to order. The warehouse has a system where goods are moved according to age. Also, people have to learn. I'm forty. When I was a kid, there were avocados sold in Ohio but not many. Now, high demand."

"Thanks for the apple."

"Local." He beamed. "And don't forget our dinner outings."

"Fair is excited."

"Another tough business, the restaurant business. Some of the places on our list I occasionally supply. I have odd fruits in small numbers, like kumquats. I can deliver if needed."

"Bet you know all the secrets."

He nodded. "I'll never tell."

18

Sunday

"That really makes it cozy," Susan remarked about the wood-burning stove in the tack room, which was two-stalls wide.

"Fair gave that to me on Thanksgiving, when it got so cold. The electric baseboards never got this room above sixty-two, I swear. I'd sit in here in winter with my gloves on, fingers cut off so I could punch keys. Once I saw how the stove company would set it on a nonflammable base, I thought it would be okay."

"Better than okay." Susan sat next to Harry. "I like looking at the flame."

Harry hated her house being an office. When she walked into the old frame farmhouse she didn't want to think of work. Fair, on the other hand, had his office at work and a small office in the house. She was getting used to the stove. It had been only two weeks since she'd had it installed. She turned it on and was warm in fifteen minutes. Plus, she was out of the house.

Mrs. Murphy and Pewter dozed in front of the red enamel stove.

The dogs, on their backs, laid under the saddle racks and stacked saddle pads resting on an ancient tack trunk.

"I had no idea fentanyl is so prevalent or lethal."

"It's in the news but usually when someone famous overdoses." Susan leaned forward, her chair next to Harry's.

"Been enough of that." Harry scrolled to a graph with statistics. "This year more people died of it than prior and the numbers keep climbing. What I don't understand even after all this reading is, don't you know it's in whatever you swallow or sniff?"

"No. That's the point. Didn't Cooper tell you about all this?"

"Not in detail. She said it was widespread and appears to be worse around universities."

"Parties." Susan crossed her arms over her chest. "I partied but not a lot. I never got drunk because I'm so virtuous. I didn't want to puke in front of everybody." She grimaced. "Enough people did. Totally gross. Of course, we had some drugs. Pot, but nothing like today. You can't sell or taste the stuff now. If someone takes cocaine, they taste bitterness. Not fentanyl."

"So why is it mixed in?" Harry wondered.

"If it is a tiny dose, I guess it acts as a mood elevator. You feel the world is wonderful and so are you. Kills physical pain, too. A good chemist can make a safe mixture, a safe pill, a safe high, if that's possible. Some mix it with heroin." She turned to her friend. "You aren't going to solve the problem."

"I didn't think I would." Harry clicked off the big screen. "I'm trying to understand it because I can't see why a middle-aged man with no papers would have it in his system."

"People who are addicts don't look like addicts for the most part." Susan reflected on those she had known. "And people with money, it is easier to hide. Think of Ballard when he was young. You aren't on the streets taking risks to get your supply. You probably have good medical care and you can hide. If you're poor, trying to escape the despair, how can you hide?"

"I guess. Three nameless men, dead. I can't say as I care so much about the two thieves, but the man we found," she paused, "bothers me. I believe everyone deserves a Christian burial or some kind of final goodbye. If I hadn't seen him I probably would not have thought much about it. He looked like a normal middle-aged man. He didn't look like a criminal."

"Well, Harry, who does?" Susan lifted an eyebrow.

"All right." Harry agreed in her way. "But I have been turning this over in my mind. Number one, how many people that we see, think we know, are on something? If they knew how to take it, when to take it, we wouldn't know. They would be functioning people."

"So you think it's possible to take drugs and not slide into the abyss?"

"Susan, how many people do we know who drink but don't become alcoholics? Peoples' systems are different and so is their discipline."

"If you had discipline, you wouldn't start," Susan said forcefully.

"I don't agree. Something relaxes you. Makes you feel wonderful, I can't think of another word because high isn't as accurate. Maybe a person can be in a light altered state as opposed to an oppressive one."

"So you admit it becomes oppressive?"

"For some people. Think of the people we have known who have gotten roaring drunk at parties, especially when we were in our late twenties and early thirties, behaved in an outrageous way, but only acted like this on rare occasions. Not binge drinkers. Just someone who gets loaded socially from time to time."

"I don't know. Most of the people we know don't party that much anymore unless you count barbecues." She smiled. "Men drink too much beer at barbecues."

"And how do we know that when they go to the bathroom they aren't taking lines of cocaine? And still seem normal. Extra happy maybe." Harry folded her hands together. "We don't know."

"But what has this to do with your, shall I say, intense interest? You know how you get, Harry."

"Well, yes." Harry knew the oldest friend in her life did know how she could become obsessed. "But this is where my mind is going. What if the man we found didn't take fentanyl?"

"What do you mean?"

"What if it was stuffed down his throat or he was given a drink with a lethal dose in it?"

Susan stopped. "Well?"

"It could happen."

"Yes." That was drawn out.

"Well, that's where I'm heading. And maybe the other two were given the stuff, too. Three men. One not of Northern European descent. Maybe that's a better description. But three men with no papers, no phones, no coins in their pockets. Dead."

"Because?" Susan obviously didn't want to be reeled in, but she was listening harder now.

"What if they knew something. Something that would destroy or ruin someone powerful? Then again, maybe they performed some service for this person. Some illegal service. See what I mean? This really could be murder."

"But so what? What has it got to do with anything around us?"

"That's just it. They were killed here, right? So I think it's possible there is some form of criminal activity making someone, maybe even someone here, huge pots of money."

"Drugs?"

"Why not? Or smuggling in illegal workers . . . or smuggling in sex workers. I'm sure there are other possibilities, but in a situation like the latter two examples, fear of the kingpin, again the only word I can think of right now, would be useful. If a few people got out of line or reached too deep in the till, kill them. Make it look like a drug overdose."

"Harry, I marvel at how your mind works." Susan shook her head.

"Okay. It's a bunch of ideas without any proof. Just ideas, but what if there are more murders?" Harry sat up straight. "Christmas is a good time to steal or kill. Everyone is focused on the holiday."

"That's a fact," Susan agreed. "We all are on overload."

"And what if whatever it is this person, or persons, is selling would sell even more units during Christmas? A captive market."

"To change the subject," Susan had had enough, "don't forget we are going to The Old Tavern in Richmond tomorrow. Should be de-lightful, if for nothing else than seeing Richmond decorated."

"Won't." Harry returned to her subject. "Just think on what we've talked about. You often come up with insights."

"Here's my insight. I'm not going to trouble myself unless there's another death."

19

Monday

Pulling her thick wool coat closer to her body, her cashmere scarf soft against her neck, Harry walked through the center aisle stable at The Old Tavern in Richmond. Fair walked with her, as did Susan and Ned. Joel Paloma and Jodie had not yet arrived. Nor had Ballard Perez.

"The owner spent money. The wrought iron, the brass newels on top of the stall dividers, the walnut roughs and stall boards." Harry was impressed.

Fair, arm through his wife's, nodded. "Well, the forests were so thick. Finding beautiful hardwoods was easy. Cutting and planing them wasn't, but as there were no power tools, no one thought they were being mistreated. Hard labor was the way of the world. And these stalls took labor."

"Skilled." Ned smiled. "A lot like the stalls at Mount Vernon."

"Those with money copied what was done in Europe. When Fair and I visited England, of course we visited big estates. All of them overwhelming, but what I really wanted to see were the stables and outbuildings. Some of the buildings we walked through had been built in the thirteenth, fourteenth century. Of course, many of the cathedrals were older than that, but to see the service buildings, that dazzled me."

"Me too." Ned agreed. "Funny what you remember, but my junior summer Mom and Dad gave me the gift of a trip to Europe. You know they didn't have much. They must have saved from the day I entered Dartmouth. I was determined not to waste their money or my time. I poked my head in every museum, public building, concert hall, but what really floored me, knocked me out was," he paused, then beamed, "the Alhambra. I know you all haven't been to Spain. You've got to go."

"If we can ever wriggle free, we will." Fair smiled.

"The only way we will get the time is if my husband takes a partner. It's not an easy decision." Harry's gloved hand reached for her husband's. "Plus we can't just be throwing money around."

"Oh, Harry, how many years have I heard that. You aren't on food stamps," Susan chided.

"That doesn't mean I couldn't be," Harry shot back.

"Come on. Let's look at the tack room." Fair headed for the large room in the middle of the eastern aisle, a wash and tacking stall opposite it. The buckets of water had to be brought in from the well. Again, you needed muscle power. Bucket after bucket of water is tiring.

"Bunk beds," Harry exclaimed.

"And a fireplace with a thick screen, slate underneath the screen. That's what would scare me. Fire," Susan mentioned. "Boy, everyone had to be extra careful." She thought a minute. "We have the potbellied stoves at school. When were stoves invented?"

"Potbellied stoves? Well," Fair thought a moment, "the Franklin stove was invented in 1742, maybe twenty-five years before this place was built. Potbelly, later. Early 1800s, I think. More efficient than a fireplace but this fireplace is made of stone, sits on stone, has a flue going up and out. It's not as efficient as the iron stoves but in this space it would keep you warm. Keep full water buckets from freezing. That would make morning chores easier."

"Come on. Let's see if the others are here." Susan led them out of the stable; they closed the doors and walked up the back way to The Tavern.

"These boxwoods are huge," Harry noted.

"Well, they're over two hundred years old." Ned, who was in Richmond part of each week because of the House of Delegates, learned about the city's history. Even though born in Virginia, he never paid much attention to the capital. He liked history, so his few years there to date gave him a welcome antidote to the fussing, deal-making at the House.

"It's one of the great things about living in one of the original thirteen," Harry said.

"Honey, some people don't know we are out of the seventeenth century," Fair teased her.

"Oh, we are at least in the eighteenth," she replied.

"Well, here we are. This really is a lovely structure." Ned opened the back door as a light snow was falling.

"Hey there." Joel, Jodie, and Ballard called to them from the front hall as they heard the door open and Fair's voice.

"What a great idea to come here," Harry complimented Joel.

"He knows everything." Jodie smiled. "If it involves food, Joel knows about it."

"Well, it is my business." He smiled back.

A well-dressed woman appeared from a side room. "Ah, Mr. Paloma. Your party's table is ready." She walked them into the dining room. Seated them. Their waiter arrived with handwritten menus.

"Before you decide, we have to pick straws." Harry reached in her small buttery-colored Veneta bag, gorgeous and costly, to retrieve straws.

She arranged them in her hand so the tops would all be even.

Joel and Jodie laughed as Susan said, "She never forgets anything."

"Ladies first." Harry indicated Jodie should pull.

She did. Followed by Susan.

Next came Ballard. "Drat. I wanted to head the table." He twirled the long straw between his fingers.

"Joel." Harry reached over to him.

"Ah." He pulled the short straw.

Fair, even though Joel had the winning straw, if it was winning, plucked the last long straw. "You're it."

Beaming, Joel announced, "As the head of this table, do study your menus."

Except for Joel, everyone looked around. "This really is historic." Susan gasped slightly. "The tables, the china, the tablecloths. This has always been a tavern, right?"

"Famous for its food and other delights," Joel informed them. "The couple that put it on the map, Eudes and his wife, Mignon, were talented. Word of the good food spread."

"Mother loved to come here. You know how she adored old gossip and good china." Ballard laughed.

"What's the difference between a tavern and an ordinary?" Susan asked Ballard. "I should know, but I don't. You know you're good at history."

"A tavern was usually able to sell food and drinks. An ordinary also served food and drinks, and might have a room or two. Taverns were often larger and while they did not necessarily have rooms for the night, they might, but an ordinary almost always did," Ballard answered.

Fair interjected, "Before I set up my practice I looked at an ordinary from the early eighteenth century in Louisa County. Thought I might be between Richmond and Albemarle but then I settled on Albemarle. So many of these places survived."

"This one certainly did. It's beautiful," Jodie enthused. "Paintings on the wall. Subdued colors. Fireplaces, one at either end. It's so well done and probably always was for the bluestocking trade."

"Yes." Joel paused a moment, a sly smile on his face. "The woman who started this, Georgina Howard, made a fortune. Not much is known about her except she was born in Virginia, on the other side of the James. Obviously a shrewd woman.

"In the evenings, she had a lady play the pianoforte, sometimes a harpist, and a singer noted for her beautiful voice. But what was not bandied about, although we know it from diaries of men at the time, this was a high-class brothel. The rooms were upstairs. All carried out with discretion."

"Sex sells." Harry laughed.

"Always and ever," Ballard chimed in. "There were even gay brothels, too."

"Well, the story goes, or the diaries go, that she first made bundles of money here. Beautiful women, good food, protection of her clients. And there were people, not women, of course, who ate here, did business here at the tables, but did not hire the girls. One of her most fervent customers was a banker, Sam Udall. She made many business deals with him. She was highly intelligent about using other people's money and she made them money. She also took a junior partner, for lack of a better word, a black woman who worked here and they started yet another brothel, down by the docks. Apparently that woman was spectacularly gorgeous. They both died very rich women."

"Are you all ready?" the waiter asked, as the drinks had already been served while they were talking.

"The menu is from the time." Joel motioned for Susan to order first.

"Fascinating." Susan then read off the menu. "I'd like the slow roasted beef with carrots, potatoes, and mushrooms. Those are roasted, too?"

"Yes, ma'am." The waiter wrote this down.

As the others ordered, all dishes from the time, Harry finally reached her decision, she had asked to be put last.

"Okay, I want the salmagundi."

"On a cold night?" Susan's eyebrows raised up.

"I love that salad and I'll have hot tea to drink."

The food was delicious and when the waiter returned to see if anyone needed anything else, Jodie asked him about a large portrait. "Is that Georgina?"

"Yes. There's not much known about her personal life. She seems to have been a woman who lived for business. She had great power in Richmond, as she knew everything." He thought a moment. "Died in her seventies, shortly after Monroe's second term, which ended in 1825."

"Do you have to learn the history to work here?" Harry asked.

The waiter grinned. "Not a problem. It's anything but boring. Two murders, maybe more. Political programs hatched. Ladies of the evening. Deals made on ships, property, who knows what else? Georgina knew how to entertain."

"She looks rather formidable, doesn't she?" Fair cast his eyes at the huge oil painting.

"Certainly well dressed, perfect hair. A good-looking lady," Ballard agreed. "I can't imagine how hard it was for a woman to be in business for herself at the time. If she married, she was chattel."

"Well, I bet Georgina didn't marry." Harry grinned slightly.

"As a matter of fact, she did not," Joel confirmed.

The waiter took their dessert orders.

A plate of orange-glazed sweetbreads, with a small crème brûlée was placed before Harry.

"Isn't that odd? That was on the menu in Fredericksburg. I've never heard of it." Susan studied the attractive plate, although she wasn't sure about sweetbreads.

"Is odd," Harry agreed.

As they all were served their desserts, the waiter handed a champagne cocktail to each guest. Sugar cubes soaked in bitters, a cherry, and a twist, plus champagne comprised the drink.

"On the house," the waiter said with a smile. "Georgina offered this to her favorite guests. Of course, she had many favorites."

As he left after thanks, they all sipped the time-tested cocktail.

Joel held up his glass. "To Dom Pérignon, a monk at the abbey of Hautvillers, he invented the drink of the stars in 1673."

"I had no idea." Susan sipped the delicious drink.

"Bless him." Fair loved champagne.

"Isn't it remarkable how much we use from centuries past? Sherbet. The Romans ate sherbet," Harry told them. "That's the only thing I know about food history."

They chatted, talked, then Joel asked the group, "Would you all like to see the kitchen? It's close to its original state."

"We'd love to," the ladies chimed in together.

The waiter, having been prepped by Joel unbeknownst to the others, as well as being tipped, led them through the swinging doors.

It was nearly original. The big difference was electricity, plus the huge old wood-fired stove had been replaced by an equally huge Aga stove. In every other respect, it was as Mignon and Eudes left it.

The group stood to the side as waiters walked in and out, plus the chef and workers were more numerous than Harry had imagined they would be. The kitchen was spacious.

"If it weren't so cold, I'd show you the icehouse, which is to the side, outside, dug deep so there was even ice in the summers," Joel volunteered.

"You must know everything," Harry teased him.

"Well, I do know many of the restaurant owners. I like the food business but the story and menu of early establishments fascinates me. The chef and his wife were not slaves. He was freeborn. He said she was, too, but many people felt she was an escaped slave. Whatever they were, they had talent. Today, they'd have their own TV show."

As they left the kitchen, Harry mentioned to Joel, "Are the workers, some of them in the kitchen, undocumented?"

A tight smile crossed his lips. "I never ask."

20

Saturday

"*Why is she looking at dogs?*" Pewter swept her whiskers forward, which made her appear inquisitive.

"*She has to go to that special class with the famous man,*" Tucker answered.

"*What famous man?*" Pewter looked over the saddle pad, as she was on the neatly stacked pile in the tack room.

"*Mr. Irish Wolfhound,*" Tucker simply replied. "*Sam Ewing.*"

Pirate, on the floor in front of the stove, lifted his handsome head. "*I have to walk and trot in circles. It's not hard but why can't I run in a field? I mean, if there are going to be shows for dogs like me, couldn't we be out in the open where we can really fly?*"

Mrs. Murphy, sitting on the large desk, peering at the computer screen, looked down at her buddies. "*He's handsome and has a big mustache. Kind of like your mustache, Pirate.*" Then the tiger cat laughed, sounding like little breaths puffing out.

"*Do you like going in circles?*" Pewter asked.

"It's okay. I'll do whatever Mom asks. I just want to be with her." Pirate, so sweet, watched Pewter's tail sway hypnotically.

"I like being with her, too, if she has food. Catnip is good." Pewter flicked an ear forward while the other one remained back.

The phone rang, an old landline on the desk.

"Hi," Harry answered.

"What are you doing?" Susan, on her cell, wondered.

"Trying to understand the Irish wolfhound standard. I'm looking at all these photographs over the years from AKC shows. Beautiful hounds, but I can see differences."

"Like what?"

"Well, some are fuller than others. The coat color might differ in the colored photos but that's accepted. I have a hard time with stills. I need to see an animal move, which is why the classes help."

"You say you aren't going to show Pirate but you sure are putting a lot of work into this to be sitting on the sidelines."

"Yeah." Harry paused. "I don't have the time or money to really show. He's such a good sport, though, my boy. I wouldn't mind some small shows, something we could do together without all that pressure. I like the other wolfhound people and if I meet people with other breeds, that would be interesting."

Susan giggled. "You think the English bulldog people will look like Winston Churchill?"

Harry laughed. "Bet some do. One of my favorite of Fair's ties is the one like Churchill's, dark navy with tiny white dots."

"Ned wears his, too. It is handsome and understated."

"I'm a little sexist, but I like men to be understated. Not sure I trust someone who calls attention to himself with loud clothing, although some of the pictures of Sam Ewing in the ring are, well, vivid."

"The breeder Linda told you about. That guy?"

"Right."

Susan pondered the clothing issue. "You know, we get to wear silk, satin, exotic fabrics, really, in all the colors women can wear. I can understand if a man wants some color, even if it's a lime green tie with a gray suit. Something."

"I guess. But for me power means understatement. And men have the power still, so why do I want to see someone in, say, a pink tuxedo? Means he isn't powerful. Means he needs attention."

"Well, Harry, why does a man have to be powerful?"

"Because we're not and I want us to have fifty-one percent of the power," Harry fired right back at her old friend. "If I have to tart myself up to be accepted, I am already on a lower rung. A man has only to wear white tie and he is the epitome of elegance."

A long pause followed this. "Well, yes, and my Ned is beyond handsome in white tie. I mean, look how many years we have been married, but in those tails, his top hat under his arm, he is to die for. And as our representative, he is serious."

"Some sure aren't." Harry laughed.

"Well, do you want political power? We used to talk about this in our twenties. Then the pressures of everyday life squashed that subject."

"No. But that doesn't mean I want to be a second-class citizen."

"Then you have to fight."

"Come on, Susan, I do, and so do you. We vote. We work for a candidate we believe in. We support the League of Women Voters, but do I want to run? No. Do I want to dedicate my life to something for which I have no affinity? No. I have an affinity for alfalfa, and orchard grass, and sunflowers. I love farming. I'd be next to death sitting in a state house or in Congress, plus I'd stand up and let it fly, you know?"

"I do. Just giving you a tweak. Wanted to push back on your pink tuxedo thought."

"Do you want to see a man in a pink tuxedo?"

"If he's having a good time, why not?"

"You're probably right. I'm being crabby."

"*She admits it,*" spoke one who could out-crab anyone.

"*Humans have moods.*" Tucker always defended Harry.

"Hold on. My other line is blinking. Ned won't give up any of our lines." Susan switched off then came back on in a minute. "Harry, are you sitting down?"

"Yes, I'm at my desk in the tack room."

"Sy Buford was found dead early this morning."

"Good Lord, but he looked healthy."

"That was Ronnie, the accountant at the orchard. She said one of the workers found him in the back of the peach orchard. If it hadn't been winter, he didn't know if he would have seen him. No signs of violence or anything. Just flat on his back, snow on him, gone."

"What terrible news, and just before Christmas." Harry thought of Sy's family.

"Ronnie also said Marjorie would have an autopsy done, as he showed no signs of any kind of illness."

Marjorie was Sy's wife.

"I guess everyone, the winter staff at the orchard, are in shock?"

"Yes, everyone is in shock. He inherited and expanded a great business. Maybe the pressure got to him. Boom. One big heart attack, and he wasn't even fifty."

"Guess we'll know after the medical examiner's report. We'll find out quickly. That's some comfort. I mean, I think it would be if it were your husband."

"Actually, Ned told me that around Christmas there are more deaths. Heart attacks. Violence. A murder or two, but mostly suicide."

"Really?" Harry was surprised.

"Not that I think Sy killed himself."

"Right." Harry chewed on this for a bit. "The statistics still show that men die before women. Heart attacks. Strokes. Suicide. Maybe that's the price of being the superior sex. Pressure that wears you down."

"Maybe so. But I don't want to be shoved aside any more than you do. I want young women to have opportunities, yet with success comes a lot of responsibility and pressure. Still, I think we can handle it better because we aren't too proud to seek help."

"Oh, I don't know. I wouldn't be so quick to go to a therapist."

"Harry, if you were in great pain I think you would."

"I'd talk to you."

"And I'd talk to you, too. We are lucky to have each other."

"Maybe Sy didn't have anyone to talk to. Maybe it all piled up and his heart shut down."

"I am sorry for this phone call. Just out of the blue. This will prey on my mind all day."

"Susan, mine, too. Hey, come over. I'll make sandwiches. You can look at these Irish wolfhound photos with me or we can sit in the kitchen and talk. I don't feel like being alone and Fair won't be home until six or later. End-of-the-year paperwork. But this upsets me. I really liked Sy."

"Are you going to call Fair?"

"No. If someone doesn't call him, I'll tell him when he gets home. No point in disrupting his day when he's on overload."

A half hour later, Susan and Harry sat in the kitchen.

The animals also sat in the kitchen; although Harry had fed everyone to deter begging, that didn't stop Pewter.

"Get all your shopping done?" Susan asked.

"Almost. Thought about books for everyone else."

"Always a good gift."

"Susan, back to Sy. Can't help it. Did Ned say the autopsy would be done soon?"

"Actually, he did call the medical examiner after we spoke and she promised they would try to do it this week, if not early next week. No point in having something like this hanging over the family. If a body comes in who has been shot, everyone usually knows what has happened, even if they don't know who did it. This is different. Could have medical repercussions."

"Never really thought about that. It's going to be a heart attack or stroke," Harry predicted.

"What if it isn't?" Susan said.

21

Monday

Stifling heat enveloped Richmond. The river made it feel worse. The girls sat in the back this late afternoon. Bodices opened a bit to catch whatever breeze might blow their way. They lightly fanned themselves; helped.

Deborah leaned back in the chair, which would have fit in on an English estate. Georgina paid attention to fashions in England and France, had them copied by workmen in the city.

Lily and Sally were both young, Lily white and Sally black; they leaned back on the bench, giggling. Beatrice, opposite them in another lovely chair, was sipping a lemonade, remembering being that young. While she wasn't old, a woman could age fast in this business.

The boss was in her office, heedless of the heat, going over the bills.

Eudes, Mignon behind him, knocked on the open door.

"Yes." She liked these two.

"Given the heat, Ma'am, might I substitute braised beef with Mrs. Purdles's spinach salad? Should be refreshing with the fruits. And we have chicken. Can't ever go wrong with chicken salad or even fried chicken."

"You're right. It's too hot for heavy dishes. Sherbet?"

"Peach, lemon, strawberry." He smiled.

"You know the Romans made sherbet."

"No, Ma'am, I didn't know that, but I expect those ancient peoples were ahead of us."

"Is there anything else?"

Back outside, a horse whinnied in the tiny paddock behind The Tavern. It was Nestor's mare. She fit right in. Most city homes had a mews with a bit of grass and flowers between the back of the house and the stables, which were often built to match the house. Nestor did not know what happened to his mare. If he did, he would not go back to Georgina's.

"Lordie, will this heat ever pass?" Fiona fanned herself vigorously.

Lily, next to her, smiled. "You're giving me a good breeze."

"Well, fan back." Fiona jabbed at her with her fan.

The gate by the mews opened with a creak. Sandy Oster walked toward the women, whose attributes were generously displayed thanks to the swelter. The girls simply placed their fans over their bosoms.

"Ladies."

"Mr. Oster," they replied, as all knew him as the constable.

"I'm calling to see if one of your number is missing?"

Deborah took over. "No, Mr. Oster."

"You may have heard that a young woman was murdered in the church on Grace Street. We picked up a man with head injuries, but he was too befuddled or frightened to tell us anything."

"Perhaps he killed her," Deborah posited.

"He swears he didn't. Declared that as he was driving a young woman out of town he was pulled from his cart by a man whose face was covered."

"Who found her?"

"The priest. Father Hinson."

"Well, the poor fellow must have suffered a shock," Beatrice chimed in. "And in his house of worship."

"Some people thought the young woman worked here. I mean resided here."

Deborah half smiled. "No. Our residents can come and go as they please, but no one is missing."

He looked from one attractive woman to the other. "I see."

Deborah asked him, "Will you be expanding the number of watchmen, Mr. Oster? Might deter these unfortunate incidents."

A long sigh escaped him. "Ah, money. We truly do need more watchmen."

"Perhaps in good time. It will help the city grow. People need to feel safe." Jocelyn smiled at him.

"Yes. Yes, indeed. Well, thank you for your time."

As he left, no one said a word until he was out of earshot.

"Nestor had the good sense to keep his mouth shut," Beatrice murmured.

"Maybe he really didn't remember. Blows to the head can erase memory," Fiona suggested.

"He was a fool." Deborah shrugged.

"Aren't they all?" Milady sniffed.

"Perhaps," Beatrice answered noncommittally.

"Let me go tell Georgina." Deborah rose, walking back into The Tavern.

The girls looked at one another.

Finally Lily snapped her fan shut for a moment. "Did she steal anything?"

"She didn't pay for her most recent dresses. At least that's what I heard." Milady shrugged.

"Mmm." Fiona nodded.

"Think there will be many callers tonight?" Sally asked.

"Too hot," Fiona replied.

A devilish look crossed Jocelyn's face. "When the night is hot and sticky, not the time to dunk your dicky. When the frost is on the pumpkin, that's the time for dicky dunkin.'"

They all laughed, then not mentioning Livia's threat, which they all knew, Fiona quietly said, "We have to stick together."

All nodded in agreement, then Fiona sang, "Auld Robin Gray."

The others joined in. No one planned to work at Georgina's. But they had landed there in one fashion or another. They did need one another, and most felt they were freer than respectable women.

22

December 13, 2021

Monday

"I'll fire up this stove now. It's bitterly cold out there and if Fair stops by on his way home from the clinic, he can stoke it again, then do it again on his way to work. Will get the chill out of the room. When it's this cold you need to keep the stove going." Harry carried a heavy hardwood log, as did Susan and Tazio.

"My weather app predicts twelve degrees tonight." Tazio grimaced.

"It's only in the mid-twenties now. Well, it's almost the winter solstice." Susan carefully placed the log inside. "It's frigid in here now."

"Sure is." Harry knelt down to wiggle around the logs so Tazio could place another heavy log on top. "Thank God for these little log starters. Helps."

"We've got enough folded newspaper in here, too. Should catch quickly." Susan brought one more log. "Tight squeeze."

Harry knelt down to slightly move the other top log. "Try again. Kick it with your boot if you have to. It will slide in."

Susan did as instructed, and the log wedged in. She pulled a box of kitchen matches out of her coat pocket, removed her heavy gloves, knelt down, and lit the paper.

"Where did you find the matches?" Tazio asked.

"In the cabinet over there in the corner. Susan is always prepared. Girl Scout." Harry smiled.

"Well, that's the Boy Scout motto but now girls can join the Boy Scouts." Tazio stepped back as the paper roared, touching off the small starter logs and other kindling. "Were you two Girl Scouts?"

"We were. Actually, I learned a lot. I don't know if I would learn as much with the boys. Then again, we don't have to find out," Susan replied.

"It's funny how the stuff you take for granted changes over time. Think of my grandparents going from horse and buggy to cars. Every generation faces change but maybe they faced the most." Harry had liked her grandparents, although they seemed so old when she was young.

Shutting the door, flipping the door lock, Tazio held out her hands, gloves off now. "Feels good close-up." She looked around. "This is a big space but the old potbelly can really warm it up over time. Maybe not in the seventies, but it gets in the middle sixties here. The schoolrooms had the kids' body heat to help some."

"Bet those teachers on the raised dais were strict." Susan also put her hands nearer the stove.

"When I drove by Buford's Orchards, I noticed the large black wreath on the door." Harry changed the subject. "Sad. And they always have the best Christmas wreaths."

"Wonder how long it will be before we know how he died?" Tazio wondered.

"Don't know, but I asked Coop if she thought there might be foul play. You know how people come up with stuff. How they could come up with anything about Sy, I don't know."

"What did she say?"

"No. But she did tell me, when I asked, what happened to the van that veered off the Miller School Road. She said it had been towed to the chained lot for abandoned vehicles. I asked her was there anything in there they overlooked when this first happened. She said no, a couple of wooden crates, empty. A few seeds. So at one time I guess there were vegetables and fruit in there."

"I have to take another step back. This thing is throwing out the heat." Tazio walked away.

"Where are you going?"

"To the bleachers."

"And."

"Still cold over here," Tazio answered.

"Bet it won't be so cold when we have our class tomorrow."

"You'll still need some kind of jacket," Susan predicted.

"Back to Sy. Thought it was wise of the family to delay a service until after Christmas. No one knows if an indoor gathering will be allowed."

"You know, no matter what the state or federal government says, people will go home for Christmas. They may not be able to fly, but they'll drive." Harry felt people could take only so much separation.

"A mess." Tazio came back nearer the stove. "Mom was not happy that I wouldn't be home. St. Louis is a long, long drive, and I don't have that much time, really. I told her once COVID restrictions were lifted, I'd be home."

"I wonder if there is a family waiting for the fellow we found? Or even the men who fled from the van?"

"Harry, you've got to forget that. You're getting obsessed."

"Well, it's sad. And if your son or husband or brother doesn't come home for Christmas, you know something is wrong," Harry fired back.

"Oh hell, he can come home and something will be wrong." Susan laughed.

23

Tuesday

"See if you can lengthen your stride, Mrs. Cobb," Sam Ewing called out. "And smile. Look like you're having a good time."

Looking at Bugsy, head carriage stiff, as Veronica had the lead too high, the woman realized the only way to lengthen her own gait would be to relax her lead.

"Better," Sam encouraged as Veronica also realized she was out of shape.

The pair stopped at their place in the lineup, with Bugsy worried about her human's heavy breathing. She nudged Veronica's hand with the leash, producing a rub on the head.

"Good girl."

"Are you all right?" Bugsy asked.

"Next." Sam motioned for Isadore Reigle to move out with Jumpin' Jack.

Jumpin' Jack never needed prodding. Inexperienced as the two were, they kept their pace steady, the big fellow showing to good effect.

Sam, under his breath, remarked to Linda, "Hound's right front paw turns out."

"It does. Affects his gait. He's got such good bone. But it's a flaw. Isadore is aware of it."

"Mmm" was the reply.

Isadore, in better shape than Veronica, was nonetheless glad to finish his trot.

"Izzy, you two looked good together," Veronica quietly said.

"Thanks." Isadore was more nervous than he cared to admit.

"Next."

Ballard, smiling at Lafayette, walked to the circle then picked up a trot. Ballard wore a coat and tie. The two then began to run in sync.

"Isn't that Candida Perez's son?" Sam asked. "She showed Norfolk terriers and Scottish deerhounds. An unusual combination back in the seventies and eighties."

"Yes. He knows how to show a dog."

"I'd like to encourage Ballard to show him."

Sam called out, "Reverse." Then replied, "Drugs? I recall he's had quite a struggle. She'd lament this at shows."

"Clean for seven years."

"Good for him." Sam appreciated anyone overcoming a struggle. "Mr. Perez. Stop. Now come up to me directly."

Ballard did so and Lafayette, that smart fellow, looked up at Sam and smiled.

"Thank you."

Ballard and a playful Lafayette returned to the bleachers.

Alice Minor, scarf floating behind her . . . she needed it to keep warm, being cold by nature . . . gracefully trotted around, looking as though she had shown Irish wolfhounds all her life, which she had not. Marvel, her dog, matched her in stride, focused, ears a bit up, wanting to please. He was a solid hound, a bit of padding but not fat. In a class with a good, experienced judge, that slight padding might keep him from the blue ribbon, but he wouldn't fall below a third or even reserve.

"Good boy," Alice praised him.

Ballard's showing abilities egged her on. She wanted to match him.

"Let's do it again," the happy fellow encouraged her.

"Use the turn to your advantage," Sam called out as Marvel took a step ahead of Alice, somewhat unbalancing her but she quickly recovered, doing as Sam said. She was able to somewhat hide the insecure footwork by catching up to Marvel on the turn.

Sam nodded to Alice then held up his hand. "He has a big stride. You're a petite lady. And you used that turn to your benefit."

"Good on you, Alice." Ballard meant that. "And good on Marvel."

She plopped next to him on the bleacher while Marvel and Lafayette watched Harry and Pirate go out.

Taking a deep breath, Alice murmured, "There's a lot to showing. I had no idea."

"Watch *Best in Show.*" Ballard laughed, as the film was beloved of dog show people.

Harry winked at Pirate. He stared at her intently.

"Let's boogie, Big Boy."

His ears pitched up, he looked up at her, then they began to walk.

"Trot," Sam called out.

"We'll show 'em." Pirate was getting into this.

Linda, knowing these two, grinned.

Sam called, "Reverse." Then he looked at Linda. "I know you like these two. He's still too weedy but when he matures he should be shown. He could go head to head with Lafayette."

"We'll see. Harry is hesitant."

"I'll take care of that," Sam, confidence always high, predicted.

Pirate, feeling the excitement, lifted his head slightly and extended his reach as Harry trotted. Given that she rode her horses,

followed behind a beagle pack on foot, plus managed her farm chores, Harry was in great shape, as was Pirate.

"How young?" Sam asked Linda.

"Year and a half."

"Good mover. Great shoulder." This was said in a low voice as the two in the ring didn't want others to hear.

"Very."

Harry and Pirate hit their spot. Harry leaned over, she didn't have to lean far, to kiss her big boy on the head.

Stepping out, Joel started before being asked, which suggested he was nervous. He was a little bit, but mostly he wanted to shine. He was competitive. He knew Ballard looked really good and Harry moved effortlessly with Pirate.

Sam keenly watched Lodestar move along. The hound's hind end showed the bit of the slope desired. Not a big drop, but a noticeable end to a long back.

"He's trying too hard," Sam, voice low, said to Linda.

"He wants to win. Likes the center of attention."

"The bow tie tells me that. Why wear a bow tie in the dead of winter? Is this his first hound?"

"Yes. Not bad."

"No. Does he have money?" Then he called out, "Stop. Now slowly reverse your course. Slowly."

Joel, a bit confused, as he thought he'd put in a good run, did as he was told.

"Lots of money. A food purveyor for central Virginia."

"All right, Mr. Paloma. Now trot. Not so fast. You want Lodestar to look relaxed, an easy way of going, as they say in the horse world."

Joel was getting it.

"Better. The slower pace shows Lodestar at a gait where I can study him.

"Thank you," Sam said as Joel returned to his spot. He reached into his heavy jacket inside pocket for a ballpoint pen. Finding it, he pulled out a Smythson small notebook from his outside pocket. He opened it, revealing medium blue pages, and began to scribble. Looking up he called, "Celtic Queen."

After a full round, Veronica was waiting.

Veronica looked up as Sam motioned for her and Bugsy to come straight to him. She walked.

"Trot."

She trotted, her face flushed, then stopped right in front of him.

"Now trot back and return to your place."

After everyone walked, trotted, loped, they now stood up as Sam carefully walked to each dog, opening their jaws, feeling along their shoulders, spine, rubbing down those sloping hindquarters, running his hands down the legs and under those long stomachs. Then he stood behind each hound, lifted the tail, and looked at the hind end.

Each human stood beside their hound and watched the process.

Satisfied, Sam scribed in his notebook.

"Okay." Sam crossed his arms over his chest for a moment.

"You can sit down," Linda told them.

Relieved, they did. Unbeknownst to them, Sam had studied them from the minute they walked into the warm building. He had a good idea of varying quality from the start. Seeing them move confirmed this.

Sam stood before the group, as Linda now also sat on the bleachers.

Before he could say anything, Joel asked, "Mr. Ewing, why do you pull up the tail?"

"Two reasons. If there is an offset from the hindquarters I may or may not see it but I can run my hand over the leg and then to the ground and pick up a paw if I want to check pads. I didn't check your pads. Given that it is winter, some are probably a bit cracked. Use Bag Balm. Helps. If you were showing, you'd want those paws firm and uncracked. The other reason is if your hound is female, I can possibly see if she can bear puppies without undue stress. Of course, anything can happen in the womb but you'd like as much assurance as possible. Breeding is a serious proposition."

Alice held up her hand. He nodded.

"Mr. Ewing, do you believe in treadmills to condition our hounds? Especially in weather like we are having."

"People use them. I don't. Unless there is a great deal of ice, I take them out in the open. If you have space and it's not near a highway, let them go. They'll run. Irish wolfhounds love to run. They are built for inclement conditions. Ice is the main culprit but extreme cold, they can take it. Not that I suggest you exercise in sub-zero temperatures for an hour. But a good run in cold snow, they need it."

"What's extreme cold?" Joel asked.

"Twenties and dropping. Let your hound run around. If you have other dogs, maybe a dog without much coat, a mutt perhaps, put a coat on that dog and let the dogs play. Hounds need physical exercise. Never forget the mental element with an Irish wolfhound."

"After a show, can I ask the judge questions?" Joel was full of questions.

"Depends on the question. If you ask him or her for suggestions to improve your hound, your showing, fine. If you are disputing a call, I wouldn't do it."

Linda interjected, "The judges want great hounds. That's why they're judges. People want to improve a breed as well as their own handling. It's a never-ending process."

"A day you don't learn is a lost day," Sam seconded her thoughts.

Isadore, feeling a bit more confident now, spoke. "Do you feel some hounds like to show off?"

"I do, and you have one."

The group laughed as they all knew Jumpin' Jack's buoyant personality.

"Do you like to judge?" Alice was curious.

"No. My passion is showing and breeding, but when Linda asked me to come, I was happy to do so. Ours is a breed without great numbers. Fewer people can adequately provide the right environment for an Irish wolfhound than, say, for a dachshund. That limits the numbers right there. And too many judges don't truly study our breed. I think that is changing but I would like to see more judges well versed in our breed's original purpose. The hound should have the speed to catch a running wolf then bring him down. For instance, look down at your hound's feet. I like to see a tight foot. What foxhunters call a cat foot, but if our hounds were truly hunting wolves, the foot might be a bit lower, not as tight, depending on the environment. Any breed is a lifetime study, but there are fewer of us so we need to make a point to teach newcomers."

The talk continued for another hour, as the people were fascinated, and Sam did want to share. He was generous with his time.

As the class ended and the people filed out into the dark . . . the sun was setting at about four-thirty . . . Harry stayed back to close up shop with Linda.

Sam helped. He was happy to pitch in.

"Mrs. Haristeen."

"Please call me Harry. It's a childhood nickname. Actually has nothing to do with my married name."

He nodded his head slightly. "Pirate is uncommonly fit. Solid muscle. He's a bit weedy but Linda tells me he is only a year and a half."

"He's a farm dog. He puts in a good day's work." She let her hand fall on Pirate's handsome head.

"Good. We see too many fat dogs today, regardless of breed. Any dog that can do what it was bred to do, or at least be outside, is a happy dog, I think. Well, not the very small ones, but everybody else." He then added, "I spend more time in my kennels than I do in the house. Training, exercise, takes hours but it makes them happy and it makes me happy." He realized he'd veered off what he intended to say. "Harry, I encourage you to show Pirate. He has quality."

Harry reached out and shook Sam's hand. "Thank you for making the trip and for your encouragement. I hope to see you again. Not only will I watch hounds more, I'll also start watching people."

He laughed. "Now, there's a judging exercise."

Harry waited until Sam and Linda were out of the building then she closed the door, locking it. Pirate ambled by her side, thrilled to get into the back of the cold Volvo station wagon. Once the motor was on, the heat came on quickly. The old, hard-used Volvo felt good.

Home, Harry plopped in her kitchen chair. Her cell, on the table, rang. She picked it up.

"I've been trying to reach you." Susan's voice was agitated.

"I've been in Linda's handling class over at the school."

"Sy's autopsy report came back. Ned had the information. Fentanyl."

Harry gasped. "No."

24

Friday

Suffocating humidity hovered over central Virginia. Bumbee sat outside her weaving cabin, linen shirts over her lap, sewing languidly. Her girls, also outside, tried to sew or cut thin fabrics but mostly they kept falling asleep.

The stables, all doors and stalls open, proved cooler than some of the pastures. The horses dozed under huge shade trees as the humans tried not to doze while cleaning bridles. Something about the air kept eyelids drooping.

Even Catherine, who could usually work through anything, would fall asleep and wake up with a start as she sat outside in an old kitchen chair dragged out for this purpose. Letters sent to her father slipped off her lap. She finally gave up and put them back in the kitchen, a cup on top of them. Returning outside, she gave in to the moment, soon to be sound asleep.

A light breeze offered brief respite.

A short distance from Catherine's pleasant clapboard house

rested her sister Rachel's house, an exact copy. Rachel, not at all sleepy, bent over her husband's drawings as the old corgi, Piglet, snored at her feet. Charles's straight lines, sense of proportion, engaged her. He never set out to be an architect but was becoming well known in Virginia. His plans, sensible, attracted those who wanted beautiful dwellings that were practical. His plans and the building of St. Luke's Lutheran Church in Wayland's Crossing made his reputation. Gray fieldstone, a slate roof, a main church, flanked by two arcades, one on each side, which ended in smaller buildings for church functions but not church services. This land fell away in terraces and quads.

Charles, at present back on the old Barracks' prisoners-of-war camp, with Ewing Garth, was trying to help his father-in-law make good use of the land.

"It's not worth saving these old log buildings, Mr. Garth." Charles still formally addressed his father-in-law. "They weren't chinked, anyway. Stuffed with branches to keep out the cold, pine branches. Didn't work. We'd stick anything we could find between the logs."

"Mmm. I never really got beyond the commandant's house."

"We did the best we could. Many died. I often wonder if my guardian angel protected me and Piglet."

"I am glad he did and also glad you realized the great task ahead."

"For all the splendor back in England, or France, Italy, Spain, take your pick, they have no idea what is here. I fought for the king. I was captured, as you know. I didn't run away but the more I saw of this country, the more I realized this is where I wanted to be."

"What did you think of the Hudson River Valley? I have never ventured beyond New York City. My father sent me on a Grand Tour as a young man but there is so much I haven't seen here."

"It's beautiful. Rich in timber. The Hudson River is mighty, a source of commerce, as are the rivers here. Not quite as temperate but a man willing to work can make something of himself there. The march from Saratoga to here was what truly opened my eyes."

"Speaking of opening one's eyes, our elected worthies," Ewing paused after worthies, "are still discussing the amendments to the Constitution. I really believe the main criteria for an elected official is good lungs."

They both laughed.

"Everywhere. Parliament is not much different. Members love to hear themselves talk."

"Before I forget, do you know where those who died are buried?"

"We didn't have one main burial ground. Men were laid to rest in a plot near their cabins, which were not uniformly laid out. Disease took away many. Our first winter in this New World shocked every one of us."

"You have winter in England." Ewing remembered being in London during November.

"Nothing like this. Our chimneys were charred logs. The trick was keeping warm while not burning down the cabin."

"Well, I do not want to disturb the dead. If you can remember, mark those areas and perhaps we can think of a way to keep them undisturbed."

"If you plow or plant, you won't disturb them."

"I hope not." Ewing turned to walk back to the carriage. Barker O, his driver, parked the two-horse carriage in the shade.

"Master?"

"Take us home, Barker."

The two men stepped into the open light carriage, a phaeton.

Being open, what breeze there was drifted over the three men. The ride back to Cloverfields would take twenty minutes at a slow trot. King David and Solomon, shining in the early afternoon light, completed the dashing picture. Phaetons were always sporty.

The two chatted while Barker O avoided what ruts and bumps that he could.

"Barker, will we ever get good roads?" Ewing called to him.

"I hope so," the powerfully built man replied.

Highly skilled, not only could he drive carriage horses, he could train them. His rival and friend was DoRe, Maureen's head stable man, who she would send to Cloverfields, as he was to marry Bettina. The date kept getting moved and the parties at Cloverfields grew weary of it. Maureen wanted more and more money for DoRe every time the subject was broached.

"I believe I will be getting two commissions in Richmond." Charles listened to the soothing clip-clop of the horses.

"Good. The city will grow."

"The river will see to that. Virginia is fortunate to have such outstanding tobacco crops, hemp, apples."

"Mother Nature is a fickle business partner." Ewing smiled.

"While I was talking to Sam Udall, the banker who wants a new house, there was a murder. A young woman killed in the church, her throat slit."

Ewing grimaced. "One doesn't think of church as a place to kill someone."

"Odd. More thefts, fights. Summer seems to inflame the passions. Sooner or later this heat will abate. Sometimes you can't breathe."

"Yes. Fortunately we get more of a breeze than they do in Richmond."

As the two enjoyed their brief ride back to Cloverfields, Martin and Shank picked up another wagon from Big Rawly to try and escape the worst of the heat. Their destination was Richmond, which could take about three days.

On the other side of Charlottesville, driving along Three Chopt Road, a young, attractive woman . . . late teens perhaps . . . was at the end of a driveway, selling vegetables.

They stopped to buy two tomatoes.

"Hot out here in the sun." Martin made conversation.

"My parasol does no good. Here you are. Anything else?"

"Do you live up this road?" Martin asked as Shank stood on the other side of the slanted table holding the vegetables.

"Yes. Mother and I farm. The apples aren't ready to pick yet, but if you come back this way in a month, we will have perfect apples."

"If you have sisters, they should be out here working with you." Shank smiled, not a very convincing one.

"My two sisters spend their time chasing after their babies."

"Ah." Martin had now stepped behind her, put his hand over her mouth, while Shank quickly bound her hands. As she was little and light, they easily placed her in the back of the wagon, stuffing a cloth in her mouth and pulling a thin blanket over her.

An hour later, as they turned toward Richmond on Three Chopt, Shank stopped the wagon, they got out, removed the blanket. The poor young girl was drenched in sweat, wide-eyed.

Freeing her hands and mouth, Martin gave her a choice. "You can lie back here or sit up there with us. If you try to jump off and run, we'll catch you. If you do as we tell you, you'll be safe."

"And you'll make money," Shank added.

She held the cloth that had been stuffed in her mouth, too frightened to protest. "I need to tell my mother."

"Once we get you settled you can write a letter to your mother or have someone write for you." Martin sounded soothing. "And if you accept our offer, you will be able to send your mother money every month."

"What do I have to do?"

"You can talk to the lady in charge when we get to Richmond. If you agree, we won't tie you up when we stay in an ordinary overnight. We'll tell people you are my niece," Shank informed her.

"How much money?"

"To start, I don't know, but once you are set you should be able to send her a hundred a month, maybe more." Martin dangled the bait, but she could only make that much if she learned how to please men. He didn't mention that.

"That much?"

"You can make money doing what you need to do. You aren't going to make money selling vegetables," Shank said.

"What's your name?" Martin asked.

"Abigail."

"Be smart, Abigail. Make money. Go where there are lots of peo-ple."

Martin and Shank would make fifty dollars apiece for her from Georgina. A young, attractive girl in her late teens was exactly what The Tavern needed. The relationship between the two women promised Martin and Shank more income. The less they knew, the better.

25

Wednesday

"Whose idea was this?" Susan asked, a stream of frosty air escaping her mouth.

"All right." Harry put her chain saw on the bar under the tractor, where she had fixed a small toolbox. Small enough to fit. "I really thought we could get two Christmas trees down ourselves."

"Climb in." Susan edged over on the tractor seat.

"I'll walk behind you. Anyway, if I fall behind, I'll meet you in the kitchen."

Popping into gear, easing her foot off the old metal pedals, Susan started downhill.

She kept it in first, old tractors don't have creep gears. Harry, walking quickly, a few sprints, only fell behind a bit when Susan reached level pastures.

"*Slippery*," Pirate, his huge frame in balance, remarked.

Tucker, having a bit more traction, agreed, then waited at the bottom of the hill for Pirate to slide down to her. Once the wolfhound tried, he did slide a bit. They then slowly ran across the pasture.

"Mom's keeping up." Tucker grinned.

"How fast do you think a human could run, say, against a dog?" Pirate, observing his human struggle with the footing, snow, and ice, asked.

Tucker laughed. "A fit person might outrun a bulldog. But no one can keep up with any other dog. Humans can sprint and they can run for endurance, but you have to remember they only have two legs. Not much balance."

Studying Harry, now in front of him, Pirate agreed. "See what you mean. Our human does good with two legs though."

"She does, but you know if we did a flat-out run, she couldn't run at her best speed for more than three minutes. Don't know why, more than it's just the way they are built. Too fragile in a way. All that weight on two feet, not four, all that pressure on the back. They can't do too much, really. It's why we have to watch out for them."

"Yes." The big fellow simply agreed as Harry still trotted behind Susan.

The barn came into sight around a corner of trees, blocking some of the view. Harry slowed. Her legs ached. Not a deep snow on the ground, it was enough to make your legs work harder. By the time she got there, Susan was already on the ground, unhitching the chain they thought they could use.

"Can't decide if touching metal hurts more in winter or blistering summer." Susan finally felt a wiggle in the chain lock.

"Got it?"

"Yep. Heavy."

"Drop it on the floor. I can lift it up later with the spike on the newer tractor."

"Why don't you do it now? If you sit down in the house, you aren't going to want to put on clothes and go out again."

Following good advice, once the chain hung in its place on the wall, both women and the dogs, grateful for the warmth, walked into the house.

As Harry made tea for herself, coffee for Susan, Susan flipped through her phone.

"What fresh hell is there?" Harry asked.

"Oh, the usual. Threats from our enemies, or should I say rivals, at the UN. COVID changing everything. Seemingly random shootings everywhere, a sign of Christmas spirit, and more snow in a few days. Not yet certain."

"The norm." The coffee emitted an aroma filling the kitchen, as Harry kept her eye on the coffeemaker and her water for tea.

"I surprise myself, getting like you." Susan put cream in her coffee when Harry placed it in front of her. "I wanted to know where fentanyl was made. Where it comes into our country."

Smiling, Harry, still at the counter, poured hot water over a teabag in a small pot, as it was just for her. "International trade isn't what they teach you in school. The illicit trade, which differs from country to country, makes huge profits."

"Most of the fentanyl comes from Mexico. Much is made in China. India makes tramadol. It's less potent than fentanyl but it can kill you. Tramadol makes people feel high functioning. They can drive, etc. People die in accidents. Cooper said over one billion pills are smuggled into the United States from India."

Harry sat up straight. "When did you talk to Cooper?"

"When I found out about Sy," Susan answered. "The black market is thriving. Like you said, international trade." Susan stirred her spoon in the cup.

"I bet we aren't the only people now interested in fentanyl because of Sy." Harry sat down, animals in their beds.

"Well, we can't be the only people wondering did he take drugs all along and we didn't know it."

"Possible." She heard a little snore. "Tucker is a touch worn out from the walk up then down." She returned to fentanyl. "People, sooner or later, get caught, or a family member realizes something's not right. Then again, more and more, odd behavior is the norm . . . my definition of odd. What if he was given a pill?"

"A pain pill?" Susan began to see many unpleasant possibilities.

"That. Or it was liquified in some way, put in a drink. What I know is, apart from the fact that we will miss a good person, we're missing something else."

"What's that line? 'Where's the money?' " Susan laughed.

"If we all knew how much money was out there by ill-gotten gain, would anyone be honest again?" Harry laughed along with Susan. "I'm looking for a connective thread."

"I can't think of a thing," Susan confessed.

"Bear with me. This is pretty thin, but we start with a van wreck. What might be undocumented workers smuggled in where we least expect them. Then we find a man in a ditch, who may well have been in that van. Then the petty crooks are found behind the BP station. And our friend dies from a fentanyl overdose. The other deaths, the bodies had fentanyl in them."

"Yes," Susan added more than countered. "The death toll from drugs is climbing. Up, up, and up."

"Meaning, this may not be usual?"

"I'd say we need to know more about the dead before we connect them with a drug, death on purpose, murder. Know what I mean?"

"I do. But what is the purpose? There's the answer. But I did fish out another idea." Harry leaned forward. "Except for the two behind the BP station, all the people work in agriculture in some fashion, more than likely. That's it." She threw up her hands.

"Thin, but I'm thinking. This will get swept away by Christmas. If there are facts we don't know, probably get swept away with the holiday."

Harry, lightly tapping the floor with one foot, responded, "It's not so much that, but every day a search slows down, or time drags on, evidence is lost or destroyed in one way or the other. But when I think of Sy, I wonder if this epidemic, or whatever the term is for high drug deaths, is making someone rich. He was never a hard partier. Had a drink sometimes. Loved good food. Grew all manner of succulent, wonderful fruit. So why? He just had a wild moment? He wasn't a drug person. Sooner or later, we would know."

"Yeah?" Susan nodded. "He could have taken a pill by mistake. Someone gives him a pill for a headache. Stuff like that."

"Another long shot. But what did he know that we don't? If this wasn't a mistake, taking a pill by mistake, where did he get the pills?"

"Right." Susan nodded. "We all aren't wildly stupid. We would have sensed something amiss; I believe it. So this odd death," she leaned closer to Harry, "is something we either can't see or can't imagine. It could be a mistake. It could be getting rid of him."

"We are a good team." Harry grinned.

"Most times we are. When I started researching fentanyl, where is it made . . . as it is a lab drug, not natural . . . I had a spasm of fear." Susan laughed.

"I always have those around you," Harry teased. They enjoyed each other.

Susan returned to their chores. "You think this can be finished tomorrow?"

"Sure. Fair and I can get those firs down here if each of us is on a tractor. We're good. I'll lean your tree against the barn." Harry wondered why she ever thought the two of them could pick two good-sized trees and bring them down. Needed more equipment, but they had selected beautiful trees. "Okay."

"It's a push to think. Is there a connecting thread? I don't know." Susan got up and pulled cookies from the cupboard. She knew this kitchen as well as her own. "It's teaching us about streams of disease, discontent, and death."

"That's a dark way to put it." Harry frowned.

"Nothing can be darker than the Curse of Atreus," Susan tossed out.

"Two and a half millennia and that story still forces you to ask what is power worth? Who are you willing to sacrifice for it and what are you willing to sacrifice? Money? Sex? Fame?" Harry knew mythology. "Generation after generation. We don't learn, do we?"

"Apparently not. But if our friend was not popping pills, then he got popped. It's not blood everywhere, but it could be something cruel, or criminal, or both."

"Do you think in some way we are in the middle of it?"

"Harry, don't say that," Susan, exasperated, told her.

"Yeah, yeah. A little dramatic. And how would we get in the middle, anyway?"

26

Thursday

"Can we fit one more in?" Harry asked Susan.

"If you hold it in your lap," Susan replied.

Joel Paloma carried the last basket from his warehouse to the Audi station wagon. "Harry, click your seatbelt, then I'll hand this to you."

She did, and the basket was placed in her lap.

Four other cars sat in the parking lot behind the warehouse, each one taking Christmas food baskets. Jodie helped her husband, as did the staff at the warehouse.

"We'll see you later," Susan, putting the window down on Harry's side, told Joel.

"We'll be here."

"Put the window up." Harry found the food basket heavier than she imagined. "Cold."

"All right. Can you see the list?"

"I remember the first call is the closest to Miller School."

"We should be able to deliver the baskets and get back for a second load in an hour and a half. We've got the western part of the county."

"And I am so glad. I don't want to wade through traffic on the eastern side." Susan, coming the back way, turned right on Miller School Road, then turned left onto a potholed, paved country road.

"Have you ever noticed that often the more modest homes are the ones with the most Christmas decorations?" Harry observed. "How can they pay their electric bill?" Harry worried about costs.

"Maybe they save most of the year for this time. Okay, here we are. You sit still. I'll get out and take the basket from you. After that we can take turns delivering."

"Okay." Harry looked to see a face behind a window, lace curtains drawn to the side.

Susan walked up, knocked on the front door. A young woman greeted her, a Christmas tree in the background. The two exchanged a few words, the young woman smiled, taking the basket from Susan, who wished her a Merry Christmas.

"That was fast," Harry noted, as often the elderly recipients could rattle on, they were so lonely.

"Baby wailing in the background." Susan put the car in drive and they headed down the road.

"It's incredible that Reverend Jones and St. Luke's raised enough money for five hundred baskets. And other churches matched us. Maybe people are finally waking up to how much need there is in our county, rich as it is."

"It's easy to overlook the poor. Ned sometimes takes out maps, the big DMV maps of the surrounding counties, as well as our own, and shows me the poverty pockets. Living in the country, the poor aren't as visible as in cities. You see the homes but they aren't necessarily run-down. Some are, of course."

"Usually older people. They can't work anymore."

"With kids on Christmas vacation, maybe they could tidy up the yards of the elderly, or even put up Christmas trees."

"Never thought of that."

"Me neither. It just popped into my head. After this Christmas we can talk to Reverend Jones about it. Bet we can all come up with something. The least we can do is praise the kids for helping others."

"Mom and Dad always did. I don't know, as I was selfish, but I spent my time with you, my classmates. I sure didn't think about people, poor and alone."

"If it weren't for Grandmom and Mom, I doubt I would have paid attention. Remember the first time we delivered baskets? Our junior year? As I recall, you moaned and groaned because you wanted to play basketball with the boys."

A slight flush colored Harry's cheeks. "I did. But I shut up eventually and never missed a Christmas after that. Even during college, because we all came home."

"Okay. Lorraine Thigpen." Susan turned into an unplowed driveway, west of Batesville, a small clapboard house at the end. "Glad I have four-wheel drive."

"Me too. At least there are tire tracks. Someone comes in and out," Harry noted as Susan stopped, threw the shift in clutch.

"Your turn."

Harry got out, opened the door to the backseat, where three baskets rested, the rest being in the far back. She wiggled one out, walked to the front door carefully, as it was packed with snow.

An older lady answered the door. She wore sweatpants and a sweatshirt. A wood-burning stove sat at the rear of the small living room.

"Hello, Mrs. Thigpen. I'm from St. Luke's Church and we want to wish you a Merry Christmas."

"Oh my." She reached for the basket. "It's heavy."

Fortunately, Harry hadn't let it go. "Would you like me to put it somewhere?"

"Yes." Mrs. Thigpen walked to the rear of the house, where a kitchen table, an old refrigerator and stove shared the space with a smaller wood-burning stove.

"Your stoves keep the house warm." Harry set the basket on the table.

"I wouldn't trade them for anything. I grew up in this house. Everything still works from when my mother was alive. She was born in 1907. Married William Thigpen. Love at first sight, he said. Mother didn't say much, but they got along. So many Thigpens in Virginia."

Harry, hoping to stave off a genealogy recitation, agreed. "There are. It's an old Virginia name. An important name."

"My married name, but my maiden name was Fleming. We used to argue whose people got here first." As she took another breath, Harry saw her chance.

"Mrs. Thigpen, it's good you got here whenever you did. Merry Christmas."

Finally back in the car, Susan looked at her. "A near miss?"

"About to get the ancestor parade."

"Must be hard to be alone."

"Guess that depends on the person." Harry pulled the seatbelt over her. "This thing is hard to pull."

"It is. Car's getting old. Little things are starting to go or be difficult. I always thought the seatbelts were hard."

Two more stops and they emptied out the backseat.

"Five more to go. These are big baskets."

Susan replied, "They are. Joel and Jodie did a great job."

"And they threw in fifty baskets from their company. Can't hurt business to have the churches using them this year. The apples are big and red; the oranges, lovely. Cans of Virginia peanuts, carrots. Stuff one can cook or not cook, too. Makes it easier since some of our recipients probably don't cook anymore, if they ever did."

"That's the thing about old men. There's so much they don't know how to do for themselves. Their wives always did it."

Harry agreed. "Division of labor. Is it sexist? Maybe it depends on the labor."

Susan thought about that. "Maybe. I'd never get anything done if I worried about was it a man's job or a woman's."

"Me neither. Hey, what's going on?"

Susan slowed as one ambulance, two sheriff's cars, lights flashing, parked in front of a well-to-do house, just outside of Crozet, not far from Wavertree, a big place. Cars were parked everywhere.

"Looks like some kind of Christmas party?" Harry watched. "That's Coop's SUV. Maybe there was a fight."

Susan was doing her best to move on. Cars had slowed and sirens were heard in the distance. She wanted to get out of the way. "Must be some party."

"Let's hope no furniture was destroyed." Harry smiled. "That house has to have good furniture."

Finally clear of the impediment, Susan reached the next destination in ten minutes. This time it was a ranch house on an offshoot road of 611, a road that ran south from Batesville.

"My turn." Susan parked, went around to the back, flipped up the hatch door, pulled out a basket. She knocked on the door. No response. The Christmas decorations, mostly garlands and a ribbon on the door, meant someone was keeping the season. She knocked again. No reply, so she left the basket by the front, card taped to the cellophane.

Harry looked up from her cellphone. "Bulletin. The place with the cop cars, three dead kids."

"What?" Susan turned the car around, as the driveway had a nice turnaround. "Dead?"

"It just says a party of college kids, parents not home, called an ambulance when three got sick."

"That's all it says?"

"For right now. They won't release the names. Wasn't a fight or anything like that. Some kind of sickness."

"Booze?"

"Unless a person guzzles a fifth of whiskey, I doubt they'll die from drinking. Has to be drugs. I mean, what else could it be?

"The word used is *unresponsive*. I said dead, the bulletin didn't."

Harry clicked off her phone. "This isn't the Christmas I thought it would be."

Back at the warehouse after dropping off the last of their baskets, Harry and Susan went inside to pick up more.

Jodie rushed up. "Karen McLachen rushed home. Her son threw a big party at the house when he knew she'd be away. Three kids died."

"That was the McLachen house?" Harry was surprised.

"They moved over near Wavertree. He's a professor at UVA," Jodie informed her.

"I've seen them from time to time. I can't say that I really know them," Susan offered.

"She is on the St. Mary's committee for Christmas baskets. I drove her home. No way would we allow her to drive." Jodie's face looked ashen.

Harry replied, "That poor woman."

"The officer who came here said Karen's son told him where she was; he offered to drive her, but I volunteered and said it might be better if one of us did it. He led, siren screaming. Karen sat there almost immobile. I don't know that she believed it, and yet on one level she did. Joel took over here. He's out delivering baskets, since Karen can't obviously."

"The officer didn't say anything about violence?" Susan asked.

"No."

"Drugs?" Susan stated.

"It so often is." Jodie shook her head. "When I walked her into the house, the place was jammed with college kids, sitting, some crying. The sheriff was there. He thanked me, so I left. I've been back here for maybe twenty minutes. The ambulance was gone, so I didn't see anything else."

After talking to the other people there and making sure Jodie was all right, Susan and Harry picked up two baskets, all that was left for their quadrant. They delivered them, then Susan drove Harry home.

"Would that party be called a rave?" Harry asked.

"No. A rave is high tech. A DJ, lots of lights, often in big spaces. Warehouses or abandoned buildings. The McLachen party was a bunch of young people, booze, drugs."

"Music. Bet they had music. Remember back in the '80s there would be these parties where everyone brought drugs? What they could steal from their parents' medicine chest, or what they bought from a dealer. They'd drop the pills in a big bowl, and when you walked into the party you'd grab a drug, you didn't know what, and you'd take it. There'd be lines of coke on smooth surfaces. Lots of ecstasy. Indiscriminate. There'd be some deaths but not like what we're seeing now." Harry looked out the window at darkening clouds.

"I never went to one but I remember. I mean, I remember hearing about it."

They drove in silence then Susan turned onto the farm driveway, plowed of snow, long and winding.

"We deliver baskets every year and I look forward to it," Harry remarked.

"I do, too," Susan said.

"We've seen a lot in our years of deliveries. People crying because they are so happy to have food. People with one drink too many. Kids left alone. Old people desperate for someone to talk to. And most of us pass these people every day but we don't really know them. And I have not one idea how to make their lives better, because much of what we see is out of their control. I mean, Susan, for a lot of people alcoholism is out of their control, and that's legal."

"That or an eighteen-year-old with three little kids. Did she know what she was doing? Maybe not for the first one." Susan remembered past deliveries. "Mouths to feed. Who is to say they won't have a good home, if not a stable one financially? I don't know."

"I don't either, but I do know this is the first delivery time we have ever shared together when three young people died."

27

Thursday

Jeddie walked with Barker O up to the large building where the carriages were built. DoRe accompanied them, John lagged a bit behind, as he walked with Jeffrey. Stepping inside the building, all windows and doors opened, Jeddie marveled at the three carriages under construction. Having never seen the phases of building from the bottom up, he was amazed.

"Something." DoRe smiled.

Jeffrey's workers now numbered six in this building and four in the wagon building.

Pointing to the wheels affixed to the axle, Barker O squinted at the juncture. "One inch off and the ride would be a tooth extractor."

DoRe nodded. "I think that's our biggest problem. Finding a method for the axles and wheels to absorb some of the bumps. Don't have it yet."

"Well, if anyone can figure it out, it will be Mr. Jeffrey," Barker O complimented the man who had just walked into the building.

"You've made progress since I was last here." John admired the activity; building, marching, planing timberwork. He liked to see it. Be in the middle of it.

"Yes, and I need more workers. I can't train them fast enough; Toby helps." He cited Toby Tips, one of his most accomplished slaves. "He can make these things simple. He can teach. I don't know how to do that, I only know how to build."

John smiled broadly. "Yes, you do."

As the men studied each carriage in a different phase of building, Jeffrey, at the most completed one, said, "Putting on the dashboard. Has to withstand pressure."

A man on each side of the large wooden panel, covered with hard leather where the coachman placed his feet, dropped it into place.

"I try to keep these carriages light as I can. The dashboard bears great pressure from the coachman, and on the outside it gets all the dirt and stone. That's why I use this wrought iron to affix it." He indicated the thinner strips of black iron. "The axles are heavy iron, naturally, but they bear the weight. The carriage has to be sturdy but not heavy. It's too hard on the horses and more than difficult when weather and road conditions are wet, and snowy. In some areas, I use more wrought iron instead of wood. Heavier by a bit but almost unbreakable."

Seeing Jeddie ponder the graceful curve of the dashboard, Toby, who had walked over, said, "We bend the wood. Soak it then bend it, holding it into place with vises. There are other ways to do it. Some people even use strips of wood then sand it and paint it, but those dashboards never have the strength that this does."

"My goal is to see these carriages in the hands of their owners and not see them back here for repairs from faulty construction. A wreck, a tree falling on it, that's different." Jeffrey beamed.

"My wife, in thinking about your work, mentioned to me how beautiful your carriages are and how distinctive."

"She is very kind." Jeffrey smiled.

"And she thought if our government needs carriages, should they not be the same? Should not people recognize when the president or vice president is calling? She thinks of things that never occur to me. She said our flag should be painted on the side with gold lettering underneath."

Jeffrey thought about this, quickly perceiving the advantage of an arrangement with the federal government.

"One would need good political connections for something like that."

"Well, Percy Ballard has them, as does Zachary Thigpen. If Zachary buys one of your coach-in-fours, many people will see it because of his stagecoach line. As for Percy, his family has ever-growing power here."

"Percy has bought a coach-in-four, as you know. Give him a month or two, then ask him how he likes it?" John sensibly suggested. "Of course, I will recommend this once Percy remarks on how much he likes the coach. But I can tell you the state of Virginia may not pay for your sturdy wagons; however, given that they have a military purpose, I think someone will help pay for them. Then, in good time, once our elected officials realize this will reflect positively on them, perhaps the state will order some."

"Ah." Jeffrey smiled. "Thank you for thinking of me."

"As you are building a forge to help our militia, I think some benefit to you is not out of the question."

"John, I am not a political man, but I do know it is an exhausting business."

"It is. That's why I leave it up to Percy. He's made for it."

They both nodded in agreement.

Dragging his leg, William came into the shop from the wagon section. He carried a bucket of large black screws. Seeing Jeddie, he looked away. Handed Toby the bucket then turned and shuffled away as best he could.

Jeddie stared at him.

DoRe, observing Jeddie, remarked, "He got what he deserved."

Jeddie's hand went to his shoulder, the one William broke when he pulled him off Black Knight. He said nothing.

Barker O shrugged. "People who think only of themselves come to a bad end."

The white men hearing this nodded also. For them the depth of William's betrayal wasn't quite as obvious as what he did to Jeddie, then later what he did to Sulli. But Jeddie understood. You never jeopardize your people. Watching William painfully drag away, he felt no pity. He did get what he deserved.

Abigail did not think in terms of what she deserved. She weighed the choices before her yesterday when Shank and Martin dropped her at Georgina's. She could run or she could be locked up until sufficiently beaten down. She could agree to Georgina's terms and make money. She wanted to make money. She wanted free of a life of drudgery. Her mother, her sisters, already looked older than their years. Rarely laughing. Working their fingers to the bone. Respectability be damned. She wanted money.

Beatrice was in charge of her. As it was another hot afternoon, there were no customers; the evening would no doubt see some, but the two women could sit in the backyard, and Beatrice showed Abigail how to mend slips, lace slips, a costly item.

"You don't want the thread against the skin." She put her hands over Abigail's to guide her.

"Yes, Ma'am." Abigail was a quick study.

A light breeze brushed their faces. The house and dining room were being cleaned, set up. As each woman finished her task she came out back to sit in the breeze. The dining room group took longer, as Georgina was a fanatic about her china, glass, and utensil settings.

Fiona, watching Abigail's hands, asked, "Did you sew at home?"

"A bit." Abigail smiled. "I liked it better than pulling up carrots." The women laughed.

"Sally, go upstairs and bring down Lily's nightgown," Fiona suggested.

Lily, sitting under the pine oak tree, waved Sally off, indicating this was fine.

Shortly, the thin young woman returned, the lovely gown draped over her arm. She held it for Abigail, who placed it on her knees.

"This is . . . ?" She couldn't think what to say.

"Silk," Lily informed her. "Paris. I have a caller who likes me in refined garments."

"See-through is a better description." Fiona laughed.

"How long before I have a gentleman caller?" Abigail asked.

Milady, now outside also, said, "I was fifteen but I looked older." She then sized up Sally. "If you don't put some meat on your bones, especially upstairs, you'll be twenty before you have any callers."

Sally blushed, said nothing. Milady could be mean.

Lily, a bit older than Sally, nineteen, told Abigail, "Men like bosoms. Sally does have some work to do there."

Abigail glanced down at her pleasing bosom, bound to grow even more in the next few years. "Ah. I think they just get in the way."

"Oh, they do," Milady declared. "But they make men crazy."

Beatrice, taking the slip, checked Abigail's work. "Good." Fiona asked Abigail, "Can you sing or play the pianoforte?"

"No, Ma'am. But I sang in church."

"Well, tomorrow let's see what you can do. Be a benefit if we had a bit more music, voices," Fiona remarked.

"How old are you?" Milady asked, back to the former subject.

"Sixteen."

"I see." Milady peered more closely at Abigail's skin. "Not a wrinkle."

"Oh, you'll get some here." Fiona sighed. "What you should know is we never use last names. We never reveal our customers to anyone outside of the house. We never steal another woman's client, although they can change partners. But often a client becomes attached. You always smile at every man who is here, whether he is in the dining room or sitting back while Fiona sings. Smile. Act as though you are thrilled to see him."

"Yes, Ma'am."

Milady added, "Your client is always right. No one is allowed to hit you. Nothing like that, and if anyone does, Christopher, at the stable, takes care of him. But clients can be very peculiar."

"Yes, Ma'am." Abigail couldn't imagine.

"Some want you to lavish attention on them while they lay there. Others are at you the minute the door is closed. No matter what they do, you always tell them how wonderful they are." Beatrice's voice was soothing.

"Some want you to think they are masterful and know what they are doing. You go along with it. The truth is, very few of our clients know anything about women, but they need relief. If they've had a good time, they think you've had a good time," Fiona pitched in.

"Yes, Ma'am."

"I take it you know little about men." Milady almost purred.

"Not much."

"Pretend he's wonderful. He can be the biggest bore in the world with the smallest member, you pretend he's wonderful and that part of him is big. He'll believe you and he'll often give an extra tip."

Jocelyn, who had joined them, thought this an amusing discussion. "It's the money that counts. His dick is the way to money."

Abigail's eyebrows raised.

Beatrice patted her hand. "Don't worry. It's easy. Most of them are lonely. They may be married, in fact most are, but they're lonely."

"Yes, Ma'am."

Beatrice began to chuckle, the others started laughing, too.

Finally, Lily, face flushed, said, "Can you say anything besides 'Yes, Ma'am'?"

Abigail laughed at herself. "I can try."

"Don't worry, sugar. You'll fit right in," Beatrice promised.

"We'll show you the ropes." Fiona meant that.

"What about me?" Sally felt left out.

Milady eyed Sally. "Eat more."

"But what if that doesn't work?" Sally whined.

"Well, we'll have to think of something. Say, we could pass you off as a young boy if a client leans that way."

"No," Sally wailed.

"Oh, Sally, we're teasing you. You'll develop where it counts." Jocelyn stared at Sally's flat chest.

"And on a hot day like today, you'll wish you hadn't," said Milady, who knew of whence she spoke.

28

Friday

Charcoal gray clouds overhead showed flashes of lighter gray; those clouds promised snow. So far no wind. The road crews were already out preparing for the snow, predicted to start at about 4 P.M.

Harry checked the clock on her station wagon: two-thirty. She should make it to her destination and back before the snow proved troublesome. On her way to Ballard Perez's place, she drove north on Route 22, a lovely road. The estate was past where Route 22 hooked east, while the straight road took you up to Gordonsville, a lovely town becoming chic. That it was becoming chic made Harry nervous. It meant housing prices would climb, shops would cater to those with deeper pockets. Then again, this was the story across much of the United States. One community loses its luster or becomes so expensive, it's frozen, and another place is discovered. The trick is to hit it at the right time.

Anything along Route 22 was foolproof in real estate terms, and none more so than Lone Pine. She turned left off the road, drove a half mile, then turned right, through the large fieldstone pillars, the name Lone Pine engraved on a brass plaque set in the stone. The tree-lined driveway, huge red oaks denuded in winter, remained impressive. Each of the drives on Lone Pine was lined with a different tree, such as pin oak or old shortleaf pine; the special summer drive was lined in now enormous crepe myrtles. The Ballards had begun planting before the Revolutionary War. Each subsequent Ballard generation landscaped with enthusiasm. Being rich helped. The last Ballard by surname was Ballard Perez's mother, who married Bernardo Perez, handsome, wealthy, always ready for a good time or a good deal. He evidenced an alarming or fabulous spontaneity, depending on your point of view.

To some extent Ballard possessed his father's spontaneity but not his business sense. Hence slipping into drugs, given his father's disapproval. He finally conquered the drugs, but never really found his way.

His sister absconded with much of the family fortune. No one had heard from her, not even a sighting. Ballard, knowing Constance too well, was aware that she had fashioned a false identity, was probably living high on the hog in Italy, a place she adored. Then again, who does not?

These thoughts flitted through Harry's mind as she passed the main house, a true Georgian gem, followed the central farm road back to a tidy clapboard house once the abode of the head of the stables, a prominent position. The Ballards wanted to keep their help happy. They hired good people.

Pulling up in front, she cut the motor, clucked to Tucker and Pirate; opening her door, then the back door, the three approached the front door, already open.

"Oh, you are so punctual." Ballard smiled at her.

Lafayette stood behind his master. *"Pirate, I have toys."*

"Our big boys like each other; Tucker will fit in."

"That corgi of yours would be beloved of the queen. Tucker is such a social butterfly."

"Here." Harry handed Ballard the book by Sam Ewing that she had pulled from her library. "You'll devour it."

"He is an impressive man. Mother would have fussed over him. Well, she loved her Scottish deerhounds and there are some similarities between the two breeds by the bloodlines that they would have captured Mom. You know how she could go off on horses."

"She was one of a kind."

"Come on. Let's sit in the little library. Would you like anything to eat? Cookies?"

"No, thanks."

She followed him down the center hall, stepping into a room with club chairs, a table that would not have been out of place at White's, the famous London club, and she sank into the embrace of the leather club chair.

Click. Click. Click.

They both heard three sets of claws coming down the hallway.

"You all go play. Or lie down." Ballard gave the order.

"*Play.*" Lafayette charged, Pirate in tow.

Tucker sat by Harry's feet. She reached down to rub that smart head.

"*They are so immature.*" The corgi sniffed.

Scooter, the big ginger cat, came into the room, beheld Tucker, then leapt into Ballard's lap.

"*What are these lower life-forms doing here?*" came the imperious question.

Ballard tickled Scooter under her chin.

"*And another huge dog. Isn't Lafayette enough?*"

"She's talkative," Harry observed.

"I like to think that she's a good conversationalist." Ballard laughed.

"How are you doing? I know getting this place in order and on the historical estates list took so much time," Harry inquired.

"People who like history, architecture, they are pretty easy. Even the state organizations like our historical society are easy to deal with. Where I run into problems, and it's the last place I should, is with the Board of Supervisors for Albemarle County. Everything is too complicated."

"Don't I know it? I subscribe to KISS. Keep It Simple Stupid."

They both laughed.

"But I'm okay. Of course I miss Mother terribly. She spoiled me, I know she did. But if not for Mother, I never would have survived rehab." He shivered slightly. "You get yourself frozen, in a sense. I finally understand why Dante had the Devil encased in ice."

"Now, Ballard, you are hardly the Devil."

"Well, I wasn't doing much good in this world." He rubbed Scooter again, rewarding her purrs. "How do you like our special dinners?"

"It makes Fair happy. I don't mind eating, but I'm not terribly interested in haute cuisine. But some of what has been on those menus has stayed with me."

"Like what?"

"When we were at Fredericksburg, the grilled young squab with seared foie gras nesting on rhubarb compote."

"How did you remember that?"

"I didn't. I wrote it down on the way home. I mean, who would think of something like that? Food as status."

"Always has been. Think of the dinners kings and queens provided for other kings and queens, their own nobles. It was food as politics."

"Sure must have been for Henry VIII. He was huge." Harry curled her lip.

"Didn't start that way. Some people think he had Cushing's disease. Others syphilis. Others think the accident he endured jousting affected his mind. Some severe form of concussion perhaps. But he certainly turned into a cruel, self-centered man."

"Guess there will always be a number of those. Women too." Harry felt Tucker plop across her feet.

"I'm surprised at how much Joel knows. Granted, he is in the food business, but he likes culinary history as well as these complicated recipes."

"Being in the food business takes brains. Growing food is one kind of brainpower, but then knowing what to provide to supermarkets, organic markets, is another. How do you store some of these things? How much money do you pay for what needs to be frozen while transporting it? I don't think I could do it. I mean, I can farm, but I can't do the rest of it."

"No, I can't, either."

"You've certainly secured this place, so your mind works in a different fashion. You know architecture and history."

"My people did. I'm more or less copying what they did. And now having a foundation for Lone Pine has saved it. Even if Constance hadn't made off with Mother's jewels, sold artifacts . . . well, you know, even if I still had those things, a place this large is a money drain."

"Different times. Back when all this was built, you had people to work. You needed outbuildings and a lot of rooms in the house. And you had enslaved people. That took a lot of energy."

"Why?"

"To keep them healthy. Takes a lot of energy for women and indentured servants, who work long hours. Sometimes alongside slaves, sometimes not. Which isn't to say there weren't benefits to decent housing. Think of a lady's maid living in the big house. Better there than where she came from?"

"I don't know. The struggle to survive was hard even if rich. Factor in being uneducated and poor, if white, what could you do? Farming, serving. Stuff like that. And for slaves, anyone who had a gift, a specialty, had some hope of maybe buying their freedom. I doubt too many owners looked forward to that, but it could be done."

"Ballard, they were businessmen. They'd let them go when they began to age. Hard-nosed businessmen."

"Yes. Well, isn't that still with us? Profit as the good?"

"Yes." Harry smiled stiffly. "Doesn't matter what century you study, there are always people using others. We've inched forward. Something, I guess. But tell me how you like being in this house, which is truly cozy?"

"I like it a lot. The big house was Mother's. I moved out once I finished college. And Constance got married, so it was just Mother and Father left. Then when he died, she reigned there like a dowager queen. Mother knew how to spend money, not make it. I love the beauty of Lone Pine, the marble fireplaces, the extraordinary floors and molding, but it's overwhelming."

"It would overwhelm me, but I'd try to get used to it." Harry laughed.

"Are you sure you wouldn't like some tea?"

"No."

"Well, now that we're here and it's just us, tell me what you think of Sy Buford's death."

"Ballard, it seems so out of character."

"As a former drug prince, I can tell you if you are smart you can hide it for years. Finally gets you though."

"But Sy Buford. And fentanyl?"

He rubbed his chin. "I don't know. I have two of his former workers in one of the back cabins here. They left him. Took up and left, and I knew Cabo and Sargento."

"And?"

"They wanted a pay raise. He refused so they left. That's what they told me, and given that it's winter, I don't have much for them to do, but come spring I'll put them to work."

"Are they legal?"

Ballard paused. "You know, I never thought about that. Guess I'd better find out."

"You can get in a lot of trouble if you don't. Do you think Sy had or has undocumented workers?"

"I have no idea, but given how hard it is to find labor, get proper documents, plus pay them, I'd be surprised if a lot of people don't have undocumented workers. What's immigration to do, comb every field in our state?"

"They only have to find a few to make an example out of them."

"Harry, I think that makes people more devious. Prevent someone from making money and you can create havoc, but ultimately you will fall. Otherwise our government, any government, would need to have people on their payroll to do nothing but spy on others."

"There are always people who will do that."

"Yes, but it isn't practical. Even Russia and East Germany, tight though they were, couldn't pull it off one hundred percent."

"Ballard, it is an awful thought. Spying, I mean. I never got the feeling Sy was on drugs or doing anything illegal in his business."

"Me neither, but that doesn't mean he didn't do it."

"Did you ever do fentanyl?"

"No. That became a problem after I cleaned up. But were I still doing drugs, how do I know it wouldn't be laced into cocaine or pills? I could have taken it unwittingly."

"Do you have any idea how it gets here? I mean, I know it's smuggled in, but do you have any idea who might be selling it?"

"I don't. Most of the people I knew who sold drugs are dead and gone."

"Overdose?"

"Users, sure; but dealers, no. Some were shot, not here but in Richmond or Washington. Others died of natural causes. You can make a lot of money selling drugs, but you may not live long unless you are the overlord."

"Those guys rarely get caught."

"A few do, but they have so much money they can buy their way out of most anything. Even if they go to prison, they can buy off guards. Might not be an entirely miserable existence and they can run their empires from the cage."

"Anyone sell here in Albemarle County?"

"A few. The usual. Weed. Coke. Sometimes muscle relaxers. Most had legitimate business here. They made extra money then got out. I'll give the dealers here credit; they know when to leave. But the kingpins? Still in our country, I think. The drugs are coming in from India. Mexico. Maybe Canada. But most of the kingpins are here."

"It truly is a business." Harry sighed.

"It is and it's run like a business, although sometimes you have to enforce your will with guns. You especially do that if someone betrays you or squeals. There will always be criminals who are smart."

"I guess."

"Joseph Kennedy, apart from his other businesses, was a successful bootlegger. His son became president. Profit, Harry, profit."

"Okay, Ballard. How would you bring drugs into Charlottesville?"

"Same way you would anywhere else. Mules. People who carry the stuff in. There is always a chain of distributors in a university town. There are bright kids who get in on selling. It's not some Mafia character driving around in a black Tahoe with tinted windows. It's people you know at the lower levels."

"And law enforcement can't stop it?"

"Not really. They'll catch a few. They might find a truckload of coke or pills. Weed is easier, obviously, and some of it is now legal. But this is a worldwide business with unbelievable profits. We are never going to end the drug trade."

"That's an awful thought."

"It is. The only way to end the drug trade is for people to stop using. And as long as someone wants to feel powerful, sexual, without pain or care, drugs will sell."

She looked out the paned window. "Getting darker. I'd better be heading home. And where is my dog?" She looked down at Tucker. "You're such a good girl."

"I *am*," she answered.

"Pirate," Harry called.

"Lafayette," Ballard in turn called, then whistled.

The two large boys padded into the library. Lafayette had a large red ball with a handle on it, which Pirate was trying to snatch from him.

Ballard smiled. "Stole that from the barn. That's Reggae's ball."

Reggae was his steady mount for just about everything.

"A thief in your midst."

A sad smile crossed Ballard's face. "Maybe it's in the blood."

As they walked to the front door, Ballard handed Harry her coat from the large hall closet.

"Thanks. Have you noticed the dessert on each of our menus? The orange-glazed sweetbreads and crème brûlée?"

"Can't say that I have. I know it was on the menu at The Tavern in Richmond. An old combination."

"Is. Well, good to spend time with you. I'll see you at our next culinary feast, and then with Lafayette."

In the car, dogs settled in the back, Harry turned for home, straight west. The sky spit a little. She was glad to have seen Ballard, impressed that he had worked so hard to save the estate. Hearing his thoughts on the drug deaths alerted her to how naïve she was.

29

Saturday

"One hundred thousand deaths, almost." Harry sat in front of her computer with Susan and Cooper.

"We'll surpass that number next year," Cooper confidently predicted.

"Ned thinks so, too," Susan said.

The stove provided a welcoming temperature. Each woman wore a sweater, but there was no need for other layers or keeping their coats on.

Mrs. Murphy and Pewter spread out on the large old tack box while Tucker and Pirate sprawled on the floor not far from the propane stove. The flickering lights shifted shadows on their fur coats.

"You're good to come over here on your day off," Harry thanked Cooper.

"My pleasure. Have stuff to talk about, too."

"Tell us now." Susan perked right up. "I mean, we can talk about drug deaths all day."

"And probably will." Harry sighed. "Or maybe not."

"I visited Reverend Jones last night after work. You know, I've never been in his house there. It's beautiful. All the same materials as the church and the old stables, not the garage. I wouldn't want to leave there, either."

"And?" Susan wanted to get to the point even though she wasn't sure what the point would be.

"He said he would think about selling me the home place. He knows I would take good care of it. He had no idea what it is worth and would need to talk to a few realtors. Jane Fogelman, the Wiley Brothers, some good ones to choose from. Right now it seems prices are fluctuating daily."

"They are," Susan affirmed. "But you know Reverend Jones is not out to gouge you. If he talked to you and said he might be willing or he'd think about it, he will. He will never leave St. Luke's."

"They'll carry him out feet first." Harry smiled. "He loves it. The last thing he would ever want to do is retire."

"So you want to buy it." Susan had to restate the subject.

"I do. Harry has helped me so much; Fair too. They've taught me about the soils, about the drainage and runoff, about what to plant and what to harvest when. I'm almost a country girl and I do love the house. Sometimes at twilight I look out the window and see those changing colors of the sky reflected on the tombstones of the Jones's family. It's not creepy. It's comforting."

"It is. There's a peaceful feel to the place. And your neighbors all farm. That's a help. There are no five-acre cutouts from our farms, so no new person will call the police if you happen to walk through or a dog does. You need a dog, Coop."

"Well, if they call the police, that will be me."

They laughed.

"Let us know if there is anything we can do. Reverend Jones will listen to us," Susan bragged.

"He will listen," Tucker agreed. *"Doesn't mean he'll do what you want."*

"Yeah, he will," Pewter argued. "He's a big softie when it comes to women."

"He loves everybody," Pirate said. "He lets me in his office sometimes even though his three cats hiss. They settle down."

"Do you know," Pewter declared in her most confidential voice, "Elocution, Lucy Fur, and Cazenovia eat communion wafers. I have seen them do this with my own eyes."

Lucy Fur, Elocution, and Cazenovia were Reverend Jones's three cats.

"The reason you saw them eat communion wafers is that you were eating them, too." Mrs. Murphy turned on her side to better see the dogs.

"You ate them!" Pewter snapped.

"I did. After all, I am a Christian cat." Mrs. Murphy stifled a giggle, for the communion raid was the best fun.

Cooper noted, "They're chatty."

"Every now and then." Harry looked at her beloved cats. "But I never know what they are saying."

"You don't want to know," Tucker declared.

"Now Tucker's getting gossipy." Susan had bred Tucker.

Her Owen was from the same litter.

Harry, still looking at her pets, turned to Cooper. "Any word on how those three students died?"

"Pills. The other partiers testified there were pills, transdermal patches, and inhalers. No one was describing the contents, but there was also cocaine, without a doubt; in my mind, at least. As for a transdermal patch, that would be for muscle pain. Maybe a deep pain. You can put opioid on a patch. You can drink an opioid, snort an opioid, inhale it, or have it as a kind of gel for a patch."

"Well, Coop, how do they do all this? It sounds too complicated." Harry's eyebrows shot upward.

"By this time, most students could pass as chemists' assistants if they are doing a lot of drugs. But mostly this stuff comes in the form in which they use it. Inhalers, for instance. Not that anyone is putting fentanyl or tramadol pure based in an inhaler. One puff and that kid would be dead in less than five minutes. But there can be traces. Those substances are painkillers. Too much suppresses respiration. It's a quick death."

"Naloxone." Susan stated the antidote.

"Yes, we all carry it now, but by the time we reached the party we were way too late," Cooper said.

"But naloxone can save someone?" Harry didn't know there was an antidote.

"It can." Cooper leaned back in the chair. "You need to inject the dose. Should begin to work in two or three minutes. If it doesn't, inject another dose, and some people try breathing into the victim's mouth, but if they took a larger dose than anyone realized, that respiratory work can kill the rescuer. If the victim doesn't start to awaken, give another shot. Usually the stuff works and it works fast. Most people call it Narcan. You can buy it at the drugstore."

"No kidding." Harry was impressed.

"It's an opioid binder so it reverses the drug. It is an antagonist."

"Cooper, can't you shoot the stuff up their nose?" Harry asked.

"Some of us have the nasal spray, but most have the needle, and a bottle of Narcan. We've saved so many people with this if we got there in time. Although if we can't get naloxone in quick order, they will suffer brain damage even though we'll bring them around. Timing is critical. Someone starts to go into convulsions and we need to be there within five minutes. Or the ambulance crew."

"So someone can be impaired for the rest of their life?" Susan's voice rose. "Why fool around with the stuff?"

"Because no one thinks they will die. They believe they are taking safe cocaine or safe heroin, if there is such a thing. Well, if it's relatively pure it is somewhat safe if you discount the addictive properties." Cooper had seen a lot of drug overdoses in her law enforcement career.

"What got the partiers to call?" Harry wondered.

"The first kid went into convulsions, then the second and third," Cooper said. "Seeing anyone go into convulsions for any reason is frightening. And one has to think fast, which whoever picked up the phone did. But it was still too late. The road to Wavertree doesn't allow for high speeds."

"Don't you find it odd that there have been so many deaths this season?" Susan asked.

"I do. I also know Christmas lends itself to all forms of overindulgence. And young people want to be together. They come home from college and I'm sure they are glad to see their parents. Then they want to go out with their friends. No one wants to sit with Mom and Dad." Cooper was sure about that.

"Do you think the stuff was always here?" Harry asked.

"I do, but not in such quantity. Fentanyl is a growing business." Cooper shook her head.

"To sort of shift the subject, you all questioned the Bufords, right?" Harry prodded.

"Of course."

"Did Marjorie or any of the managers speak of disgruntled workers?"

Cooper thought a moment. "Not plainly. His peach manager said that occasionally a worker would leave because he or she felt they could get better pay elsewhere. And he said they couldn't up the pay for one person. They'd have to bump up all of them."

"Keeping costs steady is a losing battle," Harry commiserated. "You raise the hourly wage, I'm not opposed to that if the owner does it. I am opposed if the federal government does it, because I don't think one size fits all."

"Yeah, but Harry, so many workers like fruit pickers or fast-food employees are underpaid." Susan felt strongly about this.

"I'm not arguing the point." Harry then added, "But if the federal government passes a nationwide, no exemptions raise, what happens if you are a farmer and your fields just flooded? Or your bridges washed out on the farm? There is no insurance for bridges. So you must pay this higher salary. Even if you can offer lodging and transportation, you pay the same as an urban company. How can you keep your head above water? The only way is to let people go and hope those you have left can help repair the damage. When things look better later in the year, or by next planting season, you can hire more people."

"Well, what happens to the people you let go?" Susan sat up straighter.

"My point exactly." Harry allowed a note of triumph in her voice. "Not Sy, at least I don't think Sy, but most bosses or owners will cut staff first. Higher wages. More unemployment."

Cooper, listening, shrugged. "Try being a so-called public servant. We don't have the money to hire more people. We hear, but not too much around here, 'Defund the police,' then when there is a crisis, we aren't there. People are outraged."

"If you had more people, could you have gotten to the McLachens' faster?" Susan asked.

"No. It is in the western part of the county and the roads while paved are good, they are also narrow. The only way those kids could have been saved was if someone had Narcan on them."

"Well, maybe the first step is to encourage the young to carry it." Susan just thought of that. "It may freak out their parents to know they have Narcan with them, but it might save another person's life or their own. We aren't going to stop partying."

"No, we aren't," Cooper agreed. "This would take a big education effort. I know Sheriff Shaw would be for it. But again, an educational campaign will cost the county money."

"It will, but if people like my husband say one person is worth the cost, saving your child, I think people will do it."

"No one thinks their kids are on hard drugs," Harry countered.

"Some do, Harry," Cooper said. "They just don't know what to do about it. The wealthier ones might haul their son or daughter to a therapist or go with them. Hope that helps, but having every young person and maybe not a few old ones carry Narcan could save many lives."

"Worth a try," Susan agreed.

"Back to the deaths. We don't know anything about the men with no IDs. We don't know anything about the kids except they were partying and someone brought drugs. Probably more than one. We'll eventually find out. The only person we know is Sy."

Cooper lifted an eyebrow. "I'm listening."

"Maybe we need to know more about Sy," Harry finished her thought.

"Let me start with the people with whom he did business. I prefer not to disturb his wife right now, but I can start at the outside and work in," Cooper reasoned.

"We can sniff around." Harry felt a little buoyant; she could do something.

"Harry, keep out of this. If these deaths are related, this is a bigger problem than we anticipated. If not, it's a large coincidence."

"Cooper, save your breath," Pewter counseled.

"It's too late now." Mrs. Murphy spoke the truth.

30

Thursday

A flash of lightning turned the night sky electric blue then subsided.

Beatrice, entertaining Bayard Ernst, glanced out the window, as did he.

"Thunderstorms make me amorous," Beatrice cooed.

The temperature plunged twenty degrees. The effects of the storm were appreciated. The fierce winds now subsided to ten miles an hour. While this stiff breeze felt cooling, you could hear it rattle boughs. Before that, trees cracked. The extent of what damage there might be wouldn't be known until sunup.

Beatrice, next to Bayard in another dress, was glad for the sudden coolness. The dress made her perspire. Why he wanted to roll around with that much clothing on was his business though. She would accept his peculiarities.

Hale Van Vlies wrestled with Milady in the adjoining room. Freed from clothing, the window open, then closed somewhat because of the rain, he felt a slight chill. He pulled up the sheets as Milady wrapped her arms around him.

Those men enjoying the ladies tonight liked the thunderstorm for its cooling properties and because the woman whom he was spending money on clung tight to him because of the violence of the storm. A few actually were afraid, but most knew only too well how being frightened or needing something moved or picked up appealed to their client. The men felt happy this Thursday night and the women received fat tips. Everyone was happy.

Abigail and Sally ran up and down the stairs to deliver candles or lamps using a mixture of oils. The candles provided the most pleasing effect. Those candles removed a few years on the women getting older.

Abigail knocked lightly. Milady had requested another candle, as the wind blowing through the opened window blew out what she had. Abigail quickly entered when Milady told her to do so, placed the lamp on the table close to the bed, then turned and left.

She met Sally in the hallway, as they had more lamps, thick candles inside, to deliver. They stepped on the stairs lightly. Both had listened when Fiona told them no man likes a heavy step. So they tiptoed.

"Beatrice's client wears a dress," Sally whispered.

"What?"

"A dress. Beatrice says not to tell. He needs it to get hard. Strange."

"Yes." Abigail was learning fast.

Mignon and Eudes had prepared the lamps. They'd cleaned the kitchen, leaving out fruits and small pastries, should anyone be hungry. A large jug of sun tea, with a light towel over it to keep the flies off, also sat on the table.

"Here. Tell you what, Sally, we'll leave four on the table here should anyone run out or need more. The lamp oil is on the table on the other side of the room."

Eudes chimed in, "Don't want to take the chances of anyone spilling oil on the food. Least we don't have to worry about that with candles." He wiped his hands on his apron with a bib. "Some storm."

The two young women left. Mignon and Eudes finished up the last of the cleaning.

"If this cool weather holds, those who spend the night will have larger appetites."

Eudes smiled. "Depends on how successful they are tonight." He then put his arm around her waist. "Something I never worry about with my angel."

She didn't reply but patted his hands with her own. They complemented each other, a lucky pair. Those upstairs may have never complemented anyone, or if they did perhaps it wore off. Then again, if like Van Vlies, the captain, they were far from home, that person needed some specific comfort, and women were comfort.

Sally emerged from Jocelyn's room as Abigail left Lily's.

Abigail whispered to Sally, "They were standing up. No clothes. It's cool in there."

"Oh, they'll cool off when they're finished." Sally then added, "You'll be amazed at some of the stuff people do. Well, they pay for it."

"Do you know how much?"

"Abigail, Georgina will tell you when she thinks you're ready. But depending on what they do and who they are with, some of our girls make a lot of money. Deborah makes the most."

"Because of the banker?" Abigail was catching on.

"Yes. He now has her exclusive attentions. He pays Georgina a sack full of money and he pays Deborah, too. We aren't supposed to take money directly from the men, but most everyone accepts a tip or jewelry. Sometimes the men fall in love with their dove. I heard one man tell another down by the music room that the girls are soiled doves."

Abigail raised her eyebrows. "Do any of the girls fall in love with the men?"

"Every now and then. We had a popular girl here who ran off with a man who said he would marry her." Sally stopped herself because she couldn't and shouldn't discuss Livia. "Sometimes it works. They live far away. But most times it's a lie. He isn't going to take her away, marry her."

Shrewd for her years, Abigail intoned as they reached the bottom of the stairs, "People believe what they want to believe."

Sally considered that. "I guess. Do you like it here?"

Abigail walked down the front hall to look out the door and the long side windows along it. "I do. Still raining."

"Is. How did you get here?"

"I was selling vegetables by Three Chopt Road and two fellows kidnapped me. Can't think of another word. They didn't touch me. Took another two days on the road but they brought me here."

"You weren't scared?"

"I was more afraid to stay at home. Sooner or later I'd have been beaten up or killed, I think."

"Why?"

"One of my sisters married a rough man. She had a baby straight-away. Got a little fat. He started hanging around me. He even took his thing out to show me and told me what I did to him. Sooner or later I figured he'd hold me down. And if my sister found out, she'd blame me. She believes his lies. So does my mother. He makes money in the lumberyard. They like the money. He doesn't drink it, anyway."

"Was your mother cruel to you?"

"No. I don't think she cared one way or the other, but when I start to make money I'll send her some. She's bent over now. Hard work. Too much hard work."

Sally thought about this. "A lot of people get bent over when they get old. Jocelyn says she worries about her older customers. Says she has to work hard to get them ready, but she did say if she can do that, they become faithful to her. Will buy her anything."

"Aren't a lot of these men married?" Abigail asked.

"Seem to be. Guess their wives figure they have enough work without getting them hard." Sally laughed.

Abigail laughed, too. "Let's hope we don't find out, at least not for a while. I don't want to go to bed with some old man."

Sally wrinkled her nose. "We'll have to do it. Milady says old men pay for young women. Think it keeps them young."

"I guess it depends on how much." Abigail's mind was not far from money.

As the two young women, nineteen and sixteen, stared out the window and talked, wondering how long before they could turn in for the night, Georgina and Deborah sat in Georgina's office, the window opened a crack, the air fluttering pages on Georgina's desk. She put a paperweight on them.

"Cary Street." Georgina repeated the name of a street above Shockoe Slip. "Not far to walk from the ships."

"I asked Sam the price. He said he would look into it. The Murphys, the people who own the house, haven't made up their mind yet."

"Let me know the minute he knows." She listened to the rain then pulled on her light shawl, the one for cool summer nights. "Aren't you a little cool?"

"No. If I get there, I'll have one of the girls fetch my shawl."

"How do you like the new girl?"

"Abigail does what she's told. Learns quickly. And she's pretty. She's nothing like the last girl Shank and Martin brought here."

"Livia wasn't born with the sense God gave a goose." Georgina half smiled.

"That she couldn't help, but if she had even a grain of sense she would have learned something. But this one, she's smart. I don't think she'll be consumed by a dream."

"Good." Georgina wrapped the shawl a bit tighter around herself as a stronger gust of wind wedged through the crack. "Maureen Holloway told me something interesting the last time we met at

Sam's office. She has her tentacles all over Europe and the Caribbean. She told me in England's Parliament last May a man stood up for three hours to denounce the slave trade. Curious. It's a big business for investors not just in England but Spain, Portugal, some in Italy and France. If one of those countries has colonies or even one colony, it makes tremendous profits buying from West African tribes. The spoils of war. One tribe conquers another, takes them as slaves, saves some for themselves, and sells the rest to the Portuguese and now the English."

Deborah, born into slavery, listened. "No one gives up what makes money. Slavery is here to stay."

"I quite agree, but is it not interesting that a man would stand up and argue against something so important to his country's economy? You know people have been talking about money since B.C." She laughed.

"Nothing ever really changes. Men paying for women's bodies. Slavery. War. I don't much care. I want to profit from what's out there that I can manage. I can't build a ship. I can't run a market. But I can look at a woman's body and I have a good idea of what she'll bring over time."

Georgina smiled broadly. "I think we both do. And we both know how to please our clients. Give them a place to eat, listen to music, take care of their physical needs. The place should be attractive and the women even more so. Plus Eudes and Mignon work wonders in the kitchen. No one comes close to what The Tavern can offer."

"Yes." Deborah inhaled the odor of wet leaves and crepe myrtles. "Thinking about slavery, I wonder if we can offer refuge to those who run away? I will need pretty girls once we get the second house."

"I don't know how we could let it be known without risking ourselves," Georgina replied.

"What I was thinking is, we need a few more men like Martin and Shank, men who can find girls who want to profit but do less work than being in the field. Running away is difficult enough, but if you have nowhere to go, what do you do?"

"I see," said Georgina, knowing Deborah once faced this problem. "This is something we have to keep between us. Using Martin and Shank can only work if Maureen knows nothing of their business while using the wagons her husband builds. We need other men."

"If word would filter throughout the plantations that there is refuge for young, pretty women . . ." Deborah's voice trailed off; she shrugged her shoulders.

Georgina silently considered this then spoke. "If we don't do this, somebody else will. Now that you mention it, it's obvious. But I think many a young woman might find her way to us as well."

"We have to feed them and train them. Not everyone can start work immediately." Deborah was already figuring costs. "Most of our girls came here with some knowledge," Deborah stated.

"They did. And all have a story. No one grows up thinking she will be a prostitute. I prefer the term *paid companion*." Georgina said this, giving the last an uplifting sound.

"Then that's what we shall use. Let's watch Sally and Abigail, neither of whom came here with any training and know little about men. Even though Sally does not appear to be a good candidate now, she might surprise us."

"True, but some men want a woman who is boyish. She may yet have a real clientele. I don't think Sally will develop as ladies do."

"Abigail is already there."

They looked at each other, pleased with their ideas, thinking about the future.

Then Georgina warned, "Maureen must never know."

31

Sunday

Windows and doors were wide open for whatever breeze there might be. As it was noon, a midday meal was served for men who stayed at The Tavern. The number remained small in summer. The regulars who lived in town would be at St. John's Anglican Church or the other attractive churches in the growing city. Family was their focus on Sundays. It was important to be seen with the wife and children. These languid Sunday mornings and afternoons allowed the girls to do whatever, be it sitting outside, hemming a skirt, or doing nothing.

"What's worse, the heat or the cold?" Jocelyn wondered.

Fanning herself with an elegant, expensive fan, Milady answered, "Heat. At least we can put on layers in winter. And having to service our clients takes stamina in the heat. If they're hairy, it's even hotter."

Fiona laughed. "True. Breathing in winter feels good. The air tingles your lungs, you exhale and can see your breath; I like it. I'd like it better if I could figure out how to keep my feet warm."

"Farm boots," Beatrice said with finality.

"Can you see us greeting our customers wearing farm boots?" Milady giggled, which made the others follow suit, as Milady wasn't really a giggler.

"Who cares? You take them off the minute you're in your room." Beatrice felt she was being sensible.

"Well, what about those men who want to flop on you while you are wearing your shoes?"

"Oh, Jocelyn." Sally was scandalized.

"True," Beatrice said with finality. "Of course, none of us is going to wear warm shoes, no matter what, but stockings, wool, and a thick shawl can keep you warm. It's only the shoes that fail."

"Well, any of our customers with a bit of wit would declare he will keep us warm," Jocelyn murmured.

"Here you are." Lily came out with a tray of drinks, followed by Eudes. "You all look as though you need a libation."

Lily put one tray on the white table outside. Eudes put his down, too.

"Not much going on today?" Milady asked Eudes.

"Quiet. Heard there is a preacher from Philadelphia at St. John's and people who rarely go to church have gone. If it cools off tonight you all will have some business."

"Oh, I wouldn't mind a day off," Fiona said longingly, then she looked around, taking the drink handed to her by a polite Sally. "Thank you, dear. An extra day off sounds wonderful. Some days my bones creak. I need a rest."

Deborah came out, took a drink, and sat down. "Fiona, did I hear you say you needed a rest?"

Fiona knew not to trust Deborah. "Oh, every now and then an extra day. If for nothing else, to tidy up my wardrobe."

"Don't say that. I am so far behind." Beatrice's eyebrows knitted together. "I'd buy a few new things, but the heat deters me. Come fall, I will bedazzle you." She laughed.

"Beatrice, you always bedazzle us," Jocelyn complimented her. "You can deal with anyone. I remember years ago the little jockey fellow who wanted you to pretend to be a horse."

Beatrice lifted her chin. "Yes, I was truly ridden."

"Did he use a crop?" Abigail, who had been silent, was astonished.

"No," Beatrice answered. "There are a few customers, fortunately not mine, who enjoy inflicting pain, or they want you to give it to them."

"Oh yes. Old Roger Pokenham still wants to be tied up and tortured," Fiona announced.

"Still? I didn't know that." Deborah liked to know the customers' proclivities, especially as she was planning the second house.

"Still. He wants you to smack his bottom until it's bright red and then he wants you to squeeze his family jewels until they hurt. Screams with pleasure and asks for more." A pause and then Fiona in her most ladylike voice declared, "Who am I to deny a city father pleasure?"

They all laughed.

"And they pay more." Deborah nodded. "Anything out of the ordinary raises the price."

"Hmm." Sally was putting this together. "So if I specialize in being a horse or giving pain, I'll make more?"

"Sally, you need to grow a bit first." Deborah was firm. "Georgina has strict standards. As you still look so young, she wouldn't want anyone to think we had children here servicing men."

"People—" Abigail's mouth hung open.

"They do." Deborah answered before she finished the question. "As I said, Georgina has strict rules. We have to dress a certain way, always smile, do what our customers want, and it doesn't hurt to make small talk."

"That's the truth," Beatrice affirmed Deborah. "You learn a lot."

"Hales Van Vlies, the ship's captain, when he's here he tells me what's come in at the slip. Who has brought good furniture. Who has some items he might sell cheap. And the other thing, Sally and Abigail, men love to talk about themselves. All it takes is one or two questions."

"I know some women who like to talk about themselves, too," Lily added.

"Well, I can tell you something unusual I learned from Sam Udall." Deborah kept her voice low then stopped.

All eyes were upon her.

"Well?" Fiona asked, which was what Deborah wanted.

"Sam, who follows such things, said there was a member of Parliament in London who spoke for three hours about ending the slave trade. Three hours."

"Won't happen here," Jocelyn stated simply.

"Wouldn't it be better if it did?" Sally, who was black, innocently asked.

Beatrice, pondering this, replied, "Sally, honey, I think that depends on your line of business. For us, we don't need it but if we grew tobacco, we might feel differently."

Fiona, thinking on this news, nodded. "As long as people can buy themselves out of slavery, maybe that's a kind of answer."

"Takes forever," Deborah flatly stated. "My thought on all this is, I don't want to be anybody's slave whether it's a white person or a Negro man. I am not taking orders from a man, so don't get married girls. If you marry, he thinks he owns you."

Beatrice leaned back, took a long sip of her drink. "Well, legally he does."

Abigail, taking all this in, said, "I don't want to get married. My sisters are married. I'd die of boredom."

"You can do that here." Jocelyn laughed. "Sometimes when one of my customers is on top of me, I think of other things. When you get right down to it there isn't a lot of imagination to, shall we say, being close?"

"That depends." Beatrice beamed. "Sometimes there is a lot of imagination. Then again, we see what wives don't. You keep a man happy, he keeps you happy. Look at the gifts we sometimes receive."

"True, but there are those who think of you as a beast of burden. You are nothing to them." Lily, young though she was, had her share of men wanting a young, pretty woman and that's all they wanted.

"I have an idea." Deborah smiled. "There is a steeplechase race in Albemarle County in September. Sam told me. It's a new thing. I don't know that I can explain it. They run and jump. You bet, of course. Well, if you give me enough time maybe I can convince Georgina we all need to go. We'll meet new customers, we'll have a day by the mountains; and who knows, we might find some new," she thought a long time about this, "sisters."

"Really?" Lily sat up straight.

"It would cost us a few days of profit, but I believe we can make it up there."

"Deborah, how can we do that? We have no place to," a long pause, "entertain," Jocelyn said.

"Yes. But if we all go, properly dressed, we will certainly be noticed. It's open to all. Let me talk to Sam. If he goes with his wife, of course, that doesn't mean he can't introduce the men he knows there to us. The wife will be busy being an important lady with other important ladies. And this will take more work, but if we rent a house for the evening of the race, I know we will have a lot of business."

All sat in silence.

"You think Georgina will go for it?" Beatrice warmed to the idea.

"If there is money to be made, she will. And if we are successful, a few of those well-heeled men will find their way to Richmond from time to time." Deborah slowly smiled. "I'm here for money. Aren't you all?"

A chorus said, "Yes," with a few also nodding.

"Well, you make money by finding more buyers for your product. That's what I want to do."

"What will I wear?" Lily sounded panicked.

"For God's sake, Lily, we have a few weeks. We will all look alluring, at the height of our allure." Deborah beamed.

Milady, a touch of her vanity showing, said, "I think I am more alluring out of clothing than in clothing."

Deborah, not Milady's admirer even though she did bring in business, purred, "Darling Milady, you know perfectly well how to use your assets to best effect. They will want to rip your clothes off."

Beatrice, laughing, quoted Caesar, as she was quite a reader. "*Alea jacta est.*"

"What?" Abigail was confused but liked the idea.

"Julius Caesar broke one of the rules of Rome when he crossed the Rubicon River. He knew it would lead to trouble, possibly civil war. So he said, 'The die is cast.' Meaning he had thrown the dice. Bold."

"Well, girls, let's throw the damned dice." Fiona laughed.

32

Sunday

The seven friends studied their menus at the table. The restaurant in Staunton was crowded. Had Joel not made the reservations they would have had a long wait, as so many people came home for the Christmas holiday.

"Any idea?" Fair asked Harry, who was assiduously reading the menu.

"Well, I like shrimp cocktail."

"What about a sole basted in white wine for your entrée?" Joel, glasses on, looked up from his menu.

"You know, I want a ribeye steak. Something plain," she replied.

"Béarnaise sauce?" Joel's eyebrows raised.

Ballard peeked over the top of the large menu. "I'm starting with the mussels and then I want pompano. It's been years since I ate that and I forgot how much I like it."

After enough time, all came to some conclusion, and the waiter took the order.

"All right." Harry bent down, picked up her purse, and pulled out the straws, which she carefully arranged in her hand. "Ladies first."

Jodie reached up as Harry left her seat to walk around the table so no one would need to reach over their drinks.

"I'm okay." Jodie smiled.

"Next. Aren't you pleased I'm considering you a lady and I've known you since year one?" Harry watched as Susan plucked a straw.

"As to year one, do we really need to go back that far?" Susan pulled another long straw. "Not me."

"Ned." Harry stood by Susan's husband.

"Got it." He held up the short straw in triumph. "As the head of the table, I hope you will enjoy your libation."

Harry sat down after collecting the three straws, put them back in her purse.

Joel watched this. "Cotillion made a great impression on you."

"Did." She reached for her Perrier with lime. "You know it still goes on. Usually called cotillion in the South, but dance school elsewhere. If your parents railroad you into it while young, those lessons stick. You are usually relaxed because you know just what to do."

Jodie put her finger to the side of her nose. It stopped there, as though she'd forgotten it. "Well, now that you mention it, they do."

Fair shrugged. "I had to go, but really my mother and aunts beat those bad manners out of my skin all on their own."

They laughed, especially Harry, who knew the formidable ladies. "Honey, you were already growing into a big man. This was their only chance to tower over you."

"Oh, they didn't need to tower. Scared the bejesus out of me sometimes." He smiled, remembering his family, whom he loved.

"Joel?" Ballard asked.

"Given that I had to attend Sunday school and be part of a religion class, then catechism, I got away with it. The nuns managed to impart what was correct. Used rulers, too."

"Now they'd be arrested." Jodie turned to smile at him.

"If only they were arrested then." He squeezed her hand.

"You all knew Mother." Ballard sipped his whiskey sour. "Joel and Jodie, you only knew Mother at the end, but you walked a fine line with her. So yes, I was beautifully mannered, but still mucked up my life."

"Now, Ballard, you got back on track," Ned praised him.

"The only things I didn't do were grand theft and murder." Ballard shrugged.

"There's time," Joel teased him.

"I'll drink to that." Fair held up his glass, and they all clinked glasses.

"How was everyone's week?" Susan asked.

"Still cleaning up downed limbs," Ballard answered.

"One of the advantages of living in Ednam." Joel named an exclusive suburb of Charlottesville. "We have to manage the lawns, but anything on the road, the homeowners association gets. Same with snow plowing. We pay for our driveway but the road is cleared."

"Yes. I can see the advantage of that. You are looking at our snow-plow person." Harry held up a hand.

"You don't do it?" Joel pointed a finger at Fair.

"Now, just a minute. I do, but when I'm called out early I have to go. Like any doctor, you go when needed. My patients are on four hooves but they are still my patients, and Joel, we have two tractors, so my bride and I often do it together."

"Is this what togetherness in marriage means?" Jodie had a devilish twinkle in her eye. "Honey, maybe we should get two tractors."

"Well . . ." Joel's voice trailed off. "Isn't this why we bought winter property in Florida?"

"Joel, you're smarter than the rest of us." Ned laughed. "As I am in Richmond so much, I've hired a service. Susan, even though her mother and grandmother also have a service, usually goes over there to check on them, especially if the power goes out. Owning anything costs more money than you think. Services are raising prices." He looked at Joel. "Food prices are rising."

"Ned, I have to pay them, too. We've got some problems with COVID, now truck drivers. People leaving work. A lot aren't coming back. And just a heads-up, I don't think food prices are coming down for some time."

"He's right." Ned affirmed this.

"Are you all talking about it in the House of Delegates?" Jodie wondered.

"Talk is the operative word."

"Can anything be done?" Ballard asked.

"It will take time. My party will take the high road, so they think. The other party will be willing to sacrifice children. You get the idea." He inhaled, paused, then continued, "Yes, something can be done but not until many of my esteemed colleagues can figure out a way to use this impending crisis to their political advantage."

"What about the governor?" Ballard listened intently.

"If he throws his weight behind those in need, many of whom are already in trouble given rents, etc., yes, it will be resolved as best we can, faster. But you have to remember, he's a new governor and he has to throw red meat to his ardent supporters."

"People don't count anymore, do they?" Susan sounded a bit wistful.

"Their votes count, then they are forgotten." Harry, who hated politics and everything about it, groused.

"Harry, you're a cynic." Joel said this without rancor.

"I am," she confessed.

"Here's the thing. As your representative, even if you didn't vote for me," Ned smiled, "we can fix this, but the posturing has got to stop and it will only stop if the resolve comes from the people. Citizens must demand services, roads, bridges, good schools. You elect us to run the state as smoothly as possible. Our roads, wildlife, forestry department, they may not be at the top of your list, but they make our lives easier."

"What about health?" Fair finished his drink.

"Unfortunately, that has been politicized, starting in Washington.

Our outgoing governor, as a physician, I do think did his best despite the misinformation. Our current governor, not a doctor, obviously isn't out to get us all infected, but his focus is more on business. Getting people back to work."

"It's a conundrum," Jodie remarked.

Harry, factoring all that had been mentioned, offered an idea. "It is. But it has given us the opportunity to plan for the next catastrophe, be it weather, disease, or even a spike in violence. Plan now. We have enough information where we are weak."

"Harry, that sounds hopeful." Susan sounded surprised.

"With Ned as our representative, I am hopeful."

"Thank you, Harry." Ned was as surprised in his way as Susan was in hers.

Ballard waited for Ned to finish, then he said, "Joel, if it's a bad winter, I'll come down to Florida. I don't want you to miss me too much."

Jodie laughed. "You are so thoughtful."

The topic changed to football, both college and pro. The whole group loved football. Harry liked baseball more, but she could get excited by a football game. The playoffs had everyone's attention, and soon all the college games after Christmas . . . the large number of bowls . . . would mesmerize people, but most especially the alumni and alumnae of the competing institutions.

"William and Mary." Susan appeared hopeful.

"They have a chance." Fair was not about to say anything negative about Susan's alma mater. "William and Mary is so outstanding academically, but some of the teams are also good. Really, I think football comes down to the coaching staff. A university might have one or two stars, but mostly those kids will graduate and go on to their professions. A few will go to the pros, but none of our schools here are on par with Ohio State or Nebraska. Just a different world."

"We've had UVA men go into the pros. Go back to Nelson Yarborough. Frank Quayle a little later, the Barber twins, and I know I'm leaving men out." Joel was a football nut.

"UVA has times of being terrific, but in the main, it just muddles along." Jodie took a breath then smiled. "Now, Virginia Tech—"

This was interrupted by Joel. "Honey, we're eating."

Jodie twirled her fork for a moment. "I need to go to one of my Alpha Chi Omega meetings and remind the alumnae we should tell our girls at Tech not to marry a UVA man unless she's considered what football season will be like."

Joel just grinned.

Fair said, "Honey, how do you think Smith will do?"

This got everyone away from predictions and rivalries.

When the dessert menu came, full though they were, no one could resist.

"Apple crisp with ice cream. Almost as American as apple pie with ice cream." Ballard picked out his dessert.

"Hey, here it is again. Orange-glazed sweetbreads and crème brûlée." Harry added, "Maybe it's become some kind of in thing. I mean, I do not remember this ever until we started our dinners."

Ballard leaned her way. "Didn't you say there seemed to be murders after you discovered this dessert? Did I get it right?"

"Well, sort of." Harry blushed slightly, as she didn't want to look like a woo-woo person or someone who leaps to odd conclusions.

Ballard held his menu up. "Murder menus."

They laughed, and Joel pursed his lips a moment then spoke. "Odd, but stranger things have happened, I'm sure."

"Well, what about that great Hitchcock TV show, about the woman who murders her husband with a leg of lamb, then cooks it and serves it to the police." Susan loved watching old TV shows.

"Now, there's a thought." Jodie laughed. "I'll remember that when Tech plays UVA."

The group, in good humor, fed, and happy, nattered on finally leaving, braving the cold, all driving home.

Harry, Fair, Ned, and Susan drove in Ned's car. They took turns driving to save gas, but also to be together. Old friends . . . family, really . . . and they loved one another. Ballard drove with the Palomas, and it was his turn to drive.

"Harry, is it true about the orange-glazed whatever?" Susan asked.

"Well, I thought there was an oddity there, but mostly I thought the dessert was odd. But hey, while we are on the subject of murder or overdoses, whatever, I bought Narcan. You should, too."

"Really?" Susan exclaimed.

"Honey," Harry looked at her husband, "I bought some for you, too. Did it this morning after my chores. Listening to what Cooper said about the fentanyl epidemic . . . I guess it's an epidemic . . . I thought we should be prepared. The naloxone, if administered right away, can save people. Get them breathing."

Ned slowed for a moment, since there was more traffic than they'd thought as they got onto I-64 east. "That is a good idea. Honey, how about if I go out tomorrow, or we go together. The drugstore?" he asked Harry.

"Yeah, they have it."

"Who do we know that is going to OD?" Susan wasn't challenging, just curious.

"We didn't think Sy Buford would. Better to be prepared, and we are in a county with lots of schools plus the university," Harry reminded them. "Was it an accident? Was he on painkillers or did someone kill him, God knows why?"

Fair tried to relax in the backseat, which didn't have quite enough room for his long legs. "People who work around horses are often battling some pain. Goes with the territory. How do I know what they are taking or what someone may hand them and say, 'This will take care of it.' Running a big orchard is physical. Pain, no doubt, plus age will get you, too. So yes, I will carry the Narcan with me. Hard to believe this, isn't it?"

"It's the old saw, 'Better safe than sorry.' "

"Honey let's hope we never have to use it. I can use a needle but I sure don't want to do it."

"Practice on oranges to get used to it," Fair suggested.

"Not exactly an apple a day keeps the doctor away, but close enough." Ned thought Harry was practical. "Let's talk about other topics. How about Smith's football team?"

"I'll get you for that," Harry promised.

33

Saturday

A cerulean blue sky, a few rolling white clouds sliding in over the mountains, low humidity, and a temperature at sixty-eighty degrees, Fahrenheit, at nine in the morning presaged a perfect day. The horses to race that day had arrived the night before. Many were stabled at Cloverfields, some at Big Rawly, Ewing had a temporary pasture with a few sheds constructed at The Barracks by a narrow fast-running stream. Those horses could come to the meet the back way.

Owners, jockeys, grooms fed lightly, hand-walked a bit, then brushed their charges, who happily enjoyed the morning. Some stayed in stalls, others lingered in pastures, being carefully watched in case of a fight. The last thing anyone wanted was to make the journey to Albemarle County only to have their horse kicked in the paddock.

Maureen, walking arm in arm with Jeffrey, chatted with each person who had rented a stall or pasture. With the exception of the house for the old and infirm, watched over by Olivia and Sulli, Big Rawly burst with activity and anticipation. So did Cloverfields and The Barracks.

Any excuse to gather was usually taken by people looking for something new, new people, old friends. Travel, being difficult, meant one stayed a few days or more, depending on the relationship.

Maureen, wearing a pair of topaz earrings, flanked by diamonds and a stunning necklace to match, beamed hospitality as well as wealth.

"Ah, Zachary Thigpen." Jeffrey then introduced his wife. "Welcome. So glad you could stay with us."

"Good to meet you. John sent me over, saying we might have a few moments before the races begin." He kissed Maureen's hand after this. "They ran out of stalls. Quite a good thing for a new race. Luckily there was room for me."

"Mr. Thigpen. John speaks of your valor at Yorktown." Maureen had made it a point to learn something about every contestant.

Blushing, Zachary confessed, "Oh, Mrs. Holloway, I couldn't shoot my way out of a barrel. But I stood my ground. Were it not for John's courage and leadership, we would all be dead."

"Mr. Thigpen, you are too modest." She glowed.

"Please call me Zachary. I feel as though I know you, for John has told me so much about what you have accomplished here."

"Jeffrey has vision," Maureen simply added, and she believed that.

"Darling," Jeffrey squeezed her arm, which was resting on his forearm, "allow me to show Zachary the forge and the carriages."

"Of course. Should you all desire anything to drink or find yourselves famished, please let me know. A bit of tea never hurt anyone."

Zachary bowed and Jeffrey smiled at Maureen. "I'll send Toby to you if we do."

The two men turned toward the higher ground, walking briskly to the first stop, the wagon shop.

Zachary, a sharp eye for coaches, conveyances as well as horses, observed everything with compliments. He noticed William's bad limp. Said nothing. Then the two walked to the impressive carriage shop, all the windows open as well as the two huge doors at either end.

Walking into the large space, Zachary stopped, mouth wide open.

The men in the building noted this, and Toby, the smartest, looked to Jeffrey for a sign.

Jeffrey smiled at Toby and Caleb, both in clean clothes, which wasn't easy given their work. Today was a show-off day of men and coaches.

"My word," Zachary exclaimed.

"Would you like a closer look?"

"Indeed I would," Zachary enthusiastically replied, hurrying to a deep maroon coach finished with gold pin striping, lanterns by the doors, and that beautiful, curved dashboard, which Jeffrey and his men had enhanced and strengthened, also pinstriped.

A sleight of the hand had Toby walk over to open the coach door.

"Step up, Zachary."

The well-built man, a few pounds heavier since his warrior days, fairly hopped up. Sitting down, he inhaled the aroma of the leather seats. Saw the foot heaters tucked under the footrests.

"Even my wife could not find fault with this." Zachary laughed. "My good woman is not fond of the discomfort of travel." He stepped out.

"Allow me to call your attention to the axles. You'll have to bend a bit."

"Well, I can still do that, but I now have a creak or two." Zachary laughed at himself. "This is impressive. Does the thickness of the axles affect the ride?"

"A bit, yes. But they are quite sturdy. The boys and I keep playing with ways to absorb the shock. But a good driver and decent roads greatly add to a more comfortable ride."

Zachary stood up, a slight sheen to his brow. "Well, that's it, isn't it? Good roads."

"Yes, we have a lot of work to do. Come look at the coach that Percy Ballard will pick up tomorrow. I'm sure John told you he has a horse in the race?"

"It will be a marvel to see my old comrade. Like John, fearless. But I tell you, Jeffrey, winning a war is quite different than winning a peace."

Smiling broadly, Jeffrey agreed. "John has praised your insight."

"Ah." Zachary waved his hand as if to brush away the compliment. "Have you been to Europe, Sir? These carriages are as elegant as anything I saw in England and France when I was younger."

"I have not, but my wife was educated in France, her ideas most especially regarding interiors and colors have been so helpful. I do think women are better at those things. I would be lost without her."

"She herself is elegant and very welcoming," Zachary complimented Jeffrey on his lady, never a bad idea.

"Might you look at this." Jeffrey pointed to a tiny but lovely lone pine tree on the middle of both coach doors. The gold glittered. "Lone Pine."

"I say." Zachary grinned, as he knew the name of Ballard's estate.

Jeffrey showed him two coaches in the earlier stages of construction. Zachary crawled over them, fascinated with the advances Jeffrey had made in underpinnings and body work. The bodies, one without doors yet, were sleek, not boxy, yet they would hold six people in relative comfort.

Zachary stayed immobile for a few moments, looking around the building.

"Would you like to see the forge? By the way, we are building a large one at some distance to provide conveyances for our militia. John has spoken to me about our need to defend ourselves."

"We need a larger standing army and navy." Zachary's voice rose a bit. "Otherwise we will have fought our war for nothing. I promise you, Jeffrey, even our allies across the ocean are looking at our lands with lust in their hearts."

"Yes, yes, John has made that point. My wife feels strongly, as do

I, that those of us with some resources must do what we can until Congress realizes the potential dangers."

"Ah, some do. Some don't." Zachary exhaled. "I am supplying muskets and men. We will do our best for Virginia and pray that it prods other states. We cannot fail, Jeffrey. We cannot."

"No, Sir."

They walked outside and Zachary surprised Jeffrey by stopping and taking his arm for a moment.

"John told me you had a gift. He also said you have laid out some of the grounds here, created testing paths for your carriages. I see he is correct. I would like to order two coach-in-fours; I think they will enhance my line. You did know I have a coach service. My coaches serve Baltimore, Philadelphia, and Richmond. Over time I hope to add more destinations."

"He said you are a person with vision."

"Ah." Zachary grinned broadly. "I would like to order two coaches and two wagons. And as you know, they will be traveling great distances over variable roads. In time I hope to have a line going west through the gap. Too early yet."

"Yes, but it is growing. Frederick Town, quite a bit. Winchester. Sometimes I forget these name changes. My father always called it Frederick Town. But if roads improve toward the west, I would like to serve those towns." Jeffrey believed Virginia would grow quite a bit, the further in time the war receded.

"My wife tells me our black coaches are dull. She says people should see us coming from a distance. What do you think?"

"Your wife is right. My wife tells me in Europe some coaches are painted in the livery color of the noble, often the arms large on the side."

"Color?" Zachary wrinkled his brow then looked at the stunning sky. "Cerulean. Yes. Cerulean."

"Your wife will be greatly pleased."

"Well, let me get back to Cloverfields and see to my horse and my people."

"Your horse's name?"

"The Marquis, for our commanding officer."

"Of course. I wish you the best of luck. And you may know that Percy's horse is Big Blue. He said he couldn't use Blueskin, as that was one of General Washington's horses, but he calls his fellow Big Blue."

Zachary laughed. "That devil."

As he left, Jeffrey waved him off then hurried to the house, where he eagerly told Maureen everything.

She kissed him. "Wonderful. Wonderful."

"John, I must thank John when I can."

Maureen, happy to see him so happy, replied, "The Garths are good neighbors. Perhaps we, too, should be leaving for Cloverfields."

By eleven, the day sparkled. The humidity, pleasingly low, made the day seem cooler. At seventy degrees, the temperature was pleasant. A hint of fall was not yet in the air but the deep green of the leaves on the deciduous trees gave an announcement it would not be far off.

Almost 120 people gathered at Cloverfields. The course, well marked, had been laid out so one could see it especially at the start and finish. The backside, a bit of a slope, could be viewed if one walked down toward Ivy Creek and stayed out of the way. Given that no one knew what a steeplechase course was, few onlookers dared to move too far from the crowds.

The starting line, powdered white, was to the right of the main stable. One side was fenced, which helped the jockeys keep their horses in check until they passed that large pasture. The hope was to simply drop a rope and they would be off. The finish line was the same line and the horses would have run an oval of one or two miles, depending on the race. Catherine and Jeddie felt four races was quite enough, especially since everyone was doing this for the first time.

The crowds consisted of everyone who could manage to make the journey. Rich people, poor people, white, black, free, and enslaved. A spectacle like this drew many people and since one paid just a penny to get in, most people could pay that.

Ewing told his daughter spectators must pay something, no matter how small. A penny had some purchasing power, so fences could be mended if needs be. It was the idea not really the amount.

The entry fee was five dollars, a bit stiff but this helped weed out unconditioned horses. Catherine was adamant about bringing in the best. Those with money tended to use good horses.

People arriving in coaches had a special section near the finish line. One could sit up next to the driver and enjoy an expansive view.

The first race to go off at noon was a one-miler. The jumps took thought. Catherine felt three feet was enough. Maybe after this first race in coming years, if all worked well, the height could vary, but for now three feet. The first jump was a simple post and rail. After that the jumps became more creative. The two of them planted boxwoods, a long line of boxwoods. They built . . . with help, of course . . . stone jumps, and Catherine wanted a ha ha jump but she wasn't certain how it was built. So she had a ditch dug of only two feet width and one stride on the other side to a line of boxwoods. She thought the sight of this more imposing than the jump itself. Nor was she afraid of some of the hard work, which upset Barker O and Jeddie. They didn't want her to hurt herself and they didn't want to look as though they were dumping the work on Cloverfields' great lady. She was their great lady. She thought of herself as a horsewoman. She wanted to work. Femininity had no interest for her at all. Still, she did as a lady should most times. Given her extraordinary beauty, Catherine could get away with a lot.

Ewing with his best friend, Yancy Grant, sat in a temporary stand also to the other side of the finish line.

"A success even before the first race." Yancy patted Ewing's back.

"All Catherine. We really don't know what they do in Ireland, but we know what we are going to do here. And by the way, your Black Night can't run of course due to his old injury, but Catherine is certain one of his foals will be ready in a year. Two now on the ground. Good for you."

"Yes, I've been keeping my eye on him. She has a knack, doesn't she? She sees things we don't. Pairings. And who would think of doing something like this?"

"Father." Rachel and Charles walked by then stopped. "Would you like anything before we settle down?"

"No. Where are the children?"

"With Ruth, Father. Charles and I felt this was too much for them at this age and Marcia is especially bullheaded. I'd spend the day running after her."

"Wise decision," he agreed. "Where are you going to wait?"

"With Barker O on the carriage. Best view."

"It is." He checked the pocket watch his daughters gave him for his fiftieth birthday. "Soon time."

She agreed, Charles took her by the arm, propelling her to a Cloverfields carriage not quite as spectacular as the one Maureen and Jeffrey were sitting in.

Her husband helped her up and Barker O also took her hand. She sat on the driver's long seat.

"Your carriage is long in the tooth," DoRe called from his spectacular carriage, built by Jeffrey, of course.

"You're getting long in the tooth," Barker O shot back.

The two drivers, outstanding with four reins in their hands, were old rivals and friends. Bettina could not sit with her fiancé, as Maureen would never allow a slave to sit next to her. Her driver was one thing, Bettina quite another.

So she had a chair not far from the carriage, where from time to time she looked up at this burly bear of a man and he would wink at her. She pretended she was shocked. Here they were in middle age, having lost spouses to disease and accident, and love found them. Getting to live on the same farm was proving difficult but in time it had to happen. For one thing, Ewing, Catherine, and Rachel were running out of patience.

Catherine, her long stride covering ground, wore a simple green dress. The other ladies were more resplendent in their attire but if anything needed to be done, Catherine was not going to do it burdened with jewels and flounces.

Maureen looked down at the woman going from owner to owner for this race.

Jeffrey said, "A triumph for her. Let's hope the day turns out to be without accident."

"That will be a miracle." Maureen paused. "Will any of us ever forget that flat race down by Richmond when William pulled Jeddie off his horse. He could have been killed."

"I always think, my dear, that anyone who throws their leg over a horse needs a bit of courage. And might I add you look splendid when you ride."

"Now, Jeffrey." She loved it. "You flatter me."

"Not nearly enough. We are in the last race, are we not? I've been so busy in the shop I have not paid enough attention to our training for this day."

"Samson," she answered. "I thought about entering Valentin and Louis the Sixteenth but let's see what this steeplechase really is. Next time, and don't fret, dear. You know driving horses. This is different."

"Of course. What do you think, DoRe?"

"Good for horses. See and be seen," the driver responded.

"And look at how many people have walked by your coach." Maureen nodded as Zachary Thigpen hurried by to reach his jockey before the race.

Tulli, dressed as a little jockey, all of twelve, had an important job. He would blow the cow horn to alert people that the race was about to begin. Small, though he was good with a horn.

"Tulli, are you ready?"

"Yes, Miss Catherine." His face shone with excitement.

"All right. Give me your best."

He put the cow horn to his lips and blew mournful notes in rising tones. Low, but the tone carried for a distance; the crowd silenced. The horses, led by grooms, jockeys up, walked to the starting line.

Cager and Mr. Percy, Bumbee's husband, behaving for now, held the thin rope. As all the horses lined up . . . two jigging, but they were there . . . the two men looked to Catherine and nodded; they dropped the rope and the crowd roared.

Sam Udall had a sleek chestnut in this race, as did one other Richmond owner; the field was comprised of six horses. One of the owners, Mr. Finney, made the trip from Maryland, his farm, Royal Oak, just on the other side of the Potomac.

The horses took the jumps better than many of their riders, but all stayed on until the next-to-last jump, which was a series of three fences, each three strides apart. One jockey came off, unhurt. His horse finished the race.

Sam Udall's friend, the investor Desmond Huff, won.

As it would take twenty minutes to a half hour to prepare for the next race, the crowd took the opportunity to walk about, talk to one another, meet new people, greet old friends.

Jeddie and Catherine, on their calmest horses, rode out to check the jumps, make sure nothing had been knocked down, no big gouges in the turf.

As they did so, Georgina and her ladies, impeccably dressed, chatted with the men who came by. If they were married, their wives were not at the races or were otherwise engaged.

Deborah elicited many admirers. Sam, in a fit of generosity and as always meaning to impress Deborah, had rented a house for three days for the ladies. They had arrived on Thursday during the day and could stay until Sunday. Georgina, never one to waste time, was having repairs done on The Tavern while she and the girls were in Albemarle County. She left Sally and Abigail, feeling they were too young

for business, and under Mignon and Eudes's guidance they couldn't go too far wrong. Any caller would be told repairs would be finished by the sixteenth and to please call then and enjoy the improvements.

Sam, ever clever, had the Philadelphia preacher at his house. His wife, thrilled with the status of her guest, didn't mind not traveling to Albemarle County. Sam, having entertained the man throughout the week, left on business. No one seemed to mind.

Georgina and Maureen did not acknowledge each other. Maureen thought it interesting that Georgina and her girls attended the races. Then again, anyone could and Georgina's mind rarely strayed from profits. Maureen's opinion of Georgina rose steadily the more she knew her.

Back at Big Rawly, the people relished time without Maureen. Jeffrey had given the men in the shops time off after Zachary Thigpen left. The house staff faced fewer chores without Maureen lashing them on. Her lady-in-waiting, Elizabetta, loathed by the other slaves and the freeborn, too, used the time to sit under a tree with embroidery. Calmed her nerves.

At the Yellow House, the name of the home for those failing in health with no family, or born simple, as people thought of their minds, Olivia and Sulli put cold dishes on the outside table. The number of people in the Yellow House had fallen to five plus little Sophia, the blind child a bit over one year of age. The very old inhabitants died off, so the oldest now was Eli, who lost an arm years ago in a farm accident. Olivia would cut his food for him while Sulli taught Sophia how to eat, as best you could with a one-year-old. But as the child was born blind, she willingly learned and had sharp senses.

Everyone else could take care of their own basic needs.

"Olivia, how long do you think Maureen and Jeffrey will be away?" Sulli, in private, never called them Master or Mistress.

"All day. Mistress won't pass up the opportunity to shine."

"Um." Sulli watched their charges eat and babble among themselves. "Let me clean up and then I am going to walk around a bit."

"Stay away from the house. Elizabetta will find something wrong with you roaming Big Rawly. She'll be sure to tell the Missus."

"Elizabetta can go to Hell," Sulli cursed.

"She might." Olivia slightly smiled. "She will never forgive you and William for running away when she was in charge of the estate. Another period of Mrs. Selisse's absence. She paid for it."

"We stole a few baubles and coins. The woman before Elizabetta had stolen so much more."

"Sheba. Yes. She made off with a fortune in jewelry and has never been found. She had been Maureen's personal slave, her lady-in-waiting since childhood. Even went to France with her and spoke French. My guess is that's where she fled and she'll have enough money to live well. People will assume she's a crook, which she is." Olivia grabbed a glass before Sophia knocked it over. "What Mrs. Selisse sees as betrayal we see as freedom."

"Free to do what? I was free when we were at Royal Oak. I liked it, but William made my life miserable. I don't think women are ever free."

"I don't know and I'm too old to care," Olivia honestly answered as they cleared the table with help.

"Done. I won't be long. I would like to walk without worrying about Maureen seeing me. She'd find some awful task for me."

"That she would."

Sulli walked down the path, passed the large coach building. She was eighteen now. Strong and good-looking. Usually people like Maureen used the good-looking women in the house, but she would never use Sulli that way. Sulli would be at the Yellow House until the day she died.

Birds sang, flitting about, catching bugs in the air.

Big Rawly, well laid out, French in its influence, delighted the eye. Maureen's first husband, Francisco Selisse, wanted a grand estate.

He felt the climate was not hospitable to Spanish architecture, and being from the Caribbean like his wife, he copied France. He was a man with a need to look important and be important. He built on Maureen's father's bank, creating a money-lending business here. Discreet. He doubled the fortune and kept enlarging it. The trees had been planted in rows along every drive. The garden, while no Versailles, was formal.

Sulli absorbed this without knowing history. But she did know that Big Rawly looked different from Cloverfields or the few other estates she had seen.

Reaching the smaller building, the wagon building, she looked for William. Not there. Back outside, she stopped herself. Walked back in and picked up the andiron leaning against the fireplace, so useful in the winter. It was heavy. Back outside she looked for William. He was nowhere in sight. She thought, where might he be? Certainly not in the big house, where he was as hated as she was. If Elizabetta could kill them, she would.

Perhaps the stables. William had been a good rider. When they found jobs at Royal Oak he worked the horses once the farm manager saw his skill.

Quietly walking into the main stables, she found him sitting on a trunk in the aisle.

"What do you want?"

"Revenge." That fast she ran toward him; he couldn't run from her very well, as his one leg was hamstrung from when he tried to escape their captors. He stood up, turned away from her. She swung the andiron full force, catching him on the side of the head. Down he went, struggling to get up. She hit him again and again.

"This is for every time you beat me."

"Sulli—" He had no time to beg.

She hit him in the mouth. His teeth flew out and he spat blood. He couldn't fend off the blows. Filled with the power rage gives one, Sulli smashed him to death. When she was done, William's face, a bloody mess, was barely recognizable.

She threw the andiron down. Started to walk away, then picked it up again. She threw it at the back of the stable and walked to the Yellow House the long way around.

Even if someone saw her, she doubted they would care. William was despised, as he had put every slave at Big Rawly in jeopardy . . . but then, so had she. If anyone knew she killed him, perhaps they would beat her. Then again, maybe they would think he had it coming.

Sooner or later scores were settled.

She noticed she had some blood on the front of her skirt. Reaching the Yellow House, she stripped, gathered her wash and some of the others', and washed.

Olivia, who had been picking peas for the evening's meal, came back. "I would have helped."

"I needed something to do."

As Olivia walked away she heard Sulli singing to herself. Odd, for Sulli had been at the Yellow House for close to two years now and never sang, hardly smiled. Hearing that made Olivia smile. Perhaps Sulli's embitterment was fading. Olivia began to sing. Sulli heard her, so they sang together, one in the house and one out.

"I had no idea Bayard has horses," Beatrice mentioned to Lily. "I know he's rich but he never speaks of racing or driving."

"With you he has other things on his mind." Fiona adjusted her broad hat. "And his wife, so well dressed and so fat." She burst into laughter, as did Beatrice.

"Two fortunes united at the altar, what, ten years ago? Everyone talked about it." Beatrice scrutinized Mrs. Ernst.

"It's the way of the world," Georgina commented.

"Their world." Deborah kept watching Jeddie, who was again on horseback to calm Percy Ballard's horse as he led him to the starting line for the fourth race. "Who is that boy?"

"One of the grooms or jockeys. I bet you Sam Udall would know." Lily took a deep breath. "Handsome."

"It will be a festive night tonight." Jocelyn made a bet with Lily on this race.

"Remember the flat races? Two years ago? Oh, I think it was two years ago." Fiona thought. "Anyway, there were betting agents there. None here."

"I heard from Sam," Deborah said, "that since this is a new type of race, the Cloverfields people thought it better we all gamble among ourselves. No telling how the races will turn out. But I think this is more exciting."

"Me too," Lily enthusiastically agreed.

"She is beautiful, is she not?" Jocelyn, next to Georgina, indicated Catherine, talking to one of the owners, Percy Ballard, as his horse was calming thanks to Jeddie.

"Yes. And I hear she breeds superb horses. Sam is a font of gossip, although Deborah gets the best of it."

Deborah shrugged.

"Bayard is a font of information about fabrics." Beatrice tried to sound impressed but then she laughed.

"He pays well," Deborah simply replied.

"That he does. One can never have enough money, although when I look around I wonder." Beatrice absorbed the gleaming four-in-hands, the matched horses, those horses racing, the clothing of the ladies, the daytime jewelry exactly right for the occasion, expensive but not too large. The men might have a gold ring, gold chain across their chest if wearing a vest, and a watch. Given the warmth and the slight breeze, fabrics were light but well cut.

On the ground, Catherine walked from owner to owner, then signaled to Tulli to blow his cow horn.

By now Tulli felt he was an expert. He didn't sound bad.

Big Blue, Ballard's horse, and The Marquis, Zachary's horse, faced Mr. Finney's gorgeous stallion from Maryland, Rory O'Conor; Bayard's horse, Royal Assent; and Maureen's Serene Samson, a stallion out of her great mare Serenissima, sired by Catherine's Reynaldo. This looked to be a good race.

The crowd quieted. All those sitting on coaches sat up straighter. Little Tulli, after blowing the horn, ran to Jeddie, again on the ground, and they moved to higher ground, the midpoint of the two-miler.

Cager and Mr. Percy, holding the rope, having practiced and now having done this for three races, spoke calmingly. They figured it was as good as it was going to get and dropped the rope, to the roar of the spectators.

The field, bunched together, sped along the fence line. Clover-fields' horses, in their stalls, would not upset the running horses. Catherine and Jeddie really had thought of everything.

The Marquis took the lead. Big Blue stayed in the middle of the group and Serene Samson brought up the rear.

Jeffrey wrinkled his brow. Maureen noticed, took his hand.

"Don't worry, he's being held back. This is two miles."

Jeffrey looked relieved. DoRe offered more relief: "Mr. Jeffrey, Samson has the power of Samson."

The first jump, a simple fence, offered no problems. The jockeys could hear the swish, swish, swish as their horses' hind hooves brushed through the next brush. They couldn't brush their hind hooves on the solid jumps or the jarring would dislodge their jockey and possibly tip the horse over.

The pace, fast, was not blinding.

The next jump down a slight hill sat at the end of the hill. The horses had two strides on flat land to find the spot and go over.

No jockey used a whip. There was no need and the soaring of the jumps made them timid. This was new to them and the horses.

The flatland allowed them to pick up some speed. The Marquis kept the lead. No changes in placement.

The next set of jumps would test balance and the jockey's eye as well as his leg. Three jumps in a row . . . square, solid thick legs . . . were placed so the first jump was easy to spot. The second one was three strides after and the last two strides after that. The jockey had to keep his leg on. Rory O'Conor's jockey did not, so the horse was stranded between the second and last jump as the others flew away. Taking Rory to the jump behind him, the jockey then turned the 16.2 hand horse around, smacked his whip hard on his flank, and the animal lurched over the fence. The jockey, another Irishman like his boss, was smart enough not to try to catch up but to creep forward at pace. It would be a long race.

Catherine, positioned so she could see the last two jumps, John beside her, heard hooves before she saw the horses.

"Isn't that something." She loved it.

"When I've heard that I've been in battle." He put his arm around her waist.

"Honey, you never talk about that."

"I thank God I'm here. I lived and married you."

On the horses came and closer. It was like thunder.

The Marquis had Royal Assent by his side. The jump was a simple low fence. All made it. The next jump was what Catherine and Jeddie had built thinking it was a ha ha fence, but it wasn't. Still, it took some figuring.

All cleared the ditch, which was two feet wide and two feet deep. Then one stride to a row of tight boxwoods to clear. Catherine chose boxwoods figuring if the sight of this caused problems, the horses could drag their hind legs through if they were wobbly. All cleared it and slowly Rory O'Conor was making up ground. Serene Samson was third.

The crowd screamed as the horses flew by, the last jump being where the finish line would be after this next half of the race.

All the horses were decently conditioned but the pace picked up. Each jump was met by cheers. Percy, Zachary, Mr. Finney, Bayard, and Maureen were riveted. Maureen did not wish to shout, as it wasn't ladylike, but she held her husband's hand so tightly he winced.

Rory gained ground. The Marquis began to fall behind. What

horse could lead for two miles and take those jumps? Again, this was the first time anyone had raced in this fashion, but the lessons would be learned.

Big Blue, running second, also began to flag a bit. His jockey should not have stayed so close to the leader.

Now at the bottom, all took the jumps. The next jump, a zigzag fence, easy enough, caused The Marquis to rap it and his jockey shot off. The horse stopped. He didn't keep running with the others. Jeddi, seeing this, ran to the barn where Miss Renata, a steady Eddie, waited. As she was tacked up, Jeddie mounted, rode toward the fallen jockey. The field was not a quarter of a mile away.

One quarter of a mile remaining.

The Marquis faded, Big Blue now ran in third place but he hung in there. Bit by bit this became a two horse race. Bayard's Royal Assent against Serene Samson.

People screamed. The horses, lathered in sweat, stretched out to their full length and even found an inch or two. The big chestnut of Bayard's against the dark Serene Samson guaranteed this would not be the last steeplechase in Virginia. People went wild as the two took the next-to-last jump, neck and neck. And that final tricky jump, neck and neck until Serene Samson just nudged over the finish line painted in the grass.

Pandemonium.

Maureen couldn't contain herself. She threw herself into Jeffrey's arms. She shook DoRe's hand, as he had helped condition Samson. People were running up to her carriage to congratulate her. Bayard also accepted congratulations, for second place. He would win a bit of money but this got his blood up. He would win next time.

The Marquis and his remounted jockey walked to the finish line, which Rory O'Conor and Big Blue had crossed.

"Well done," Mr. Finney said as he patted Rory's neck. "Quite different."

"Is." His breathless jockey slid off.

Zachary and Percy, comrades, shook each other's hands, both

vowing to think about breeding to Catherine's Reynaldo or Black Night.

"Stamina," Percy said.

Zachary nodded. "Stamina and speed. That's the way."

Jeffrey swung down from the coach, reached up to help his wife down, a nice show of manly strength, which she greatly appreciated. Beaming, they walked over, crowded now by well-wishers, to where Catherine and Ewing stood.

"Well done." Catherine meant that. "Well done," she repeated herself.

She handed the silver cup to Maureen; the envelope with her winnings was in the cup.

Maureen took the cup, surprisingly speechless.

Bayard took his second-place mint julip cup, which shone in the light. An envelope was in it.

All the people who entered horses who didn't come in first or second were given a good bridle of English leather with an English bit. Catherine and her father wisely knew good prizes lifted spirits and the word would get out. In fact, it would go up and down the original thirteen colonies.

Sam Udall managed to reach Deborah and the girls. "I look forward to seeing you all tonight. The house will be full. There is a cook and," he looked at Fiona, "a harpist to accompany you."

"I do so hope this will be a big night. You are so generous," Georgina cooed.

"It will be a night we will all remember." He winked at Deborah, who pretended to be thrilled.

Ewing had drinks for everyone, spirits as well as Bettina's sweet tea. She also made unsweet tea for those who didn't like sugar. Unsweet tea was called untea. Bettina and her girls worked. The day was exciting, and egos being what they are, Bettina was more than happy to serve biscuits, little ham sandwiches, and corn bread. Her skills, legendary though they were, rarely failed to make other ladies of quality jealous. Why weren't their cooks as good as Bettina?

Each of the owners shook hands with the others.

Given the size of the crowd, not everyone was able to talk to everyone else. An event like this allowed people to mingle together, though, slave and free. Horses let them focus on something most admired. Granted, the respectable women, slave or free, did not speak to Georgina and her girls, but many of the men did, even those with wives might slip off for a minute. Other than that, the newness of the event provoked ideas, business. As Catherine had hoped, owners wished to breed to her stallions, whom they had seen the day before the race and that early morning. Horsemen always find their way to a horse.

"Tell me, Catherine, why did you not race Reynaldo?" A flushed, overjoyed Maureen asked once she reached Catherine, now at the front of her stable, Jeddie nearby.

"Since we built the course it did not seem fair. We would have been able to ride it, familiarize ourselves and Reynaldo with it. This way, no one could feel at a disadvantage. And your Serene Samson was superb. That lovely shoulder of his and his heart girth. He took so much of the best of your Serenissima."

Glowing, Maureen answered, "I hope so, but I am mindful of his sire. I will bring a few more mares over, but I have a feeling you will be besieged with mares."

"I hope so." Catherine laughed. "Ah, here's Zachary. He said he ordered two carriages and two wagons, and the carriages will be cerulean blue."

"Indeed." Zachary liked being surrounded by women as much as he adored his wife.

"My Jeffrey and his axles." Maureen laughed.

Mr. Finney came over to join them. "Having seen your carriage, Madam, might I visit tomorrow to see more?"

"Where are you staying?" Maureen asked.

"We haven't gotten that far yet, I fear. But Mr. Ballard said there was an ordinary not far."

"Nonsense. You will stay with us. Then you and my husband can talk. He will go on about his axles, wheel fittings, lanterns. It's over my head."

"Madam, I doubt much is over your head." He half bowed.

"Well, that's settled, then."

As the group was feeling the effects of a drink or two, the breeze, the sun nearing the horizon, Mr. Percy, Bumbee's husband, noticed Martin and Shank back with a group of poor whites.

"Bumbee, those are the men I saw dragging the young woman away at St. Luke's. Remember, two years ago? Think it was two years."

She squinted. "Say nothing."

"But remember after that people said Livia Taylor was missing? They took her."

"Percy, let white people take care of white people. And if you want to take care, you won't be shining on any young things today."

"Me?" He was notorious.

"You."

Later, Mr. Finney, his jockey and groom, Rory O'Conor walking behind the carriage arrived at Big Rawly. DoRe climbed down from his driver's seat as he led the Irishmen over, and he took Rory to put in a stall and set the groom up.

"Caleb."

Caleb, who lived near the stable, called back from his cabin, "DoRe."

"Give me a hand. I don't know where the boys are."

As Maureen hurried up to the house to alert Elizabetta there would be an important guest, Jeffrey, DoRe, Mr. Finney, and the jockey, a slight Irish boy, Niall, walked into the stable.

"Good God," Jeffrey exclaimed.

William lay at the end of the aisle, smashed in the face, one leg crumpled under him, blood everywhere.

DoRe ran over, knelt down. Then he stood up.

Mr. Finney walked over, more out of curiosity than anything, then blurted out, "I know him."

As the boys, Caleb quickly rounding them up, took Rory and unhitched the carriage horses, DoRe and Toby Tips each lifted an end of William and set him outside.

DoRe, voice low, ordered Caleb, "Bury him as quickly as possible. No service. Just get him in the ground."

DoRe walked back in the stable.

"Niall, this should prove accommodating." Jeffrey, a bit shaken, showed the jockey that nice room in the tack room, fortunately far away from all the blood.

Jeffrey walked to Mr. Finney. "How unfortunate that you should see that, but as you have no doubt surmised, he had enemies. Please follow me to the house and if I might ask you, say nothing to my wife. I'll tell her later. You said you knew him?"

"He worked for me. I usually hire Irishmen, young fellows who have sailed over. I like working with my own people, but William, that was the name he gave me, showed up at my farm with another young man and a pretty girl. I assumed they were runaway slaves, but both the men were dab hands with a horse."

"He was trained by DoRe. Was a runaway. You're quite right, but my wife, incensed by his actions, hired slave catchers, and they found William and Sulli, who he took with him."

"They disappeared from my place Christmas. The other boy, Ralston, remains. Is the girl here?"

"She is."

"No need to see her."

"You have no people?" Jeffrey used the euphemism for slaves.

"I do not, Sir. I believe that a man will work if he has incentive. Slavery removes the incentive. It may be that some people in bondage find work they enjoy, are trained, but I think all would rather be free."

Jeffrey was liking Mr. Finney more and more. "I do, too. But let us not talk of this in front of my wife. She has a different attitude from you and I. She believes slavery is accepted in the Bible. We live in interesting times, do we not?"

"We do, Sir. We do."

34

Thursday

The overhead lights shone brightly, for Harry had turned them up full blast, as instructed by Linda. Three director's chairs sat at the end of the bleachers. The stove had been stocked when Fair came to the school after work, then Harry drove to the building before her morning chores to feed it again. The hardwoods burned long, so when she and Pirate as well as Tucker came at four to stoke it again, the place remained warm. All that nighttime chill vanished, which was one of the reasons to keep a fire burning. Even if they are easy to restart, a chill often has developed. Winter is merciless.

Since she was already there, Harry took out her notebook, a hardback, and wrote more Christmas cards while Tucker and Pirate slept at her feet. She'd brought her bag and another thin briefcase. Going through ballpoint pens, as she had so many cards to write, a handful of those rested in the briefcase.

"Did I forget my stamps?" She spoke to the dogs.

"No." Tucker had observed her. "*You put them in your bag instead of the briefcase.*"

She opened her bag, too big to be a real purse but too small to be a backpack or large shopping bag. Like most women, Harry forever searched for the perfect purse. It eluded her. Her attempts to solve this frustrated her, as it amused her husband. At this point she used an old L.L.Bean canvas bag. It looked very uncool but it held her needs, including Chapstick. There's never enough Chapstick.

Rooting around in the bag, she found the roll of stamps. "I'm not thinking clearly. This should be in the briefcase."

Plucking out a mascara tube, she dropped it back. Her address book, far too large, made the bag heavy, but she could never get all those addresses on her cellphone. Besides, what if she lost her cellphone? It was easier to keep a clunky address book in view than a cellphone, she thought. She picked up the Narcan and the needle taped to the tube.

"You know, I made Susan buy this, too. We'll never use it, but Coop put the fear of God in me. Anyway, there are no cookies in my bag." She paused, lifted an eyebrow. "But for good dogs there are cookies in the truck."

"*I am good,*" Tucker stated definitively.

"*Me too.*" Pirate echoed his mentor. Knowing Harry had no idea what they were saying. "*Tucker, does she have credit cards in there?*"

"*In her wallet.*"

Pirate stuck his head in the open purse.

"*Pirate, what are you doing?*"

"*I want a credit card so I can buy bacon and treats.*"

"You get out of there." She pulled her bag away from the large animal, who had his nose in it, hoping to insert his entire head.

The quiet time in the big building gave Harry time to reflect. Christmas wore her down. She still did not have all her gifts and she was running out of time. As for running out of money, well, she had those credit cards. Much as she hated to use them . . . most still sat in the freezer . . . she was glad to have them. Still, just being able to

buy something on the spur of the moment nettled her. She needed to think things through, unlike her husband, who was too impulsive, she thought.

Returning to her task, the briefcase serving as a bolster for cards and notebook, Harry lost track of time. Twenty minutes later the dogs looked up.

"*Someone's coming,*" Tucker announced.

The door opened. Linda King came in, as did Sam Ewing and a third man, whom she didn't know.

"Oh, it's so pleasant." Linda smiled. "Harry, this is Liam O'Clery. He's going to judge our impromptu show."

"Show?"

"Linda and I will sit at the ends of the oval and Liam will be in the middle," Sam informed her. "Each hound will get a thorough look-over and we can discuss this at the end."

Linda soothed Harry, as she could see the surprise on her face. "Sam thought, and I agree, if we told everyone about this, you would worry. Maybe Alice might get cold feet. This way, you are all even. No time to plan."

"Okay." Harry stood, putting the briefcase on the bleachers.

Walking over to Mr. O'Clery, a medium-sized man with curly black hair and bright blue eyes, she extended her hand. "Thank you for being here. We are all novices."

"Yes. Sam and Linda told me, but they also said there are some very nice hounds in this group. The age difference also intrigues me. Your fellow is still young."

"Sort of third grade." Harry smiled.

"I see." Liam smiled back.

"Linda and Mr. Ewing have helped us all, not just in handling, but in what to look for as though we were judges."

"There's variety here," Linda added.

As they talked, the door opened and Isadore walked in with Jumpin' Jack. One by one the others came in and Linda told them all the plan.

"I didn't groom Bugsy," Veronica worried.

"Your hound looks fine," Liam pacified her. "Irish wolfhounds need a rough coat and . . ."

"Bugsy." Veronica supplied the name.

"Bugsy has a good Irish wolfhound coat."

"Take your coats off, get comfortable, sit down with your hound, and pull a chip out of the hat." Linda walked first to Joel Paloma, carrying a lumberjack hat upside down. He reached in and pulled out a chip with a number.

"Three."

Alice, next, pulled out a five.

Ballard, coat carefully laid on the next bleacher step up, hesitated then reached in. "One. Darn. I hate to go first."

"Ballard, you'll get it over with faster." Joel shook his head with good humor.

"He's right." Harry pulled out four.

Isadore was two and Veronica was six.

Linda set up the director's chairs at the ends of the oval should she or Sam wish to sit. Liam would stand in the middle of the oval. Fortunately, the space was large, larger than wolfhounds often get in indoor shows, so the hounds could move better, more room to stretch.

Joel wore a nice V-neck sweater with a bow tie, while Sam wore a V-neck sweater with a regular tie plus plaid pants. Isadore and Ballard wore no ties and wondered if they should have done so. Then again, this was sprung on them, but Isadore wanted to ask, after the exercise, what should a man wear in the showing. He thought it was easy for women and they thought the same about the men.

Ballard grasped Harry's hand. "I'm so nervous. You know how I get if there's competition."

"Sweetie, this isn't really competition."

"Tell that to Joel." He rolled his eyes in the direction of Joel, who was fussing over Lodestar, then messing with his own tie.

"Maybe he'll put the bow tie on the dog," Ballard said under his breath. "I'm sweating. I wish this sweater weren't so heavy."

"Ballard, honey, you're going first. It will be over soon, and Lafayette is such a handsome fellow. Even if you fall on your face, the dog won't."

Ballard's expression changed. He looked into Harry's eyes. "I can always depend on you to make things worse. Now I'm terrified about falling." He burst out laughing.

She did take the edge off a bit.

"Just go do it. For one thing, you're in better shape. Joel's getting a pot gut."

"Ha. Getting a headache."

"Number one. Lafayette," Liam called out.

"Go do it." Harry kissed him on the cheek.

Ballard walked out, acknowledged the judge, which is what one does in a horse show. Many forget it now, but in the old days you took off your cap for the judge. The argument was, do you do it in the beginning or at the end? Well, Ballard nervously did a small bow to the judge, as he wore no cap.

"Mr. Perez, please walk around clockwise."

The two did this and Lafayette showed well. He picked up on Ballard's nervousness and, being the loving dog that he was, wanted to comfort his human.

"Now reverse," Liam called out.

Lafayette changed direction before his human did but Ballard covered it well.

"Now walk toward me. Stop. Then walk away."

Dog and human did this.

As they stopped and waited, the judge walked to them, as opposed to them walking to him. He felt Lafayette, checked his bite, lifted his pads. Lafayette thought this ridiculous but he stood still.

"All right, Mr. Perez. Trot for me half the length of the oval. Stop and trot back."

Lafayette stretched his stride, moved well, and Ballard huffed and puffed because he was nervous.

They stopped.

"Thank you."

The two returned to the bleachers.

"You showed well." Harry petted Lafayette, whom she liked. "Good dog."

"*Thank you.*" Then the older animal said to Pirate, "*When he goes along your backbone, he squeezes. It tickles.*"

"*Okay.*" Pirate took that in.

As Isadore and Jumpin' Jack took the ring, Jumpin' Jack wanted to show. He was an exuberant dog, and Isadore struggled to keep up with him. Clearly the dog loved being the center of attention and Liam noticed, naturally, just as he noticed Isadore did not. A professional handler would bring out the best in Jumpin' Jack, but then again, owner and dog were a team. If Isadore wanted a house full of ribbons, he'd figure it out. As it was, he was learning new things, spending more time with his dog.

"Harry, I have the worst headache." Ballard picked up his coat from the higher bleacher, rifled his pockets. "Damn."

"Need an aspirin?" Joel asked, as Ballard's sweating was obvious.

"Got one?"

"Think so." Joel dug into his pants pockets. Not there. He picked up his coat and shook it. Heard a rattle, as there was no longer cotton in the bottle. So he put his hand in the inside pocket, retrieving a bottle of Advil. He took out two pills, handing them to Ballard, who had walked over.

"I've got a water bottle." Veronica handed Ballard an unopened bottle.

He popped the pills, took a big swig, and then another. "I owe you a bottle of water."

She smiled. "On the house."

Joel left them, as he was number three. Isadore returned to the bleachers.

"Jumpin' Jack was on," Harry complimented him, and the others agreed.

Jumpin' Jack, maybe not outstanding, had presence. He would have beaten better-conformed dogs sometimes in the ring.

Joel, leash up and loose, wanted to be the best. Lodestar, a good dog but not outstanding, showed well and anyone would have been happy to have such a good dog, but then wolfhounds tend to be good dogs.

Sam took notes at his end, and Linda at hers.

Finished, Joel came back as Harry went out. She and Pirate felt great. Who knows why. Pirate reached effortlessly, his stride so fluid.

"*Come on, Mom,*" Pirate urged Harry.

Smiling, they stopped as instructed. Liam walked over, feeling Pirate.

He looked closely at Pirate's facial proportions, then felt his ribs. As Lafayette had told Pirate, Liam pinched his backbone.

"All right. Half the oval at a trot, return at a trot." The two did as instructed, looking as though both had done it for all of Pirate's life.

"Thank you."

As Harry and Pirate walked back and Alice passed them for her turn, Harry smiled at Ballard, who had his thumbs up.

Suddenly his face changed, he grabbed his throat, dropped to the floor.

Lafayette licked his face.

"My God." Isadore dropped to his knees.

Joel dropped on the other side, trying to hold Ballard still. The poor man struggled to breathe. His rasps echoed through the building.

Thinking quickly, for Cooper had described how fentanyl kills, Harry vaulted to her bag, pulled out the Narcan and needle. She pushed up his sweater sleeve.

"Hold him as still as you can." She calmly filled the needle then stuck it in his arm.

Isadore, now sweating himself, kept holding Ballard, as did Joel.

Sam, Liam, and Linda ran to help.

Sam, with presence of mind, immediately called 911. Linda knelt down, as Lafayette wanted to be close to Ballard.

"It's okay, Lafayette." Harry comforted the dog as she waited for the dose to work. She only had the one needle, so she prayed there had been enough naloxone in the needle to save him.

Ballard's gasping turned to large, ragged breaths.

Harry silently gave thanks and made a vow to carry more of the stuff. Enough for two shots, if need be. Ballard's collapse was exactly as Cooper had described. Had she not known that, she may not have jabbed him.

Ballard tried to get up.

"Here, lean on me but stay down." Sam, on his knees behind Ballard, leaned the man against his thighs. Lafayette could now lick Ballard's face.

Ballard still couldn't talk, but he reached up and touched his dog's face.

As they were not far from Crozet proper, the ambulance wailed in the distance. Within minutes Alice was at the door, opening it.

"Ballard, don't worry, I'll take Lafayette." Harry looked up at the ambulance. "Where are you taking him?"

"UVA emergency."

"Ballard, I'll come down for you. You do as they say."

Joel, ashen-faced, said, "Harry, I live closer to him. I can go, and if they release him, I'll take him home."

"Thanks, Joel. But we're old friends; I'll do it."

As the crew wheeled Ballard outside, the bitter air hit him in the face. He rejoiced in feeling it.

"Harry, you saved his life," Veronica exclaimed.

"Well, naloxone did."

"Why are you carrying that?" Joel wondered.

"Oh." She thought fast. "Cooper, you know Officer Cooper, my neighbor, was telling me of the high incidence of fentanyl deaths, opioid deaths. She said all the law enforcement people carry Narcan now, even firefighters. So I thought maybe I should get some, especially as much of this strikes the young. High school, college. They're partying or athletes are hoping to escape pain."

"You're right. Think of the three kids who died last week at that house party," Alice added.

"Thank God you had that." Linda took a deep breath.

"And thank you, Mr. Ewing, for leaning him against your legs so he could breathe better." Joel stood up, his knees creaking.

Sam brushed off his trousers. "You all did a good job with your hounds. Mrs. Cobb, I regret we didn't get to you and Bugsy."

"Oh, I don't mind."

The small group broke up. Harry shut down the building, as Sam had made a reservation for Linda and Liam at Duner's. She told them to go. By the time she reached the farm she was exhausted.

Fair sat in the living room, fire crackling, a book in hand. She told him everything.

"Honey, I need to go to the hospital to make sure he's okay. I really hope they keep him overnight."

"I'll go with you." He closed his book, grabbed a coat.

As the humans left the house, the two cats listened to the three dogs, as Lafayette was with them.

He lay down, so sad.

Mrs. Murphy, Tucker, and Pirate wedged next to him.

Pewter surprised the others by being comforting.

"*Don't worry. Our big human is a veterinarian. As a doctor he can take care of your human. Vets know everything.*"

35

Later Thursday

Eyes fluttering, Ballard woke up, a tube stuck up his nose, which he tried to pull out.

Fair reached across the bed, taking hold of Ballard's wrist. "Not yet."

Harry, on the other side of the bed in an uncomfortable hospital chair, smiled. "How do you feel?"

"I don't know, but this irritates."

"I'll call a nurse." Harry walked into the hallway.

The hospital, busy, meant she had to walk down to the nurses' desk. Had Fair not been there, she would have hesitated, not trusting Ballard to be alone while awake.

Reaching the cubed natural wood barrier between her and a middle-aged woman in uniform, she leaned over slightly. "Hello, I'm in room 512 with Ballard Perez. He's awake."

The nurse flipped pages in front of her. "Overdose. I wasn't here when he was brought in. We changed at six. I'll send someone down to check."

"He seems okay but he doesn't want the oxygen tube in his nose."

"All right."

"Thank you." Harry turned, then turned back. "We got here about quarter to seven. Has anyone else visited him? A few of us saw his convulsions."

She glanced down again. "Would a Joel Paloma be in your group?"

"Yes."

"He showed up right after Ballard was checked in. A neighbor?"

"Yes, he is."

"Linda King? I was here when she arrived. An Irish wolfhound person?" The nurse looked up quizzically.

"We were all at an impromptu show."

"She was in and out. Had people waiting for her but she did check and said more people might be coming by. He seems to have concerned friends."

"I would hope everyone does."

A tired look crossed the nurse's face. "You'd be surprised."

"Ah. Well, thank you." As Harry walked toward 512 she heard footsteps behind her, as the desk nurse had already reached someone on the floor.

The young woman, maybe late twenties, walked into the room. Fair stood and Harry snuck in right behind.

"Fair Haristeen. Behind you is my wife, Mary Minor Haristeen. 'Harry.'"

The young woman turned around. "You reported Mr. Perez to the desk?"

"She did. I'm fine. I can go. And take this goddamned thing out of my nose." Ballard cursed.

"Ballard, that's no way to talk to a lady," Fair sternly reprimanded him.

"Miss, I'm sorry. It's been a terrible day." He apologized, for he did know better.

"I'm sure it has. Let me check your vital signs, Mr. Perez." She stood over him, held his wrist, looked at her watch as she checked his pulse. Then she picked up the clipboard hanging on the end of the bed, checking and double checking. She removed the oxygen tube.

"Thank God." He sat up straight. "I'm fine. I want to check out."

"Tomorrow morning. Dr. Lindbeck will make that decision."

"I'm fine. Look at me."

"Mr. Perez, I have no authority to release any patient. Only a physician can do that. And yes, you do look fine, but on rare occasions, opioid overdoses, especially fentanyl, can come back on you. Very, very rare, but we must make certain. The hospital has your record. You have had addiction problems before."

"Seven years ago." His face flushed red. "I have been clean for seven years."

"He has." Harry vouched for him, sympathetic to his anger as well as discomfort.

Ballard would carry his addiction history for the rest of his life.

"Do you have any idea, then, how you came to have this drug in your system?"

"No."

"He was fine, Miss. My husband and I have known him for most of his life. The good times and the bad times. He has cleaned up."

"Then someone gave you a dose," the nurse said, but did not sound convinced. "Were you in pain?"

"Headache. I was very nervous at the show. I showed my hound. I'm not good at it."

"That's not true." Harry spoke up again. "But he was quite nervous and headachy." She thought. "Another one of our members gave Ballard an Advil. He took two of them. Right?"

"Right. Began to feel better, maybe because I hoped they would work, and then I couldn't breathe."

"I suggest you find that Advil bottle." The nurse was young, but she was tough. "And Mrs. Haristeen, you were there? Someone gave him naloxone or he'd be dead. Can you tell me what happened?"

"I told the fellows who wheeled me in." Ballard, not one to know hospital protocol, had no use for it, or much of any protocol, really.

Harry took over. "Yes. He came back from showing his hound. They did well. Well, Ballard's nerves were shot. He is telling the truth. He had a wicked headache and another of our members reached in the inside pocket of his jacket, pulled out an Advil bottle, shook out two pills, and gave them to Ballard. A few minutes passed. Ballard grabbed his throat, went into convulsions, and fell to the floor. I had Narcan, I grabbed the tube and the needle from my bag. Joel Paloma and Isadore Reigle held him still while I shot the Narcan in his arm. Another man, a visitor and judge, leaned Ballard against his legs as he was flat on the floor. This helped Ballard breathe. He did breathe roughly, then better in a few minutes."

"Why were you carrying Narcan?"

"My friend and neighbor is Detective Cynthia Cooper. We were Christmas shopping, talking about everything. She impressed upon me how short the time is between convulsions and death. She told me I could buy Narcan at the drugstore. She also said all officers carry it and so do some other public officials. Fentanyl is rampant."

The young woman relaxed a bit, spoke to Ballard. "You are lucky to be alive. You do look fine. Just spend the night and all will be well."

"I'll carry you home." Fair used the Southern expression.

Sinking into his pillow, now leaning back, Ballard looked from the nurse to Harry to Fair. "Okay."

As the nurse left, Harry mentioned, "You had two visitors. Do you remember?"

"Not really. I was so sleepy." He then reached for Harry's hand. "You saved my life."

"Thank Cooper. She was the one who told me to get the stuff."

He sighed. "Everyone will think I'm back on drugs."

"Maybe not." Fair sounded cheerful. "Honey, you go home. I'll spend the night here. I can sleep in a chair. I've done it enough waiting for foals to arrive."

"I'm fine, Fair. You don't need to stay."

"Would make me feel better." Fair walked his wife out the door. "I'll call you in the morning. I have a light morning, and I can shift those appointments." He kissed her on the cheek. "I don't trust him. If he tries to leave, I'm bigger than you. He's not getting through the door."

She kissed him back. "Okay. I'll call Cooper and tell her everything. Poor Ballard, this will make the rounds if not the newspaper."

"I'm afraid it will."

Once home, Harry called Cooper, giving her a blow by blow.

A long silence followed this. "Do you think he was on something?"

"No. He was a nervous mess but he wasn't stoned."

"I hope you're right. In my years on the force, almost twenty now, I've picked up Ballard enough times to know he was, is, a serious addict. I've picked him up passed out in the airport parking lot, his genitals exposed, babbling like an idiot. People think we see blood and guts, and car accidents. We do. But it's the domestic gross stuff that gets you. A drunk lying dead in their own vomit. A woman sobbing because she was high on drugs, went to sleep, rolled over, and suffocated her baby. That's the stuff that gets you. Domestic abuse. Teeth on the floor. Women with chunks of hair pulled out. Or he's killed her and we get there and he's crying, trying to revive her, saying he's sorry. And I've seen Ballard in some miserable places, dressed and undressed. What saved him was his mother's money."

"It did. But give him credit, Coop. He did go through the rehab."

"Three times."

"Yes, but finally it took."

"I sure hope you're right. We are facing an onslaught of overdoses."

"May I make a suggestion?" Harry couldn't imagine seeing the things Cooper did, then sitting down to eat a meal. "Get that Advil bottle from Joel Paloma."

"I was going to ask you about that. Did you see the bottle?"

"Regular drugstore bottle. The protective cover and the cotton out of it."

"You noticed that?"

"I did because Joel shook the bottle. Then he removed the cap. No cotton. It would have muffled the sound. That's all I saw. He shook out two pills, one of the ladies, Veronica Cobb, handed Ballard a bottle of water. He knocked the pills back. Five minutes later, he convulsed." She paused. "Will it take long to test the pills?"

"No, actually, it's easy. Other lab tests are not, and as you know the medical examiner can take anywhere from a few days to months, depending. But the pills, easy."

"I can't imagine why Joel Paloma would have laced pills. I mean, they looked like normal Advil pills."

"That's why this is so vicious. The stuff is well disguised."

"Yeah, but Joel Paloma? He's wealthy. When we go for our dinners, those restaurant owners know him. He makes a lot of money supplying them. He's rich enough."

"Never underestimate the Seven Deadly Sins."

When Harry hung up the phone, she reached over to pet Pirate and Lafayette. Then she got down on her knees to love on Tucker, Mrs. Murphy, and Pewter. She felt a chill go through her body. Something terrible was going on, and she hated what she was thinking.

36

"Baby." Ballard opened his arms for Lafayette to run to him.

"*I missed you. I love you.*" The big dog licked Ballard's face.

Harry, with Pirate and Tucker, watched with misty eyes. "He was a good dog but there's no place like home."

"Thank you for taking care of him." Ballard sat in the library then looked up. "Sorry, sit. Can I get you anything, Harry?"

"No. Wanted to get you Lafayette as soon as I could."

"Your husband left here not ten minutes ago."

"I know. Told him I'd bring over the big boy. You look fine."

"I am. The only substance I took was that Advil pill. I have gone over it and over it in my mind."

"I have, too. Cooper went over to Joel's last night, late, after I left the hospital. She collected the pills and jar. She hasn't called me yet, but if that bottle did contain laced pills, maybe Joel didn't know."

"Any of us could be fobbed off, but most drug dealers wouldn't make that mistake. The stuff is too lucrative to give it away or make mistakes. But thinking, remember at our last dinner when you and I got silly . . . well, okay, I got silly . . . and we talked about your constant dessert? And I made a crack about murder menus?"

"Yes." Harry dropped her hand on Pirate's head for a minute. "The fentanyl deaths did not exactly follow right after the menus, if that's where you're heading."

"It is." He held up his hand. "The menus don't presage deaths but the deaths keep occurring. So what if there is something coded? Something we don't know? It's a long shot but it's also a very strange coincidence."

"I thought maybe it was about undocumented workers."

He shook his head. "No. Wrong time of year and wouldn't be enough money right now. More in spring. That doesn't mean that those deaths aren't connected to smuggling. Let the last rung on the ladder take the chances. Deliver the goods and you'll be well paid. Maybe. Then again, maybe you'll be killed."

"Ah." Harry rested her chin in her hand. "Coop says the drugs come in through Mexico."

"The Gulf of Mexico." Ballard was on track now. "Tourists, boats everywhere. Joel and Jodie have a place at Horseshoe Beach. You can drive anywhere from there. Up into Tennessee, cover the Mid-South, Kentucky, maybe up to Ohio. Easy to come up the East Coast. A lot smarter than running drugs across the U.S.–Mexico border. Or bringing it in on planes. Small trucks and cars. No big ones. Under the radar."

"Well, you've got a point. They live well but Joel doesn't flash his money around," Harry thoughtfully said. "I guess I expect people making millions to blow millions." Harry thought for a moment. "Gulf of Mexico never occurred to me."

"Offshore accounts. Don't draw attention to yourself. Retire when you're ready, if you do." Ballard continued, "I swear to you, I am not back on drugs, but I know how it works. Think of the years when I had to find dealers. When I learned how the business really works."

"Are some of your old dealers still selling?"

"A few. Upstanding citizens. Most gave it up as they aged. Some are dead by overdose themselves or by getting in a bigger fish's way. The fentanyl had to be in those two tablets. The stuff acts quickly. It did. I think he purposefully gave it to me and I also think he has that stuff on him in case of crisis."

"Give me a minute." Harry punched in Cooper's number. "Any news?"

"Actually, perfect timing. Nothing in the Advil bottle."

"Did it have cotton in it?"

"Harry, I was getting to that. Yes, it was a brand-new jar, although half of the pills weren't there. Part of the cover stuck to it as well. You know, a little around the rim."

"It's not the pillbox that Joel used."

"That is why I'm back here at HQ getting a search warrant."

The dogs barked. Harry stood up to look out the window, as the parking behind the house could be seen from the library. "Cooper, Joel just drove up. I'm at Ballard's."

"Let me pass this warrant off to Dabney." She named another officer, young, doing well. "I'll be there."

"So you think it's him?"

"I don't know, but I don't want to take a chance." Coop hung up the phone.

A knock on the door brought Harry to the back. She opened the door.

"Saw your car."

"You're here to see the patient. He's in the library." She betrayed nothing.

As the two walked back, Pirate and Tucker followed behind Harry. Ballard stood as Joel entered the library.

"Sit down, Ballard. Please," Joel instructed him. "You've had a rough go."

"You sit, as well." Ballard indicated a wing chair across from him.

Harry sank into the club chair, Pirate in front of her and Tucker in front of the big dog.

Tucker ordered the Irish wolfhounds, *"Be ready, just in case."*

Ears pricked up.

"We were just talking about your house at Horseshoe Beach. I never did know how you found it?"

Joel put his hands on his knees. "Jodie had enough of winter. Remember the blizzards in a row?"

"We had two last year plus five weeks of nonstop wind and lots of snow." Ballard was only too familiar with the weather.

"No. Before. The weather beat us down. The power kept going out. Once we survived that, Jodie made me swear we'd find a place in Florida. 'I don't want to live in Florida,' I said. She said we could find a place away from the cities. So the search began."

"Sounds like you found what she was looking for, anyway." Ballard then interrupted his train of thought. "Would you like anything to drink?"

"No. No. I was checking on you and I'm glad to see Harry brought Lafayette home."

Harry brought him back. "Horseshoe Beach?"

"Never heard of it. But I drove from Panama City all along the west coast of the state. Some nice places. Nothing jumped out at us. Pensacola had good hospitals, that sort of thing, but too many people. We wanted peace and quiet. We have a wonderful place here, but as you know, I'm busy. Not much time to play. We stumbled upon this little town, modest. That was it."

"When are you going this year?"

"December 30. We now claim it as our permanent residence, so we have to be there by January 1. I come back in March. She stays until May usually. I love evading winter."

"Lots of boats?" Ballard asked.

"Everyone has a boat in Florida. Some of them are grand enough to live on. Go out on the ocean."

"The Gulf of Mexico is pretty big." Harry scratched Pirate absent-mindedly.

"It is. Mostly it's calm. The sunsets are gorgeous."

"Must be perfect for smugglers." Ballard was not being prudent.

"Uh, I'm sure."

"So contraband can come in from Mexico instead of crossing the border," Ballard said.

A look of recognition crossed Joel's face. "No taxes or tariffs."

"Remember when we ate at that terrific restaurant in Staunton?" Ballard pressed.

"Only too well." His face hardened.

Harry edged forward in her seat. "It seemed so unusual. The menus."

"Harry, stay where you are." Joel pulled a tiny .38 from inside his coat. "Both of you. Don't move. I'm willing to make a deal."

"Before you get to that," Ballard played for time, "tell us about the murder menus."

Joel couldn't resist bragging. "Was our dinner group the first time I had eaten in those restaurants or been in the kitchens? No. Before doing business with anyone, I make sure I know how every estab-lishment is run. The murder menus, as you called them," he looked at Ballard, "were a signal that they needed more drugs. No calls, no in-person exchanges. I would check the restaurant menu, all online now. Innocent enough. Everybody checks menus. If I saw the sweet-breads dessert, I knew to send over a shipment."

"How did you know how much to send?" Harry asked.

"The amount never varied. It was much easier that way. No new exchanges of information. Whoever he was dealing with could eat in the restaurant then take home leftover food, which would be the drugs, in the bag, that he needed for his people. As I said, anyone can check menus. Nothing unusual about that. So everyone was safe."

"That is smart," Harry complimented him.

"A deal." Ballard was surprised, as was Harry. "Let's hear the deal."

"If you all leave this alone, I will give you a small cut of the profits."

"But how do we know what the profits are?" Ballard made a steeple out of his fingers.

"You don't. But I would think an extra fifty thousand a year for each of you is worth forgoing detail. Plus you will be alive."

"Joel, if you shoot us, the sheriff will surely get you eventually. Even if that is a ghost gun."

"Ballard, I don't need to shoot you. All I have to do is get fentanyl in you. Everyone thinks you're back on drugs."

Harry piped up. "But I'm not."

"Oh, maybe one time you took a snort with an old friend. Who's to say, and you won't be able to deny anything. Be reasonable. No taxes. No work. You collect $4167 each month. I will deliver it to you in cash. Just stay out of my business." He appeared quite calm.

"I'm thinking. What about you, Harry?"

Offering hope, she grimaced. "I'm figuring out how to hide this from Fair."

"I can directly deposit cash into a personal account for you. Surely you don't mix all your funds." The gun held steady in his hands, pointing right at Ballard.

"Never thought of that." Harry lied to keep this going.

"Speaking of thinking of things, how did you come to the menus? What tipped you off?" Joel was curious, as he believed he'd thought of everything.

Neither one of them knew exactly how the menus were used, only that there was a connection between that dessert and subsequent deaths.

"Harry would order the orange-glazed sweetbreads with a small crème brûlée, an unusual dessert. But it showed up on each menu. I started thinking about it. You might possibly know your clients' menus, their chefs' creativity. Stuff like that."

"Yes." His eyes focused on Ballard.

"It was a crazy thought. And Harry kept ordering it, which kept it in my mind. What's so great about sweetbreads? A long shot. I wondered, where did the drugs come from? Opioids. Fentanyl. Tramadol. Stuff like that." Ballard paused. "I knew the big dealer had to be a local. I know from my drug experience that there was a network, a pyramid."

"Logical. Why me?"

"I didn't consider you at first. But given your business you could easily smuggle pills here. Inside melons, zucchini, vegetables like that? Slice them open, empty out some of the inside, put the pills in a plastic bag, something squishy, stuff the insides back. And whoever you delivered this to would know where to look. If you stashed the drug in fruits and vegetables, they'd know the rows. And nothing would be set off because you weren't using big trucks. No weigh stations," Ballard went on.

"You really are clever," Joel said admiringly.

"Like I said, unfortunately, I understand dealers."

"So you knew there would be no paper trail or electronic trail."

"Of course. Well, your deal." Ballard looked at Harry. "Ladies first."

She could have swatted him but she smiled. "If we're going into business together, we deserve to know the truth. Those men who were shot by the gas station, was that you, too?"

"They were just a couple of dealers who sold drugs for me. When they got picked up for that careless handbag theft, I knew Coop was going to be asking questions I couldn't afford to have her ask. And I knew no one would miss them." Harry could hear the contempt in his voice. "So. What do you say?" Joel turned to Ballard.

"Of course, I am still worried."

"Why?" Joel asked him.

"Because you tried to kill me. How do I know you won't do it again?"

"You have my word. We would both have enough on each other to create problems. Legal problems. We have to trust each other," Joel smoothly posited. "I never planned to kill you but you were beginning to make me nervous asking all those questions about the menus.

I knew with your history it was only a matter of time before you figured it out. Your headache gave me my chance. I won't try again."

"Then put the gun away," Ballard requested.

"Of course." Joel slipped it back in his coat.

"And give me the pills, or whatever you were planning to use to make it look as though this time I did OD."

Harry heard Cooper's car. She hoped it was Cooper. She knew Joel would pull the gun again if there was even a hint Cooper was ready to arrest him, or he didn't trust Harry or Ballard, but this would hold them for a time while he could kill them at a leisurely pace.

Joel stood up, saw the car, and reached again for his gun.

"Get him," Harry told Pirate and Tucker.

Tucker, a streak of light, grabbed Joel's ankle as he pulled the gun out of his pocket. Pirate hit him with 150 pounds of solid muscle. As Joel struggled to keep his feet, he lurched forward. Lafayette grabbed his arm; his hand held the gun tightly.

Cooper knocked.

"Hurry!" Harry yelled.

The door opened as Joel hit the ground, his hand still grasping his gun. If he could turn his wrist, he would have shot Harry. Tucker, low to the ground, in one stride had Joel's wrist in her mouth, those fangs drawing blood. Lafayette held his arm still. More blood.

Cooper ran into the room, her gun out.

"Pirate, Tucker. Leave him."

"More blood?" Tucker asked hopefully.

"Leave him," she commanded, and the little corgi did.

"Leave him," Ballard echoed, but Lafayette wouldn't get off Joel's back.

Ballard rose, took his dog's collar. "Come on, boy. Good boy."

"He's a bad man," the loyal dog warned.

Pirate leaned against Harry as Tucker curled back her lip each time Joel struggled to get up then faltered. The gun was on the floor but Harry prudently stepped to kick it across the room.

"Thank heaven," Harry exclaimed as Cooper walked behind Joel, handcuffing him.

His right wrist bled on the floor. He said nothing.

Ballard fussed over Lafayette.

"Everyone okay?" Cooper asked.

"Yes. He would have killed us, but not today," Harry answered.

"We'll tell you what we know," Ballard, shaken, promised. "I need to steady my nerves. If ever I wanted a stiff drink, it's now."

"Don't," Harry said. "Not under these conditions. I'm going home. Cooper, I have never been so glad to see you as I am now."

Cooper smiled. "We all got lucky."

"Wait until I tell Pewter. She'll have a fit," Tucker gloated.

Pirate, still watching Joel, didn't reply.

Once Harry got home, she called Susan. Then she called Fair, who came home immediately.

As the calls dragged on, Tucker described everything that happened. Pirate listened, nodding in affirmation.

"How brave," Mrs. Murphy praised her friends.

"I would have scratched his eyes out." Pewter puffed up. *"I'm brave. Nothing scares me."*

"What a fibber," Tucker said.

"I have never been so insulted. I'm leaving the room." The fat gray cat, head held high, swept out of the kitchen, pushed through the animal door to the basement, rarely used, and thumped on each wooden step downstairs so everyone had to hear.

The high basement windows, rectangles, allowed in faint winter light. Sunset was three hours away so she could see. She noticed a slight movement between two old trunks, big trunks, with old towels fallen between them. The cat moved toward the movement. Matilda, half hibernating, beheld the cat with her glittering eyes.

Pewter shot out of the basement. All could hear the steps thundering. She burst through the animal door; she was puffed. Every hair on her body stood out.

"A python. A python. In the basement. Death. She could have killed me."

Her wide-eyed terror gave Harry a slight scare, as if she hadn't had enough. So she turned on the basement light after opening the door, carefully going down the steps.

"*Death. Death. A huge snake. Don't go down there,*" Pewter wailed.

The other three animals followed Harry, who had her flashlight. She shined it. Matilda's eyes caught the light. Harry walked over to pet the groggy blacksnake, secure in her warmth. She wouldn't emerge until spring.

"Oh, you are big."

Standing at the top of the stairs, still wailing, Pewter needed kitty drugs.

"All right, everyone. Just leave her be. It's the blacksnake from the walnut tree. Come on."

They all walked back upstairs. Harry cut the light, closed the door, sat down at the kitchen table.

"*I'll have a heart attack.*"

"*Pewter. It's Matilda,*" Mrs. Murphy calmly said.

"*She hates me. She'll bite me. She'll wrap around me.*"

"*Pewter, she may be big, but not big enough to wrap around you,*" Tucker tormented her.

"*You are hateful!*" Pewter growled.

37

Tuesday

Catherine, Jeddie, and Ewing rode slowly toward the apple orchard bordering the westernmost acres on Cloverfields, now thousands of acres. Ewing had prudently bought up contiguous land. One of his smartest moves was buying The Barracks, as no one wanted anything to do with an abandoned prisoner camp.

In deference to Ewing, Catherine and Jeddie rode their slower horses, the ones for guests and the ones that the children would graduate to ride in time. The Cloverfields horses lived to great age. Thanks to good food, good housing, and much attention paid to their hooves and teeth.

"Father, this will be a big year." Catherine noted the bending boughs of the apple trees. "Three years and now a good harvest."

"Young, but yes, I'm finally getting some fruit. Maureen's orchard that we helped her put in also seems to be doing well. These should be ready to pick next week. It's a beginning."

"You are farsighted, Father." Catherine meant that.

"Your mother wanted an apple orchard, I planted a tree for her by the house but I didn't have the resources to plant acres. Once Dr. Thomas Walker brought back seeds after the war, I thought more about it. He still has wonderful orchards. Granted, he has quite a few years on me, but I got around to it."

"You did." She watched the breeze lift up the leaves.

"Maureen wanted Newtown apples. We'll see how they do. If Pippin is good enough for Dr. Walker, they're good enough for me."

"Father, you look comfortable on Penny."

"I am, my dear. You can find the right horse for the right person. We've been together a bit more than a year now. She puts up with me."

"Mr. Ewing, you're good on a horse." Jeddie smiled.

"Oh, maybe once. I tell you, relish these years. They fly by and sooner or later the aches and pains fly in."

Catherine laughed. "You didn't look like a man with aches and pains at the steeplechase."

He shook his head with good humor. "What a day. You were right. You took a chance and what a day. People will be talking about it forever. You and Jeddie built an interesting course and weren't you surprised at how well most of those jockeys rode it? Surprising."

"Gratifying," Catherine simply said.

"We were right to charge a solid entrance fee. Five dollars takes some thought, so we did get better horses. Very wise, and wise to charge only a penny for spectators. You created such goodwill, and think of the breeding offers. Your three stallions won over many a horseman."

"It was by God's grace that they behaved themselves in the stalls." Catherine laughed.

"You know, dear, it was good to see how many people admired Yancy's Black Knight. Restored his spirits, which can fail at times."

"The pain" was all Catherine said.

Yancy Grant, at a dinner party at Cloverfields for important guests from north of the Mason-Dixon line, drank too much and got into an argument with Jeffrey Holloway, a mild-mannered man. He did insult Jeffrey, and by extension, Jeffrey's wife. Jeffrey challenged him to a duel, slapping him in the face with his gloves. Yancy took the challenge and everyone tried to dissuade the two men, but most especially Jeffrey, who was not a good shot.

Jeffrey declared he would die defending his wife's honor. There was no turning back. John worked with Jeffrey for the week before the duel. He told Catherine that Jeffrey wasn't hopeless, but there wasn't enough time. Yancy Grant was known to be a good shot. Good friend that Yancy was to the family, no one wanted him to kill Jeffrey.

The morning came. The seconds were at the field, as was the surgeon. As luck would have it, some said Yancy stumbled, but who knows; in any case, he misfired. Possibly deliberately. He shot Jeffrey's arm; Jeffrey's bullet shattered Yancy's knee.

Once attended to, Jeffrey visited Yancy to inquire about his condition and ask his forgiveness. Yancy, realizing he'd been a fool, granted it. In time they mended their friendship. Yancy being much older than Jeffrey, he was in essence in charge. But the knee offered endless pain. Yancy walked with a cane and could no longer ride.

"Speaking of Black Knight, is it not, I don't know, fate that William would be killed on the day of the steeplechase?"

Catherine nodded. "He was reviled."

"And you?" Ewing looked at Jeddie, for William pulled him off a horse in a flat race, breaking Jeddie's collarbone. Then William kept riding on Yancy's horse, Black Knight. The horse, ribs sticking out, was finally found. Yancy gave him to Catherine, as he could no longer afford to care for him. Catherine brought him back to health.

Jeddie shrugged. "He was a liar, a thief, and cared only for himself."

Catherine lifted one eyebrow. "That says it."

"Barker O said that DoRe told him William had been killed with an andiron. They found the iron but the most amazing thing is that Mr. Finney recognized William."

"Father, you didn't tell me that."

"Slipped my mind, dear. So much going on. So many guests. But yes, William had worked on Mr. Finney's estate. DoRe believes William, the girl . . . I don't remember her name, and another youth appeared, looking for work. Do you think the other youth was Ralston? He ran with them. Why else would he run away from here? All three ran away at the same time."

"Yes." Catherine thought about this. "He can stay where he is. Ralston was a troublemaker. Not as bad as William, but bad around the women and getting worse."

"Ah." Ewing stopped as they reached the edge of the orchard. "Hopeful."

"It is." Catherine liked seeing her father happy.

They walked through the rows of trees before turning for home. Once they were back at the stable, Tulli ran up to hold Ewing's horse while Catherine and Jeddie dismounted. Ewing got off with Jeddie's help.

"Lovely ride." The older man then looked around. "Thank you, my dear. A good harvest, a successful race, it will be a good finish to the year."

So it would. An ocean away, the crisis would wash away the French monarchy and usher in a world war. Catherine, Ewing, John, Rachel, and Charles, the slaves, and other workers would feel the shift. Far away though it would be.

It is God's grace that no one can see the future.

38

Saturday

Sparkling bits of Christmas balls lay under the large tree. Mrs. Murphy and Pewter enjoyed batting them. Harry gave up on stopping this activity. Each year she bought special balls she felt she could afford to lose.

Harry, Fair, Susan, Ned, and Cooper sat in the living room, fire adding to the holiday spirit.

"Did you know you were getting a set of made-to-order clubs?" Cooper asked Fair.

"No. She fooled me."

The one putter rested under the tree, a promise of more to come, as this was not fitted. Harry figured once the set was complete, maybe she might try the putter.

Tucker rested under the tree with the two cats. Pirate laid to the side, too big to fit under the branches.

"Your Christmas news is the best." Susan looked at Cooper.

She smiled. "I think so. There's a lot to figure out."

"He knows you'll cherish his family's home." Ned spoke of Reverend Jones, who had agreed to sell his home.

"I love that place and I thank you," she looked at Harry, "for those seeds you gave me and the gardening tools."

"I'll put them in. Can't live without a garden." Harry smiled.

"As long as they have catnip." Pewter couldn't care less about tomatoes.

"Someone's coming." Both Tucker and Pirate jumped up.

"I'll get the door." Fair rose, going to the kitchen door, where Ballard was just knocking. He had stepped into the porch, now enclosed for winter, to knock on the kitchen door.

"Merry Christmas . . . a bit late, but still full of happiness." Ballard had a wrapped box in his hand with a plaid Black Watch ribbon against bright red wrapping paper.

"Come on in. How about tea, something? Everyone's in the living room." Fair then petted Lafayette. "Merry Christmas."

"Did you bring a present?" Tucker hoped.

"Daddy brought a bag for you. It's cookies."

"Tea. Hot," Ballard said, taking Fair up on the drink offer.

"You know the place. Hang your coat up, go find a seat, and I'll be right in. Dark tea?"

"Yes."

"White, sugar?"

"A little milk but no sugar."

"Ballard, come on in. We weren't talking about you, but now we will." Harry laughed as she called to him.

"The best part will be when I leave the room," he teased her as he walked in, greeted everyone, as did Lafayette.

"Ugh. Another big one." Pewter made a sour face.

"Anyone else want a drink? Tea water's about to boil," Fair asked.

Harry got up. "I'll help, honey. I know you want tea." She then indicated Cooper. "And what about you, Coop, Ned? Early sherry instead of tea?"

"I'll have tea," Cooper agreed.

"I'll get up and help Fair, too. And I might take a sip of that single malt scotch he opened." Ned rose; he needed more than sherry.

Within minutes everyone had their drink; a plate of cookies sat on the coffee table.

Pewter eyed the cookies.

"Pewter, you don't like cookies," Mrs. Murphy said.

"I can try."

Ballard handed Harry the big box and gave the bag to Fair.

Fair opened the bag. "Greenies."

"Honey, don't give the dogs cookies unless I get something for the cats."

"Okay."

"Well, open your present first." Ballard was eager to see her reaction.

"This ribbon is beautiful." She slid a fingernail under the wrapping paper on both ends, carefully pulled off the paper.

"Throw it on the floor," Pewter demanded.

Hearing her gray cat, Harry did put the paper on the floor. Pirate and Lafayette sat next to the tree to watch. Pewter immediately sat on the paper, loving the crinkle.

Harry carefully opened the box. "What is this?"

She pulled out sheets of vellum paper, the ink black, a bit faded, and the handwriting was that of another century, when handwriting really counted.

Lifting one up carefully, she read, "Fearnought." Then her eyes scanned the page. Picking up the next one, she read, "Diomed." She looked at Ballard. "Founding stallions from the eighteenth century. Good Lord. Here are the mares. Well, not to Fearnought. He was a bit before this time. What notes."

"Constance didn't get all of Mother's centuries of papers. What she didn't steal, we have copies of, and all of the Ballard papers, most of them, are at Mrs. Scott's Virginia Collection at UVA. But I stumbled on these in the pantry, back of some old crockery, of all the places. Thought of you."

Susan had risen to read over Harry's shoulder. "Ballard, what handwriting."

"Susan, can you imagine writing like this, and with a quill?" Harry looked up at her friend then back at the papers. "Ballard, this is invaluable. To a horseman. They might languish at UVA. I hope not, but who is this? An ancestor?"

"No. These are the papers, breeding line papers, of Catherine Schuyler, a Garth. She was a good friend of Percy Ballard and his wife. As you know, Lone Pine predates the revolution, but that's the thing. Percy and Catherine's husband served under General Lafayette. Subsequently, the Ballards bred horses. Catherine wrote these notes for them."

"Of course. We read about him in school. John Schuyler, the hero of Yorktown. Ballard, these are too valuable. This is too grand a present."

"Not for the woman who saved my life." Ballard rose and kissed Harry on the cheek. "A spine of steel."

Leaning toward Lafayette, Pewter intoned, *"My human can be brave but I have had to save her many times. Just the other day I saved her from a python in the basement. Huge!"*

"In the basement?" Lafayette stared at the fat kitty.

"A body bigger than my male human's wrist. Oh, you wouldn't believe it. I faced the monster down so Harry could escape."

Pirate started to say something, and Tucker, too.

Mrs. Murphy counseled the two. *"It's Christmas."*

Harry carefully put the vellum back into the box. "Ballard, I will study every page. And I'll learn more about the writer, as well."

"Do you ever feel that those who went before, are with you?" Susan asked as Harry couldn't take her eyes off the pages, the box lid in one hand.

Lifting her head up, Harry said, "I do. I think many of us do. We learn to keep quiet about it."

Ballard settled back in his chair. "My house is full of ghosts in one form or another and I thank you, Harry, for giving me the opportunity to see the unseen." He then laughed.

Fair, not the most talkative of men, reached for his wife's hand. "We think we're so smart. There is so much in this world we don't know. But here we are. Alive and well and I say let's toast to that."

They lifted their glasses and cups.

"To life."

Pewter right next to Lafayette now, purred. *"I saved them. Harry and Fair. A cat must be brave."*

The others said not a word. After all, as Mrs. Murphy said, it was Christmas.

ACKNOWLEDGMENTS

Carri Lyon graduated from Yale and New York University law school just so she could unearth eighteenth- and nineteenth-century recipes. As I have never cooked a meal in my life this was essential. I can fry eggs kindly laid by my chickens.

Linda King and Amy Benjamin spent hours teaching me about Sam Ewing, a fascinating man. I hope to use him again.

Any AKC person, regardless of breed, happily answered my questions. Dog people are terrific, the judges redefine dedication.

Rachel Moody-Tucker has covered for me on those times when I left the farm for research.

Carolyn Maki proved invaluable, yet again, laying out what is truly happening in our country with drugs.

Simply put: Don't take them.

Dear Reader,

To keep the peace we are not writing individual notes to you given one of our number's penchant for drama.

Mrs. Murphy

Pewter

Tucker

Pirate

P.S. It's not me.

Pewter

AUTHOR'S NOTE

Do the best you can with what you have.

ABOUT THE AUTHORS

Rita Mae Brown has written many bestsellers and received two Emmy nominations. In addition to the Mrs. Murphy series, she has authored a dog series comprised of *A Nose for Justice* and *Murder Unleashed*, and the Sister Jane foxhunting series, among many other acclaimed books. She and Sneaky Pie live with several other rescued animals.

To inquire about booking Rita Mae Brown for a speaking engagement, please contact the Penguin Random House Speakers Bureau at speakers@pen guinrandomhouse.com

Sneaky Pie Brown, a tiger cat rescue, has written many mysteries—witness the list at the front of the novel. Having to share credit with the above-named human is a small irritant, but she manages it. Anything is better than typing, which is what "Big Brown" does for the series. Sneaky calls her human that name behind her back after the wonderful Thoroughbred racehorse. As her human is rather small, it brings giggles among the other animals. Sneaky's main character—Mrs. Murphy, a tiger cat—is a bit sweeter than Miss Pie, who can be caustic.

ABOUT THE TYPE

This book was set in Joanna, a typeface designed in 1930 by Eric Gill (1882–1940). Named for his daughter, this face is based on designs originally cut by the sixteenth-century typefounder Robert Granjon (1513–89). With small, straight serifs and its simple elegance, this face is notably distinguished and versatile.